The King's Anatomist

"We are not privy to the stories behind people's actions, so we should be patient with others and suspend judgment of them, recognizing the limits of our understanding."

—Epictetus

A Historical Mystery Novel

The

KING'S

ANATOMIST

The Journey of
Andreas Vesalius

RON BLUMENFELD

ISBNs: 978-1-7329508-9-4 (pb); 978-1-7364990-0-9 (hc); 978-1-7364990-1-6 (eBook)

Library of Congress Control Number: 2021930840
First Printing: 2021
Printed in the United States of America

Publisher's Cataloging-In-Publication Data
(Prepared by The Donohue Group, Inc.)
Names: Blumenfeld, Ron, author.
Title: The king's anatomist : the journey of Andreas Vesalius / by Ron Blumenfeld.
Description: [Roseville, Minnesota] : [History Through Fiction], [2021] | "A Historical
    Mystery Novel"—Cover. | Includes bibliographical references.
Identifiers: ISBN 9781732950894 (pb) | ISBN 9781736499009 (hc) |
    ISBN 9781736499016 (eBook)
Subjects: LCSH: Vesalius, Andreas, 1514-1564—Fiction. | Anatomists—Europe—History—
    16th century—Fiction. | Death—Fiction. | Philip II, King of Spain, 1527-1598—Fiction.
    | Man-woman relationships—Fiction. | LCGFT: Historical fiction. | Detective and
    mystery fiction.
Classification: LCC PS3602.L869 K56 2021 (print) | LCC PS3602.L869 (ebook) |
    DDC 813/.6—dc23

Dedication

To my wife Selina, my sons Nathan and Daniel, and my granddaughter Gracelynn.

Andreas Vesalius Life Milestones

December 31, 1514   Born in Brussels. Father is apothecary to Charles V, Holy Roman Emperor.

1520-30   Primary school in Brussels.

1530-33   University of Leuven (Louvain), undergraduate degree.

1533-36   University of Paris School of Medicine. Threat of war between France and Holy Roman Empire forces him to leave Paris.

1536-37   Completes his medical baccalaureate at University of Leuven.

1537-43   University of Padua for his doctorate; immediately offered a professorship in surgery and anatomy.

1538   Creates *Tabulae anatomicae sex*—six anatomical drawings, three by Vesalius and three by the Flemish artist Stephen van Calcar, a student of Titian.

Publishes a revised edition of Guinter of Andernach's *Institutiones anatomicae* without the permission of Guinter.

1543   *De humani corporis fabrica (The Structure of the Human Body)*, published by Johannes Oporinus, Basel.

1543   Enters imperial service to Charles V, Holy Roman Emperor, and leaves his post at Padua.

1544   Marries Anne van Hamme. Anna Vesalius is born the following year.

1555   2nd edition of the *Fabrica* published in Basel.

1556   Charles V abdicates throne; divides empire between his brother Ferdinand and his son, King Philip II of Spain.

1556-59   Practices medicine in Brussels.

1559   King Philip takes Vesalius and his family to Madrid.

Called to Paris to attend King Henry II of France, mortally wounded in a joust. Works with the famous French surgeon Ambroise Paré.

1564   Embarks on a pilgrimage to the Holy Land with wife and daughter; they leave him in France and go back to Brussels. Vesalius continues on to the Holy Land.

October 15, 1564   On his return, dies on the Greek island of Zante (now called Zakynthos).

Historical Figures Appearing in This Book...

...in rough order of appearance. Other historical figures mentioned only in passing are omitted from the list.

Andreas Vesalius	1514-1564	Flemish physician and anatomist. With publication of *De humani corporis fabrica* in 1543, he ultimately becomes known as the "father of modern anatomy." Second edition published in 1555.
Antoine Perrenot de Granvelle	1517-1586	Schoolmate and friend of Vesalius; becomes a Cardinal and counselor to Philip II. One of Europe's major art collectors.
Anne van Hamme Vesalius	Died c.1600	Daughter of Brussels municipal official. Wife of Andreas Vesalius.
Anna Vesalius	1545-1588	Daughter of Andreas Vesalius.
Philip II of Spain	1527-1598	Son of Charles V; ruled Spain and the Netherlands.
Charles V, Holy Roman Emperor	1500-1558	Holy Roman Emperor from 1519 until his formal abdication in 1556.
Gemma Frisius	1508-1555	Physician, mathematician, cartographer. Friend of Vesalius. Collaborated with Gerardus Mercator.
Jean Guinter von Andernach	1505-1574	Physician and famed Galen scholar. Teacher of Vesalius at University of Paris medical school.
Jacobus Sylvius	1489-1555	Teacher of Vesalius at University of Paris; fervent adherent of Galen; launched vicious attacks on Vesalius after *Fabrica* appeared.
Ambroise Paré	1510-1590	French barber surgeon who became a pioneer in battlefield surgery and wound care.
Johannes Oporinus	1507-1568	Basel-based publisher of the *Fabrica*, 1st and 2nd editions. Was secretary to Paracelsus for several years.
Paracelsus	1493-1541	Swiss physician, religious mystic, and alchemist.

Stephan van Calcar	1499-1546	Netherlander artist from studio of Titian; artist for *Tabulae anatomicae,* and likely artist for the *Fabrica.*
Girolamo Cardano	1501-1576	Italian physician, mathematician, and astrologer; cast horoscope of Andreas Vesalius.
Leonardo da Vinci	1442-1519	Italian artist, sculptor, engineer, anatomist.
Francesco Melzi	1491-1570	Disciple of da Vinci; inherited all of his notebooks and drawings, including anatomic drawings.
Gabriele Fallopio	1523-1562	Assumed anatomy chair Vesalius vacated at University of Padua. Renowned anatomist in his own right, and a supporter of Vesalian anatomy. The two never met.
Girolamo Fabrizio	1537-1619	Assumed Padua anatomy chair upon death of Fallopio.
Vitus Tritonius Athesinus	unknown	Student and friend of Vesalius at University of Padua.
Hendrik van der Meeren	unknown	Son of a minor nobleman from the Netherlands town of Zavanthem.

List of Illustrations

(In the order they appear)

Preface

Europe entered the sixteenth century pulled by powerful crosscurrents. The continent was in a state of almost constant warfare, largely over one kingdom's claim on the land of another. Peace agreements and alliances were fragile at best. Enter the Protestant Reformation in 1517: Martin Luther and others challenged the Catholic Church over its structure, practices, and theological principles, provoking decades of religious division and violence. At the same time, the population was recovering from the decimation of the Black Death in the mid-1300s—even as plague outbreaks continued to occur. The feudal system persisted but was in decline; administrative and merchant classes grew in size and influence along with the growth of cities as population and economic centers. Advances in transportation led to increased trade and the rise of a craftsman class to produce goods.

The invention of the printing press by the German Johannes Gutenberg in the mid-fifteenth century revolutionized the spread of information, ideas, and culture. Art and architecture reached new heights. Scholars were caught up in the Renaissance obsession with the rediscovery of the lost writings of ancient Greeks and Romans, and held up those ancients as paragons of knowledge and wisdom.

In this Renaissance environment, Andreas Vesalius completed his medical training in 1536. The final authority in medicine was the Greek physician Galen, whose writings went virtually unquestioned in the thirteen centuries since his death; the Renaissance medical student was expected to gain a comprehensive understanding of medical practice as Galen originally set it down.

Galen likewise set the standard in human anatomy, though he did few human dissections, basing most of his work on animal dissections. Vesalius found himself grappling with Galenic dogma, his own anatomic observations, and how best to teach anatomy.

Part One

ASTRAL TWINS

Brussels

16 January 1565

The glimmering of first light seeping through the curtains of my bedchamber was enough to pry my eyelids open. I was loathe to give up the warmth of my quilt, but the pain between my shoulder blades would not ease until I did. I forced myself up and perched on the edge of my bed, waiting for my mind to clear. I had passed through another restless night, and my first thoughts of the day landed once more on an anguish that had been building for months.

Andreas, you are despicable. Where in hell's name are you? Had you no inclination in the past year to jot something down to me, if not to your wife and daughter? Anne, Anna, and I are forced to live with daily worry about you. When you get back from your inane pilgrimage I will embrace you and then l will thrash you bloody.

I pulled a robe over my bedclothes and made my way downstairs, greeted by the familiar stiffness in my knees. The house was cold, but in the study Marcus had already seen to the stove and lighted candles. I would snuff them out when there was enough sunlight, the clouds over Brussels permitting.

I closed the door behind me to trap the heat and sat at my desk, strewn with diagrams and calculations from the day before, none of which had advanced my thinking. I pushed them aside and opened the drawer where I kept all the letters I had ever received from Andreas. I reached for the last few from the top of the pile, but then withdrew my hand and shoved the drawer closed. I knew them by heart anyway.

Just then Marcus brought breakfast and set it down on a small table by the window, away from my books and papers; they had suffered enough from errant drips of butter or morsels of fish. I looked forward to my cup of chocolate—a smoky, bittersweet brew made with milk and ground cacao seeds from the New World that I acquired at considerable expense, and which I now find hard to do without. I brought the cup to my nose and drew in its vapors as I peered through the window at my small garden in its desolate winter sleep. A few sparrows poked at the bare ground. My eyes landed on the young oak tree in the center of the space, a gift from Andreas when I bought this house.

How we would laugh about being astral twins! In truth, we were born in the early morning hours of December 31, 1514, just a few blocks apart—the sun, moon, stars, and planets all tugging equally from the heavens at our squirming bodies as we escaped our mothers' wombs.

But astrologers might not want to hold us up as examples of the phenomenon. Out of a hundred men you would be among the shortest, I among the tallest; you are as stocky as a barrel, I thin as a fence post; your hair curly and dark, mine straight and the color of straw; your eyes dark brown, mine pale blue.

I took a sip of chocolate and watched a jay land in the tree and depart.

You charged ahead into the world, Andreas; I peeked at it from a safe corner. Your great textbook of anatomy brought you fame along with a good measure of infamy. You have served as physician to an emperor and a king. I toil with mathematics in obscurity. And yet we are as brothers to each other—or are we still? Your silence shakes my belief.

A pounding on the front door shook me from my daydream, and I heard Marcus rush from the kitchen to answer. I sighed and waited to see who would come calling at this hour.

The door opened to a booming voice.

"By the grace of the Holy See, I bear an urgent post from His Eminence Cardinal Antoine de Granvelle for Jan van den Bossche of Brussels."

Antoine never used a papal courier to post letters to me; what could it be that required such fanfare? Over Marcus' protests, the courier insisted upon delivering the letter to my hand. I went to the door to spare Marcus any further conflict with this fellow, annoyed that my chocolate would be cold when I got back to it. At the door, a gust of wind caused me to gather my robe tightly, but my bare legs felt the chill.

The courier and I examined each other eye to eye. His outline nearly filled the doorway, his uniform and red beard muted by dust. Despite the cold, his horse was lathered; it was the last of many relay mounts in a week of hard riding from Ornans in eastern France. For his part, the courier faced an unshaven man of advancing years with naked legs emerging from his nightclothes—not the image of a gentleman with whom a Prince of the Church would associate.

He repeated his message: "I bear an urgent letter from His Eminence Cardinal de Granvelle for Jan van den Bossche at this address."

"You have found him, Sir."

He broke his unblinking stare and produced the letter from his shoulder bag. He touched his cap and without another word mounted his horse and trotted off. What an odd fellow.

Marcus nudged me inside and closed the door against the cold. Standing in the hallway, I broke Antoine's seal with no small amount of curiosity. Enclosed in this letter was another, with its seal—a royal seal—already broken. Puzzlement turned to dread as I read Antoine's letter:

8 January 1565

Dearest Jan,
I weep as I write this letter. I can relay this news no more clearly than His Majesty himself has relayed it to me, nor do I have the courage to repeat it.

It is my duty to inform Anne Vesalius. She will receive a letter on the same day you read this.

Your devoted friend,
Antoine

My hands trembled as I opened the king's letter.

16 December 1564
Madrid

To His Eminence Cardinal de Granvelle,
With deepest regret, we inform you of the death this 15 October past
of Andreas Vesalius of Brussels, on the Greek island of Zante under
the jurisdiction of the Republic of Venice, during his return from
the Holy Land. The sad news of your friend and our distinguished
Physician reached us yesterday from His Excellency the Ambassa-
dor of Venice.

We are informed that Doctor Vesalius contracted an illness
at sea, and succumbed shortly after being brought ashore. He was
laid to rest with Catholic rites at the church of Santa Maria della
Grazie on that island. Our prayers include his wife and daughter,
who, as you have previously reported to us, left him in France on
the outbound journey to the Holy Land and returned to Brussels.

We are consoled in knowing that his pilgrimage will speed him
to his rightful place in Heaven, having already secured his earthly
legacy in his profession and in his service to the royal families of the
Holy Roman Empire and Spain.

With our profound condolences,
Philip II
King of Spain
Lord of the Netherlands
King of Castile
Duke of Milan

My mind fled wildly from these words, but the king's letter left me
no escape. Antoine, as a university schoolmate, and even as Cardinal,
was fond of pranks, but he would never devise one as cruel as this.

I could not keep hold of the letters; they spiraled to the floor. I
grabbed for the doorway to steady myself.

"Andreas is dead, Marcus."

"My God." Marcus gasped and crossed himself. "Upstairs with you, Master Jan."

I staggered upstairs on Marcus' arm and fell into bed. I clutched my pillow tightly to my chest and wept, squeezing my eyes shut until they hurt. I sought refuge in the darkness, but instead a vision came—I was suspended above the red-bearded courier at Anne's door and watched as he handed her the letter that would make her a widow. As she broke the seal on the letter I turned away.

~~~

I was a coddled, sniveling child born into a family of great wealth. My father, Rudolf van den Bossche, the second-generation proprietor of a lucrative trading business, possessed all the status and influence that such wealth conferred. Father saw little hope for me as a businessman, and left me to my mother while he groomed my older brother Frans as his successor. My mother, handsome even in advancing years, was the eldest daughter of a family of minor nobility fallen on hard times. The recompense for her marriage to my untitled father was a lifetime of luxury and status, albeit mercantile in nature. After the birth of Frans, the loss of two daughters in infancy before I came along made my survival a miracle to my mother, and she dedicated her life to assuring that God's grace in granting her another child would not be in vain.

As were all children of my station, I was entrusted to a governess and then a tutor, but Mother was often within earshot and would rush to my side at any disturbance. Until I started school, Mother took me to mass by carriage once or twice during the week and on Sundays with the family. She would put her arm around me when we knelt. 'Close your eyes and press your hands together like this, Jan. You must pray for God's protection, for He will not forgive me if anything happens to you.'

Other than going to church, I was taken beyond our gates only infrequently. Mother's teachings of the outside world were stark and forbidding. 'You must always hold my hand when we walk, because you can get trampled by a horse. Don't play with those boys, just sit by me, see how their hands and clothes are dirty, their games are too rough. Don't pick up anything from the ground, Jan! Don't pet the dog, Jan. He may very well bite you. Remember that all animals, especially farm animals, are covered in filth.'

It was no wonder that I came to prefer the solitary refuge of my home to an outside world full of danger and revulsion.

One day I created Jorgen, a pocket-sized boy of princely bearing in a red cap. Jorgen would sit with me as I played in my room, and listen to me talk for as long as I wished. I knew my parents would disapprove of Jorgen, so I kept him hidden and never spoke to him in their presence.

My one steady human contact outside the household was my tutor Holst, who taught me to read, write, and cipher. He treated me with kindness and praised me for taking so quickly to my lessons. One day I decided to tell Holst about Jorgen, and asked if he could sit with us.

"Of course," he said. "Is he as clever as you?"

"Oh, yes, even more. But you must keep him a secret."

"Very well. Jorgen will be our secret."

When I was five, at the end of a lesson, Holst asked me if I had heard of a game called chess. I had not, and neither had Jorgen. He took a small chess set from his bag, set out the pieces, and showed me how they moved. As a reward for a good lesson he said we would play a game.

At first I was happy just to move the pieces around the board, but after Holst showed me a few elements of strategy, I started to see the different futures that could unfold with every move. Before long I was defeating Holst more often than not. Laying down his king to concede a match to me, he would laugh and say, "How old are you, really?"

In the fall before my sixth birthday, my father announced that I would be going to school. My mother pleaded with him to let me continue with Holst, but he stood firm. A week before my first day of school Holst shook my hand, tousled my hair, and gently loosened my grip around his leg. He made a present of his little chess set and promised to visit me, but I never saw him again.

Having survived my childhood, the wealth of the van den Bossche family has permitted me to live unencumbered by profession or enterprise. My father never stopped voicing his dismay at my indifference to commerce and compared me unfavorably to Andreas, who was avidly pursuing the career of his predecessors. But in the end, my father provided me with more than enough means to follow my own path in life.

Shortly after I completed university, he developed a wasting illness with a distressing cough, bloody phlegm, and terrible bone pain. Shrunken, bedridden, and short of breath, he urged me to accept the chair in mathematics I was offered at Leuven, thinking this would at least establish me in a respectable career.

"But Father," I said, leaning closer to him, "mathematics is like the New World to me, with so much to explore and discover. You have made it possible for me to pursue my studies without the obligations of academic life, and for this I am grateful."

To my relief, he received my decision calmly, and even managed to offer faint praise.

"If you choose to spend your life with your nose in mathematics texts, so be it," he said. "You have your mother's good looks, but you can thank me for your wits . . ." He laughed, bringing on a fit of coughing. He wiped blood from his lips. "It would please me if something useful falls out of your head, and you find yourself a wife."

If something useful ever does fall out of my head, I will be happy that my father's wish came true, but I let my studies take me where they would, and they have been their own reward.

As for taking a wife, that is a complicated story.

Against my family's standards, my material needs are quite modest, so I am free of any need to further augment my own very sufficient income. Growing up, I was surrounded by servants—cooks, handmaidens, governesses, man-servants, laundresses, gardeners, and carriage-men, but I live without ostentation in a comfortable little house managed by my assistant Marcus.

I met Marcus Schoop on a walk through the markets. Wiry, tousle-haired, and not yet twenty, he was raised in a fisherman's family from Ostend, and came to Brussels to sell his family's catch. I would have a snack of herring at his stall and stay for a conversation; his calm demeanor and thoughtful manner of speech set him apart from other young men of his class. The seagoing trades batter the bodies of men and coarsen their behavior, but Marcus was spared those outcomes. He was a sickly child, and his mother did not allow him many chances to go to sea. Instead, he attended a public school for several years and learned to read, write, and do basic ciphering. Under the wing of his mother, he learned how to cook and run a household.

My housekeeper, a sweet but dimwitted girl, left my employ to marry a chandler in Ghent. On impulse I offered Marcus the position, and he accepted. The lessons he learned at his mother's side fit well in my house; I prefer his simple, hearty meals to the pretentious ordeals of my family's dining room, and he proved himself capable of managing the upkeep of my house within a budget we plan together. He has proven his loyalty to me, and provides for his kin to the extent of his abilities.

I am grateful for my life as I am living it, and unapologetic about my circumstances.

When I am not keeping Andreas company in his travels around Europe, or joining with him to smooth over one problem or another he's having, I enjoy the solitude of my studies and time spent with a few good friends. I leave the family tradition of business and profit to my brother—a responsibility that he shoulders with enthusiasm—and also the duty of legacy; he has produced three sons and two daughters by two wives. I join my aging mother most Sundays for dinner, on occasion joined by my brother Frans and his family.

It fell to me to balance Mother's accounts and resolve household problems.

"After all," Frans said, "the family business is all-consuming. As you have no job or profession you can see her at your leisure."

Ever since our dear cook Greta dropped a platter of capons and fell dead on the kitchen floor, my mother had hired and fired a succession of replacements. She would regularly dismiss one of her aging staff, but by the next day would have no recollection of it. My arrangement with them was that when she fired someone, they were to stay out of sight until the next day and go about their business as if nothing had happened.

The King's Anatomist

It was only their dogged loyalty and generous Christmas bonuses that kept them on.

I attend church less and less. I make my excuses to Mother, but I have long dismissed the value of religious observance. In the wrong hands it is a dangerous stance, and only my closest friends know.

20 January 1565

Marcus snapped open my bedroom curtains and bustled about noisily. Were it not for Marcus' cajoling ("Does Master Jan wish to piss himself?" or "You will shrivel like a raisin if you don't eat something."), I would have stayed in bed, showing no greater sign of life than a clam. I had little taste for food, nor the energy to read or write. As the news of Andreas spread, some friends came to call. I kept these visits brief; I wished only to be alone.

But this day began differently. I sat up in bed while Marcus, with his back to me, tied back the curtains while singing one of his seafaring chanties.

... Up jumps the herring, the king of the sea,
Saying "all other fishes, now you follow me ..."

"Marcus, spare me."

He spun around. Seeing me upright, his eyes lit up.

"You don't wish to hear a tribute to the noble herring?"

"No, I don't. Your time would be much better spent making me some breakfast. Go on, I will be downstairs shortly."

Marcus smiled. "I'll help you into some clothes and then ready some breakfast. I'll be back to help you down the stairs."

"Get going, Marcus. I'll need no help. I would like bread and butter with a few of your noble herring, preferably dead and smoked. And don't forget the chocolate."

"As you wish," he said, and sped off.

I got out of bed and paced around the room. My legs were heavy, my breath came in sighs, and I was still consumed with melancholy. But I arose as well with the need to find a way forward. How unprepared I was for such a loss! I had been living as if our friendship transcended time and mortality.

The Stoics, I read once, believed in mental preparation for loss by imagining it in advance, and that, given the natural place of death in the order of things, better to cherish the memory of a friend than lament his loss—an admirable but daunting practice, and at any rate too late to employ.

I made my way down to the kitchen and took breakfast while Marcus kept a watchful distance. I ate what there was to eat and went to my desk in the study. I hesitated, then pulled open the top drawer and took out the familiar stack of letters. I set aside Antoine's letter and the king's and reread the ones beneath, now a year old.

31 December 1563
Monzón, Spain

Dear Scarecrow,
Happy birthday to us, Astral Twin! It was good to have your visit. There was talk of storms in the Pyrenées. Did you get over the mountains tolerably, or were you buried up to your shriveled balls in snow? Poor Marcus, who must endure his employer's whining. I cannot imagine why he hasn't poisoned your food.

You can thank King Philip for bringing me north to Monzón for the Aragon Court, saving you two more weeks' journey to Madrid. I wrote Anne that you were coming to Monzón; I'm sure she and Anna would have wanted to see you, but the journey from Madrid is anything but easy.

I will be returning to Madrid soon. It has its charms, but hardly a day goes by without the Inquisition inflicting torture and punishment in the name of God. The Spanish take particular pleasure in human suffering, and in this their creativity is second to none. A dread hangs over the city; a bad word from a neighbor can mark you as an agent of Satan. Anna has been a joy to Anne and me, but our daughter is too pretty for her own good; Spanish boys have been sniffing around like stray dogs.

I rarely tend to King Philip here, but rather to various diplomats shitting themselves from the oily Spanish food. I was happy to see Antoine not long ago when he came for meetings with the king. He puts on an excellent show at court, but if only His Majesty knew how foul-mouthed his Cardinal gets after a few tankards of beer!

I have been scribbling in the margins of my 1555 Fabrica with the aim of a third edition, but without research the task is hard. It's a good thing I didn't get to Spain until after I finished the second edition. The Spanish physicians still think that Galen has taught them all they need to know and see no merit in putting their clumsy hooves inside a corpse. Just as well—they are revolted even more than you by the idea of dissection, and the king has forbidden the practice. At least you'd tag along to collect bones or steal a corpse from time to time, and peek inside a body cavity with a frilly kerchief over your tender nose.

I learned of late that Fallopio, the good man who held my chair at Padua, had died, and I received confidential assurances that the chair was mine to reclaim. But King Philip made it clear that he would not release me—I was "too valuable." And that was the end of it. I know Anne would prefer Padua to Madrid, but we are happy and prosperous here.

Happy birthday and happy New Year. Too bad you are losing your hair. I may have a few strands of gray at the temples, but you must admit it suits me well.

And.
Count Palatine
Medicus Princeps, Diarrhoea et Vomitus

I could still smile at his teasing and at the scorn he harbored for his Spanish counterparts. He would never let me forget that years ago, when he was in service to the Holy Roman Emperor Charles V—Philip's father—he was made Count Palatine. It did not matter to Andreas that the title was a minor honorific and that there were more Counts Palatine than stable boys. Were it not that he sent this letter privately with a Flemish merchant returning to Brussels, it would have been dangerous to post it; the king's snoops were known to intercept letters to and from his court. The merchant sought care from Andreas for a catarrh, and mentioned to me in passing that Andreas was recovering from the same illness.

There was an edge to you during this visit, Andreas, and you insisted on brushing off the lost chance to return to Padua and the academic life you missed.

I was torn about not going on to Madrid to see Anne, but I could not face a month's further travel, and I feared being trapped in Spain by Pyrenées snows.

The letter that followed from Andreas just two weeks later was posted via the usual Hapsburg courier system:

18 January 1564
Monzón

Dearest Jan,
King Philip has granted me leave for a pilgrimage to the Holy Land, which I will undertake in thanks for my recent recovery from a serious illness. Anne and Anna will join me. I will be returning shortly to Madrid to tell Anne the good news and make preparations for departure.

You have so often visited me wherever my duties have taken me—as you did here in Monzón—but it would be far too much to ask of you to join me on this journey, and I will share this rare privilege with my dear wife and daughter.

I am grateful to Our Lord Jesus Christ for my recovery, and to the king for allowing me to express my gratitude in the Holy Land.

Wish us Godspeed.
Your devoted friend,
And.

I tossed the letter onto my desk in disgust. This letter, coming as it did on the heels of the first, seemed not to have been written by Andreas, with its cold formality and with none of the usual banter. But most troubling was the sudden announcement of the pilgrimage. Unlike me, Andreas did not shy from travel, but he never had a glimmer of interest in the Holy Land; he traveled for his career and for little else. In my bones I knew something was amiss—but what? I responded to this letter the day I received it, dispensing with any caution about my letter being intercepted.

9 February 1564

Runt,

I received your 18 January letter today, so soon after your New Year's letter that I had not yet responded to it. Just as well—this one has sent me to my desk immediately.

Did something fall on your head? You have always been capable of reckless behavior, but now you have outdone yourself. The Holy Land is far away and dangerous. You said nothing of this pilgrimage while I was in Monzón. The kind merchant who brought me your last letter said you had a catarrh. I'm glad you're over your cough and snotty nose, but don't tell me that God expects your thanks for that, and to offer it halfway around the world with your wife and daughter in tow!

Why not choose a more convenient pilgrimage? The shroud of Jesus at Chambéry is quite popular. Or what of Santiago de Compostela, right there in Spain? The bones of the crusader Saint James were carried there from Jerusalem. You could ask him if he recommends the voyage.

As worried as I am about you, I am blind with fury. You cannot be serious about this plan.

With devotion and concern,
J.

I wrote to Antoine on the same day:

9 February 1564

Dear Antoine,

Something is not right with Andreas. King Philip has granted him leave for a pilgrimage to the Holy Land. He even plans to take Anne and Anna with him.

You are well aware of the dangers of this pilgrimage; many go, never to return. Despite what he thinks, he is no longer a young man. As counselor to the king, you must convince him that it would not serve the royal family to let his renowned physician undertake such a dangerous journey.

Whatever has possessed Andreas to pursue this lunacy is not clear, but I don't like this situation at all. I beg you, do what you can.

With all sincerity,
Jan

One's sense of urgency does not speed the mails. I waited as the weeks passed to hear from Andreas, but the letter was returned with an unbroken seal. The Pyrenées were impassable because of snows. My only hope rested with Antoine, and my heart sank when I finally heard from him:

3 April 1564
Château Granvelle
Ornans

Dearest Jan,
Have you heard from Andreas? I wrote to King Philip as soon as I heard from you. He was still in Monzón, and the Pyrenées were once again passable. His letter of 5 March said that Andreas had left Monzón for Madrid in January to prepare for the pilgrimage He even gave him a travel allowance and a letter of passage. During this time I learned that Andreas had been invited to return to his chair at Padua, but the king would not release him.

His Majesty did not waver from his decision to grant Andreas leave. He was moved by his request, delivered, as he wrote me, "with great passion." I beg you to understand that it is a delicate matter for a Cardinal to advise against a holy quest with Philip, who has few equals in the depth of his faith.

Andreas will reach Italy by way of southern France, and once in Venice, he will sail to the Holy Land. His royal letter of passage will ensure safe transport on a Venetian naval vessel, and an escort in the Holy Land.

Mewling infidel that you are, I suspect that you question the spiritual value of the pilgrimage (I should have had you burned at the stake years ago). But Andreas may well return a better man, and his wife and daughter better women. I will pray for their safe travels (and as always, for your imperiled soul).

Keep your spirits up, Jan. I am confident this will end well for our impetuous friend.

With devotion,
Antoine

Your prediction could not have been more wrong, Antoine.

I put the letters away and went to the table by the window and watched the bare branches of my young oak tree quaver in the wind.

Marcus came with a steaming cup of chocolate.

"Marcus."

"Master Jan?"

"Begin thinking about a voyage. A long voyage."

His expression did not change. "Our travel chests are as moldy as old wheels of cheese, and will not last two days' travel. The boots you wore back from Spain are not fit for a beggar."

"See to them, then, and anything else in need of attention."

"Where are we going?"

"Greece."

Marcus nodded, his face showing no surprise.

"Are you feeling ready for another voyage, Marcus? I know we've just returned from Spain."

"It is you who must feel ready. With respect, Master Jan, at your age travel does not get any easier. Your knees grind like millstones. The voyage to Spain was a hardship, especially the mountains."

"It was a hardship, I admit, but it was the last time I saw Andreas alive. I must make this journey to say farewell, and as for my knees, I will endure them. Don't be too smug—you're not getting any younger."

"Aye, but unlike you, I enjoy the road."

Marcus left me. Out the window in the garden, a squirrel scampered across the frozen ground, for some reason roused from its warm nest. It stopped below my window and reared up on its hind legs, its tail twitching. There was a naked scar on the top of its head. Were you in a fight, or did you fall? It fixed its gaze in my direction for several moments, then raced up the trunk of the little oak tree and along a low branch, disappearing over the wall.

"May your journey be safe and short, squirrel," I heard myself say.

I was furious at you for going on your pilgrimage, and now I will go on one of my own, to you. Our last farewell will be at your grave. I am terrified of this voyage, but I will do it. And this time I will come to you unbidden.

Then I remembered Anne and young Anna, not yet nineteen, just a few streets away reckoning with the same shattering news. I had been remiss in not going to them sooner, but the prospect filled me with apprehension because without Andreas things had become unstuck.

21 January 1565

As a cold rain fell on Brussels, I wrote a letter to Antoine:

Dear Antoine,

It is only today that I have the strength to hold a pen. I wish we were not separated by such a distance now that you have gone home to Ornans from so nearby at the Archdiocese of Mechelen. I know the Netherlander Protestants were making your life miserable, and you needed to escape to France for a rest.

I do not overlook your own mourning. He was your friend, too. Please bear no remorse for not changing the king's mind; I understand the delicacy of the situation for you. In the end it was Andreas who chose to make the journey.

I have decided to go to Zante. It is not the most rational of decisions, but I am compelled to see his grave for myself; I cannot live out my days with just a fantasy of where he will be forever.

I am not so foolish that I will travel alone; my assistant Marcus will keep me out of trouble. We will by all means pass through Ornans to see you, a visit I anticipate with all my heart.

I am summoning the courage to see Anne and her daughter Anna.

Your devoted friend,
Jan

I readied a candle to make a seal, but my wax stick was nowhere in sight. I groped under my desk for the box of sealing wax, and then got on my hands and knees to look for it. The box was far under the desk, up against something I had not seen in many years: my leather bag from primary school. I pulled it out and dusted it off with my sleeve. I opened the flap to the smell of old leather and stale air. I felt inside; it was empty except for cobwebs and an old inkwell. I closed the bag and cradled it in my arms.

The King's Anatomist

Our first day at the Brethren School was in the fall of 1520; we were not quite six years old. Mother dressed me in my Sunday doublet, breeches, and hose. She tied a cape around my shoulders, and wiping tears from her face as well as mine, put a black velvet cap on my head. Draping my new leather school bag over my shoulder, she embraced me and watched from the doorway as my father led me to our carriage at the curb. Once I was in the cabin, he leaned in and made sure I understood that my schoolmates would come from the most important families in Brussels, and that I was to represent our family in the best light.

"Off you go, then," he said, signaling to our carriage-man Roderick. I peered through the rear window as we pulled away and watched Mother recede into the distance; when I could no longer see her, I sat trembling, as alone and helpless as I had ever been in my life. In a few minutes we were at the entrance of the Brethren of the Common Life School, an aging brick-and-timber row house on Place de Saint-Géry. Roderick gave me a few gentle claps on the back and handed me off to a stern-faced friar who led me inside and up a flight of stairs. At the first floor he placed me at the doorway of what was to be my classroom, then left me there without a word. I patted my pocket to make sure Jorgen had come along.

I peered into what seemed like a vast room with two-seated wooden desks on either side of a center aisle. I counted ten desks on each side of the aisle, which meant the classroom could hold forty boys. I had never before been with even five boys at once. Many boys, neatly dressed but in everyday shirts, vests, and breeches, had already arrived and been seated; a few turned to see who had arrived at the door. I recognized some of them, but could count none as friends. One boy nearby, who I knew as Jakab, looked me up and down and snickered at my clothes. I reddened and looked away.

The air smelled of smoke and tallow. A heating stove, bookshelves, and a jumbled group of wrought-iron candle stands lined the wall to my left. The wall opposite had four windows; a painting between the two middle windows was of a golden-haloed child Jesus holding an open book as he stood before a schoolmaster.

Atop a platform at the front of the room was the schoolmaster, in a black robe and red cap, bent over his lectern. He stopped writing and peered at me, then motioned me to the front with a hand emerging from his robe. I touched my pocket for Jorgen and started down the center aisle, my footsteps seeming to crash onto the checkered floor tiles. As I neared the front, I saw tight bundles of birch-branch rods leaning in the corner, and two wooden paddles hanging on nails nearby.

I stopped under the lectern, taking off my cap and squeezing it till my knuckles turned white.

"And you are Master . . .?"

"Jan van den Bossche, Sire," bowing my head as I had been taught.

"Be seated, Master van den Bossche," he said, pointing to the desk beside me, and went back to his writing.

My desk was so close to him I could hear the scratching of his quill. I sat and slid over to the seat away from the aisle, slipping my book bag off my shoulder. Inside was a Latin grammar, a wax writing tablet and stylus, an inkwell, and my bone-handled pen with a copper nib. It was an extravagance for a child, but Mother preferred this to my having to sharpen goose quills with a pen-knife.

I heard more footsteps at the doorway, continuing without hesitation into the room and down to the front. The schoolmaster peered over his lectern at the boy standing next to my desk.

"It appears you have chosen a seat for yourself, Master . . .?"

"If it pleases you, Sire. I am Andreas Vesalius."

"I have no objection, Master Vesalius. Be seated, then, next to Master van den Bossche."

I glanced up at the schoolmaster and thought I saw a smile at the corners of his mouth.

My new neighbor bowed to the schoolmaster and sat. He turned to me and spoke, barely above a whisper, but his words rang in my ears as if he shouted them.

"Hello, I'm Andreas."

I glanced nervously up at the lectern. "I am Jan."

"Well then, Jan, we shall be friends. I'm glad to be sitting in the front, aren't you?"

The front of the room was in fact the last place I wished to be, but the friendly greeting from Andreas calmed me. He was short and stocky; seated, his feet did not quite reach the floor. Below his dark, curly hair and a wide forehead, his deep brown eyes shone with energy. Above his right eyebrow there was a dark birthmark the size of a lentil.

Andreas turned about in his seat to inspect the classroom, and noticed the painting of Jesus.

"I'll wager he never felt a birch rod on his ass," he whispered, nodding at the painting. I couldn't help but smile; he was right; who would birch Jesus?

The schoolmaster rose, came around his lectern, and cast his eyes around the room with his hands clasped in front of him. He was tall and thin, with searching blue eyes deeply set in a clean-shaven, lined face. He broke into a smile.

"By God's grace I welcome you. You will call me Brother Carel. Please stand when called so I can learn your names. And before I forget . . . there are pisspots in the rear corner, and there is a closet in the hall for different calls of nature. If you need to relieve yourself, just go quietly and return quietly."

Brother Carel called the roll in alphabetical order. Finally my name was called, and right after mine, that of Andreas. Brother Carel turned the pages of his ledger back and forth.

"I see that we have twins in this class. Look about, students, do you see them?"

Some boys did not move; others risked furtive glances at their neighbors. But my desk-mate stood and studied the faces of the other students. He then turned to the schoolmaster.

"Brother Carel, could you be mistaken? I do not see twins."

Someone behind me gasped at Andreas' insolence. Surely Andreas had earned the first beating of the school year. But Brother Carel smiled.

"Ah, but these twins look nothing like each other. For the answer, Master Vesalius, you need look no further than your own desk."

Andreas and I looked at each other, puzzled, as Brother Carel spoke to the entire class.

"Masters van den Bossche and Vesalius were born on the same day,

December 31, 1514, in their homes just a few streets apart. Alas, we are not privy to the exact hour of their births, but by the stars, they are not only Capricorns, but as united as natural twins—astral twins. And how remarkable," he went on, looking down at us, "that you are seated together! Have you known of each other before today?"

We both shook our heads.

"Then Heaven has brought about this meeting. May you both prosper from your newfound kinship."

Andreas smiled at me, wide-eyed and shrugging his shoulders. I returned his smile; I had made a friend who was my astral twin, and Brother Carel had shown himself less of a menace than I feared. This would not be the last time I would admire Andreas for his courage, though the outcomes were not always as favorable.

That my first year at the Brethren School was in Brother Carel's classroom was momentous—not only because of Andreas, but because no other schoolmaster in the ten years we spent at the Brethren School was as kind and good-humored. It was not long before I stopped bringing Jorgen to school. The birch rods and paddles never budged from their corner in his classroom, or were even mentioned as a threat. The same could not be said of any schoolmaster to follow, but by that time I had gained a foothold as a schoolboy.

Brother Carel was removed from his post after our first year. We learned that it was because he spoke not unfavorably to us about Martin Luther. It was rumored that Brother Carel had gone to Germany to join him.

The reverie over, I placed the school bag on a nearby shelf; it would not do to send it back into the shadows.

My letter to Antoine was still unsealed and open on the desk. As I readied the wax, my eyes fell on one sentence: *I am summoning the courage to see Anne.*

I would think nothing over the years of calling at Vesalius House unannounced, and since May, when Anne and Anna turned up in Brussels without Andreas, we kept frequent company on walks, carriage rides, picnics, or parlor games on rainy afternoons. On occasion she would convince me to escort her to a social event. But Andreas' death shook the ground under us; why had we not, this past terrible week, sought each other out?

The following morning I scratched out a note:

22 January

Dearest Anne,
You and Anna have been foremost in my thoughts as I grapple with my own heartbreak.
I very much wish to see you, but only when you feel ready for a visit. In the meanwhile I am at your service to be of help in any way.

With sincerest affection,
Jan

I was unhappy at resorting to this stiff little note as a substitute for taking myself to her door. But I left it as it was and sealed it.

I sent Marcus to deliver the letter. I sat by the window in the study and looked out over my desolate winter garden. It had only to wait for spring for its renewal, but there was no season for my own desolation. I hoped that going to Greece would help.

Anne responded the next morning.

23 January

Dear Jan,
Please come this afternoon. Anna and I look forward to seeing you.

Anne

I was relieved to hear from her, but her spare and detached note left me uneasy. I flipped it over to the blank side and back again, as if searching for a clue to her feelings. I stared out the window into the distance, my thoughts wandering back through time.

On a spring Sunday in May of 1541, in my twenty-seventh year, Anne van Hamme and her parents strode up to my family after mass to introduce themselves. The van Hammes had just moved to Brussels from nearby Vilvoorde; her father had taken a position in the Chamber of Accounts.

I was typically anxiety-riddled at gatherings or in making acquaintances, but Anne's striking appearance rendered me unable to meet her eyes or produce a coherent sentence. She was slender and graceful, with an engaging smile; her raven hair framed a sculpted face with eyes of deep blue set against flawless skin. I was sure she had seen enough of me, but the next Sunday she sought me out. I managed to make some conversation, and when we parted, she said, "Will I see you next Sunday, Master van den Bossche?"

Mother no longer had to coax me to go to church with her; Anne's engaging way broke through my defenses, and we sought each other out after mass. She was five years my junior, yet possessed of a keen wit sharpened by a thorough tutored education. She was thrilled to have moved from the sleepy town of Vilvoorde to Brussels, where she could take clavichord lessons and sing in a big choir.

One Sunday she asked me if I would walk her home, as her parents had gone off to visit an ailing friend. Walking Anne home from church became the routine, and after a while we would meet during the week for a walk or a carriage ride.

On an afternoon walk in a park near her house she stopped on the path.

"You never speak of your work in mathematics."

"It would only bore you."

"I'll be the judge of that." She gave me a playful shove. "Speak now or I shall never speak to you again."

"Then you leave me no choice. My main interest is in determining the precise areas of irregular flat shapes."

"What do you mean by 'irregular shapes'?"

"I mean any shape that you cannot readily name. Here . . ." I picked up a stick from the side of the path and handed it to Anne.

"Draw a shape in the path. Use straight sides, curved sides, anything you wish. It just needs to be enclosed."

"Very well." She stood for a moment with the stick poised over the surface of the path.

"Anything I wish?"

"Anything."

She traced a series of connected arcs, paused for a moment, and then joined the ends of the series of arcs with jagged lines meeting at a point below the arcs.

"There," she said.

I nodded in approval. "A splendidly irregular shape. Let's call it an 'anne-agon' in your honor. So, how would we go about finding the area inside your anne-agon?"

Anne cocked her head. "I don't know."

"You're not alone. Now, suppose you had drawn a regular shape that has a name, like a square, or a rectangle . . ."

"Now I am in familiar territory—the area would be the product of two sides joined at a corner."

"Right you are. Unfortunately there is no such rule for your anne-agon, but there is a way to approach the problem. With geometry and algebra, one can calculate the areas of regular shapes like rectangles, parallelograms, triangles, polygons, rhomboids, and circles. But there's no method to determine the areas of irregular shapes—shapes for which ordinary rules do not apply."

"Intriguing. How did you arrive at this problem?"

"The butcher shop on the way to school had a sign in the shape of a pig; what was the area within that pig? My toy boat had a lateen sail— three sides were straight, but one was curved; what was the area of the sail? As I sat with my mother in church, I had the same problem with stained glass windows that had parallel sides rising up until they curved toward each other and came to a point."

"Hmm. Rather unusual dilemmas for a young child." With the stick, she rapped me gently on the seat of my pants. "And you were naughty for not attending to your prayers."

I laughed and blushed, snatching the stick from her.

"So, then," she said, returning the laughter, "back to your problem with certain stained glass windows."

"Well. It came to me that the stained glass windows were composed of smaller pieces of glass that together made up the whole. I imagined that if those pieces were all of regular shapes, their areas could be calculated and summed to get the area of the window. Here, let me show you on your anne-agon."

Using the stick I began to draw lines within the shape. "Look, we can start to break it up into triangles, rectangles, and circles . . ."

"I see what you're getting at. What a clever boy you were!"

"Not as clever as you think. When I presented my discovery to my tutor, he praised me for being ahead of my lessons, but that I was seventeen centuries late to the idea. The Greek mathematician Archimedes had come up with the same technique; it is called the 'method of exhaustion.' You fill an irregular shape with the biggest regular shape possible, then start filling the remaining spaces with smaller regular shapes—but you can only go so far; you are always left with a number of small irregular spaces. If you ignore those, you can arrive at the approximate area of the whole shape, but not the precise area."

"But then you can fill those small irregular spaces with even smaller regular shapes."

"Now who's being clever! But you can never fill the spaces completely with regular shapes, even if you kept going down to the tiniest imaginable level."

"I would think that at some point you would be satisfied."

"For many purposes, yes, but wouldn't it be much more satisfying to know the precise area? And there may be good reason someday for that level of precision. At any rate, think of the tedium of adding up the areas of countless shapes, and still be left with only an approximation."

"Well then, the 'method of exhaustion' is aptly named."

I laughed. "It is indeed."

The King's Anatomist

"And besides, Jan, there is no end to the infinite. With this method, how would you ever get to the precise area?"

"That's the crux of the problem—Archimedes was trying to describe a way to reach the end of that infinite series of smaller and smaller shapes."

"How can there be an end to an infinite series? It is a troubling notion. It sounds like no more than a logical contradiction. It gives me a headache to think about it."

"It is the same headache I have," I said. "But I believe there must be an answer."

As we continued talking, Anne was equally interested in hearing about my travels to France and Italy, which led us to my long friendship with Andreas, hard at work in Padua teaching medicine and writing his textbook of anatomy.

"I'll be happy to meet this professor friend of yours who lures you away so often."

"You'll meet him, I assure you."

Mother, meanwhile, had put Anne under immediate scrutiny after that first encounter in church and did not hesitate to make known her assessment. One Sunday she saw us exchange smiles across a row of pews as we filed out of church.

"You can do better than Anne van Hamme," she whispered. "She is rather small-framed, don't you think, and quite free with her tongue."

"Don't worry, Mother. If I marry, I promise it will be to someone plump as a hen and quiet as a mouse."

Mother's disapproval, her most potent weapon of control, could still wound me, but not enough to cripple my friendship with Anne.

A letter came from Andreas in August of that year asking me to come to Padua; he was struggling with his as yet unnamed book and feuding with the artist, a Netherlander named Stephan van Calcar. Anne insisted that before I left I spend the day in Vilvoorde at her family home.

We took a rowboat out on the pond behind the house and then walked for a while. We were nearing the house when she asked me if I was ready for the voyage.

"As ready as I can be," I said. "It's a long way to Padua."

"Are you sure you must go, then?"

"Andreas sounds desperate in his letters. He needs me to steady things between him and his artist Calcar, or the whole project will be in peril."

"How I yearn to see Italy! If I were a man, I could go with you without raising an eyebrow," she said. She suddenly skipped ahead a pace and whirled around to face me, blocking my way. We were only inches apart.

"Did you ever want to kiss me, Jan?"

The idea had occurred to me more than once, but I had not dared to try.

She wrapped her arms around my waist and pulled herself to me. She rose up on her toes and kissed me, her lips softly on mine for several long seconds.

"There," she said, letting go and stepping away. "If you won't take me, at least take that to Padua. I will miss you." She took my hand. "Come," pulling me through the gate, "we're late for lunch."

I left mid-afternoon after a foggy succession of lunch, some songs in the parlor from Anne at the clavichord, and another boat ride on the pond with the van Hamme family. Anne stood with her family and bade me goodbye as I rode off. I was back in Brussels by sunset, and two days later on my way to Padua with Anne's kiss still lingering on my mouth.

The looming visit to Anne at Vesalius House pushed these memories aside. Still in my hand was her note, a far cry from the letters she wrote during my year in Padua with Andreas; they were at once revealing, startling, and admirable, and deepened my feelings for her. A few snippets jumped out at me:

> ... I much enjoyed reading your letter packed with news of Padua, and of your valiant efforts to keep the peace between your headstrong friend Andreas and the equally headstrong artist Calcar. But with you as mediator, I am certain the fires of conflict will yield excellent results, as copper and tin yield bronze...

. . . My parents don't know what to make of me, nor I them. They have provided me with an excellent education, and I feel as learned as the men I know—excluding you, of course—yet they would have me aspire to no more than finding a husband, running a household, and having children. They are not satisfied when I tell them these will come in their own time. . .

. . . Meanwhile, I try to fill my time with worthwhile endeavors. I am preparing for a recital on the church clavichord to take place next week. My uncle has agreed to teach me chess so I can humble you when you return . . .

. . . I have decided to hold a salon at my house, a salon for women. There are a few women at church who, like me, find tiresome and restrictive the usual patter and gossip that passes for conversation among women. We would rather discuss issues of the day, or books we have read. I quarreled with my parents before they consented, and of the six women who expressed interest, three have been forbidden by their husbands to attend. But I will hold the first salon nevertheless . . .

. . . Are the irregular shapes in Padua just as baffling as those in Brussels? I am teasing, but someday I would like to find out for myself! The argument that travel is too dangerous for women is specious. I can ride a horse and walk all day. And I will use a dagger If need be . . .

The stream of letters that year between Anne and me did not escape Andreas' notice.

"Who is this Anne van Hamme?" you asked. "You write to her more than you write to your mother."
"She is new to Brussels. We have become friends."
"Friends?"

"Friends. We would be better friends if I didn't need to be here keeping you out of trouble."

"Duly noted. I'll wager she runs away screaming when you talk about mathematics."

"She has more interest and aptitude for it than you."

"If that's true she must be quite clever. Is she as comely as she is clever?"

"You can judge that for yourself when you meet her."

"So I shall. Say, what does your mother think of her? Not that I don't know the answer!"

I pushed open the wrought iron gate of Vesalius House and walked up to the massive oak doors. Mounted above them was the Vesalius family crest, a shield with three weasels in full extension stacked in a row.

It wasn't enough that you married Anne. You had to build this, too.

The house Andreas erected in honor of his marriage to Anne was a three-story stone monolith with a large central courtyard, looming over most other houses in the vicinity and rivaling my childhood home in every way. Within the walls of the property were servant's quarters, a carriage house, and a garden with fruit trees. While Andreas had no shortage of money—his imperial physician's salary was augmented by family assets—I had urged him to reconsider the scale of the project, showing him that the construction and upkeep of the house would put a strain on his finances.

To this Andreas merely shrugged. "I won't live in an airless little hut like yours." He went ahead with no change in the plans.

I smiled at the sight of the bronze door knocker. Andreas had designed it himself—an idealized proximal shaft of a human femur that hung upside down and swung away from the door, allowing the ball-shaped head of the femur on its return to strike a cup-shaped strike-plate, itself fashioned after the acetabulum of the pelvis. "Is this house inhabited by cannibals?" Anne complained when it was installed, but she had no choice but to accept it.

A handmaiden well known to me let me in and took my hat and cloak. The ghostly outline of a painting that had hung in the front hall caught my eye; it was now propped up under the stairs.

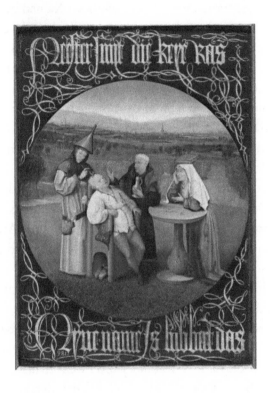

"The Extraction of the Stone of Madness" was a wedding gift from Antoine, who had found time to become one of the great art collectors in Europe. His eye for talent guided his selections, trusting that the value of his purchases would declare themselves over time. In this painting, a charlatan doctor wearing a funnel for a hat probes inside a man's head to remove the eponymous and mystical stone.

Antoine, ever the prankster, had selected Hieronymus Bosch's superb and bitingly satirical painting for Andreas knowing that he would love the joke, but could not have foreseen it ending up in the front hall.

Anne did not disguise her dislike of it, and even amidst the turmoil of the past week she seized the opportunity to take it down. I wondered if the door knocker was next.

I took myself to the sitting room and sat down on the edge of a chair near the large hearth, recently set with a fire. Above the hearth Andreas had awarded his three weasels a commanding position. A vaulted ceiling towered over the room; a row of large windows framed by floor-length curtains took up much of the wall opposite the hearth. The architect correctly sensed in his client an opportunity to embellish the sitting room with wall moldings, mirrors, and wall panels painted with pastoral scenes. Andreas' appetite for ostentation had been whetted by my childhood home; I had had more than enough of it, but Andreas had not yet gotten his fill.

Too anxious to sit, I paced back and forth in front of the hearth. The sitting room door at last opened to admit Anne and Anna, both wearing black brocaded mourning dresses closed at the neck with lace collars. The full-length sleeves ended at snug, lace-trimmed cuffs. For warmth in the chilly house they wore black caps and short capes. Anna, the very image of her mother, rushed past Anne, and abandoning formalities embraced me, resting her head on my chest.

I put my hand gently on her head. "I am so sorry about your father. We will all miss him terribly."

Anna burst into tears. Finally she let go and backed away, realizing that I had not yet greeted her mother. I looked beyond Anna to Anne, standing a few paces back. Without a word I went to her, and we shared an awkward embrace. Our eyes were both filled with tears.

"It is good to see you, Jan."

Dabbing her eyes with a handkerchief, she turned to Anna. "Uncle Jan and I must talk."

"Mama, can't I . . ."

"Anna."

"Yes, Mama." She turned to me. "Goodbye, Uncle. Will you come again soon?"

"Of course," I said. "I have some puzzles for you to solve, but they may be too easy for you."

She managed a smile and left the room, closing the door softly behind her.

We stood in place, avoiding each other's eyes, until Anne went to a chair near the hearth, gathering her cape around her shoulders. I started for the seat next to her but veered to a chair. I leaned forward with my elbows on my knees, looking at my boots and back up at Anne, who gazed past me.

She seemed to have aged very little since that Sunday in May twenty-four years earlier. She still moved with the grace of a young woman, and the streaks of grey in her hair and the faint lines at the corners of her eyes burnished her features.

The fire in the hearth crackled loudly. It startled us both and shook me into finding something to say.

"It was kind of Antoine to write us with the news," I said, "as hard as it was for him. He was a good friend to Andreas, and was honored to conduct your wedding. Few people are married by a bishop, let alone one who becomes a Cardinal."

My chatter echoed about the room like a misplayed chord. I fussed with the cuff of my doublet until I found more pertinent words.

"How are you faring?"

"We are holding on. The only relief is that the waiting is over. But you and Andreas spent your lives together, and you were astral twins," she said, managing a smile. "I have heard the stories."

"And you had the patience to listen," I said, smiling back.

The smile vanished from her face. "The waiting would have been much harder to endure without you."

"I feel the same."

These months with Anne since her return to Brussels have passed happily, even as your silence hung over us. We were with each other as we were before you entered her life, with the added joy of Anna, the image of her mother with a talent for mathematics, a talent that did not pass to her from her father. It becomes increasingly difficult to think of Anne as just a friend. In truth, I suppose I never did.

Alive or dead, Runt, you make things very difficult for me.

"In a short while I will leave for Greece."

She looked up in surprise, but her expression quickly softened.

"It's fitting that you go; he was your best friend. You understand that a voyage like that for Anna and me is out of the question."

"Of course. And I'm not sure it is the wisest decision for me, either."

"It will be a long journey. I almost wish you wouldn't go . . ."

Before I could think of something to say, she added, "Besides, given your distaste for travel, Andreas will be all the more surprised by your visit."

We shared a moment of strained laughter. I decided to venture a question I had avoided for months.

"What of the pilgrimage, Anne? You don't like to speak of it. You know how shocked I was when he wrote me of his plans, so shortly after I saw him last year in Monzón. I heard the usual complaints about the Spanish physicians, but otherwise he seemed like his old self."

Anne pulled at the edges of her cape. "You know as much as I. He groused to me as well about the Spanish court and Philip's ban on dissection, which he dared not violate. When we lived in Brussels—before Philip took us to Spain—nothing could keep him from his cadavers in the cellar." Her face contorted. "God knows how he got them."

"You know how he got them."

She conceded the point with a shrug. "He could be down there all night and come up in the morning bleary-eyed, smelling of them. I have never once been down to the cellar. He wanted to take Anna down, but I would not allow it."

"Anatomy was his passion."

Anne did not know you when you kept body parts under your bed.

Her voice rose. "Where was his passion when he quit Padua to serve Emperor Charles, and then his son Philip after Charles abdicated?"

Her face was flushed, but she quickly regained her composure.

"You were asking about Spain. I wanted to visit with you in Monzón, but I could not . . . arrange for the journey. When Andreas got back to Madrid, he mentioned he had been sick." Her face darkened. "In the next breath he told me of the pilgrimage. With the king's blessing, we would go to the Holy Land."

"You had no other words with him?"

"We had quite a few words. But you know Andreas; it was a settled matter. He told me only what he told you—the pilgrimage was in gratitude for his recovery. As for me, I was fearful of such a long voyage to a barbarous part of the world, especially with Anna . . ."

She stopped mid-sentence. "The truth is that I loathed Spain, and any respite from that country seemed worth the risk. I stopped arguing with him."

"Andreas told me only that you felt homesick sometimes. Your letters never . . ."

". . . I did not want to trouble you."

"If I knew you were unhappy I would have come to Madrid."

We sat in silence until I spoke again.

"Did he say anything about Padua?"

"Padua? Only that he wanted to show us the university as we passed through to Venice."

Did you not tell Anne about the offer to reclaim your anatomy chair in Padua, and the king's denial?

I was relieved she did not press me. I lacked the will and the heart to open that Pandora's Box.

Anne stood. "I must not keep you any longer," she said, "and I could use a rest. I'll walk you to the front door."

She took a step toward me. "Anna would be happy to see you again soon. She is very fond of her Uncle Jan." She glanced away from me and back again.

"You need not ask," I said.

At the front door I took her hands in mine. "May we both have the strength to see this through."

She squeezed my hands, her eyes searching my face, then laid her forehead on my chest. We embraced each other for a long moment, at which time she turned and left me without looking back.

The sun sat low above the rooftops, but the evening chill had not yet settled over the city. I decided to take a walk before going home.

My legs took me to Place de Saint-Géry. I crossed over to the Brethren of the Common Life School and sat down on the steps. The chill of the coming dusk crept under my cloak; I pulled the collar tight. A few carriages pulled up as the doors at the top of the stairs flew open. Students poured out onto the street, sidestepping me. The carriages took on their young passengers and rode off, leaving a few boys laughing and shoving each other on the sidewalk, but in a matter of minutes they had dispersed.

Without you, Andreas, this place would have been a living hell for me; even with Brother Carel, my fragile spirit would have been shattered into a thousand pieces. You were my first friend, my only friend. I devoted myself to please you always, and displease you never—to be a perfect friend. I did not understand what you saw in me—as inept, quiet, and fearful as I was—but I was grateful beyond knowing for your friendship, and I strove to be worthy of you.

I was an easy target for bullying, but you kept the bullies away, even fought with them. I followed you like a stray dog and copied what you did: playing schoolyard games; shoving back when shoved; elbowing my way to the food bowls on the dining hall table to serve myself, something I had never done. I learned from you that farting and throwing food was funny, even at the risk of a beating—a risk that, unlike you, I was rarely willing to take.

You always admired the bone-handled pen my mother got for me. I loved that pen, but one day I gave it to you. "Are you sure?" you asked. "Yes, it's a gift. I want you to have it." A few days later I told my mother I lost it. She was very cross. For a while I used quills, but she got me another pen. You were careful not to use it in our house until years later; by then, she had forgotten the incident.

I fought with her to let me walk to school with you, and she would not have relented had my father not interceded on my behalf. It was a while before I moved as confidently as you through the clamor of horses, wagons, beggars, street vendors, mud, and filth, but I learned that in those streets there was freedom in disorder; we made our way to school and back as we pleased, not always the same way, stopping to watch workers dig a hole or to peer into a store window—especially the butcher shop that fascinated you so, with its trays of bloody kidneys, livers, brains, and hearts on display.

On the more leisurely walks home we would sometimes talk about our families. You told me that your father was apothecary to Emperor Charles V, and that your grandfather, great-grandfather, and great-great-grandfather were imperial physicians.

"What does your father do?" you asked.

"My father and grandfather call themselves traders."

"How does that work?"

"I'm not sure exactly. They buy and sell things that come and go on wagons and boats. I also hear talk of boats that bring savages from Africa across the ocean to labor in the New World, where they are traded for things that come to Europe."

"Well, however it works to be a trader, it's made your family rich."

The square was now dark, and I could no longer sit on the cold steps. I stood to leave, not without objection from my knees, and set out for home.

From you I learned the ways of a schoolboy. But I needed no help with my lessons; Brother Carel discovered why, even before I told you.

In primary school, individual students were called to the schoolmaster's lectern for instruction while the rest of the class worked. The first time Brother Carel called on me to do sums, he handed me a wax tablet with a column of numbers and a stylus.

"Do the sum on this tablet; use the abacus if you wish," he said, and turned back to his ledger. I looked at the slate, inscribed the sum at the bottom, and handed him the tablet. He put down his quill and frowned.

"Are you jesting, Master van den Bossche? You could not have completed this sum so quickly."

I felt my face flush. "I am sorry, Brother Carel, but this is the answer."

He did the sum himself, glanced quizzically at me, and with the broad, flat base of the stylus, smoothed over the wax to erase the first problem and composed another. This time, he watched me. I again looked at the column of numbers and wrote down the answer.

"Here, let me have that." He did the sum himself and put the tablet down while I stood anxiously by. Finally he said, "How, my son, do you do these sums?"

"I look at the numbers and they just—arrange themselves."

"They just arrange themselves."

"Yes, Brother Carel." I was about to cry. "Is this is a sinful thing?"

He put his hand on my shoulder. "On the contrary, Master van den Bossche. God has granted you a rare gift. Tell me, when did you find out that numbers can . . . arrange themselves?"

"When I started doing sums with my tutor. He never knew I could do sums this way. His sums were very easy."

"Have you told anyone else about this?"

"No, Brother Carel."

"Not your parents?"

"No, Brother Carel."

"Why not?"

"Because I fear my mother will think it is magic, and she believes magic is sinful."

"I see." Brother Carel cocked his head and leaned toward me. "Do you have any other . . . abilities like this?"

"No, Brother Carel. Except, well, I remember things."

"Remember what things?"

"Like pages in a book, or what someone says."

"How long can you remember them?"

"I never don't remember them, Brother Carel."

He sat back in his chair. "Very well. You may sit down."

The next day, Brother Carel called me again to the lectern.

"Can you tell me what the last sum was that you did with me yesterday?"

"Yes, Brother Carel." I told him.

"So it was." He picked up a tablet from his desk. "Could you do a sum if you did not see the numbers, but just heard them?"

"Yes, Brother Carel."

"Let's see." He read a series of numbers from the tablet. I gave him the sum.

"Correct."

He set down the tablet. "Master van den Bossche, have you ever seen different kinds of mathematics?"

"Different kinds?"

"Kinds that are not just sums, subtraction, and so on—kinds that are used to solve problems."

"No, Brother Carel."

"Very well. There is a kind of mathematics that has been known in parts since before Christ, but Persian mathematicians made an entire discipline of it. They called it 'algebra.' I would like to teach you what I know of it."

Brother Carel kept his promise. When he could, during recess, he sat with me and showed me how a letter could stand for a number, how these letters were used in mathematical sentences called equations, and how equations could be used to solve problems. My heart opened to this new language.

Andreas asked me what I was doing with Brother Carel during my absences from the courtyard. "Learning a kind of mathematics called algebra," I said.

"Oh," he replied with a shrug.

Near the end of the school year, Brother Carel told me that he had taught me all that he knew.

"I wish I had more to offer you, Master van de Bossche, but I will think about how we can continue your studies."

Brother Carel bid his class goodbye on the last day of school without another word to me about mathematics. But when I got home that day, my father led me into his study and presented me with a 1494 copy of *Summa de arithmetica, geometria, proportioni et proportionalita* by Luca Pacioli. The *Summa* was written in Italian, but my father also acquired a translation.

"I gather you have shown some talent in mathematics. This book has sections on algebra and geometry. The bookseller looked doubtful when I told him you were seven years old, but I told him he had not met this seven-year-old."

He gave me a pat on the head. I clutched the books to my chest, overcome, until I could say, "Thank you, Father."

He looked away as I wiped my tears with my sleeve.

"There is also a chapter on business accounting," he said. "Be sure to learn that—it may be useful later on."

"Yes, Father, I will."

"Ah, one other thing. I have arranged for a tutor to spend some time with you at school every month to help you along. He is most interested to meet you."

Then, he crouched down to whisper in my ear.

"We will not tell your mother about any of this, will we? Your... way with numbers might make her uneasy."

By the following spring I had gone through the book with my tutor. It went well beyond Brother Carel's lessons, and at the same time, I developed a familiarity with Italian. To this day, my childhood copy of the *Summa* rests on a nearby shelf in my study. It holds nothing to offer me now, but I would never part with it.

With Mother's wary consent, Andreas and I started to visit each other's homes.

On his first visit I led Andreas through the gardens and stables and took him to my room, but he insisted on a tour of the house to inspect the ornate furniture, paintings, and tapestries. In a hallway we made room for two housekeepers scurrying past us with armfuls of bedding. He turned to me and laughed.

"There are far more servants in this house than people who live here."

I shrugged. "I suppose so."

When invited to stay for dinner, he rose to the occasion with respectful conversation and impeccable table manners—a far cry from his mealtime behavior at school. My mother was not swayed by his show of breeding and would remain forever suspicious of Andreas, but my father took a keen liking to him.

The Vesalius house was just as eye-opening to me, but for different reasons. It was well-appointed, to be sure, but Madam Vesalius did not aspire to my mother's standards of housekeeping. Did the two housekeepers not see the fingerprints on the furniture? Did they not know where butter knives are placed in a setting? Did they not see the dust balls gathering in corners? To my astonishment, the three Vesalius boys—Nicholas, Andreas, and young Franciscus—were permitted to run through the house and raise their voices. If Andreas' room was in disorder, it was his job, not a servant's, to put things right.

Andreas' father was often away on campaigns with Charles V, leaving Madam Vesalius to preside. At meals she expected good table manners but dispensed with formalities; she permitted, and often provoked, raucous debates that would horrify my parents.

But my greatest wonderment was entering the Vesalius library for the first time. It was smaller than ours and sparsely furnished, designed for study rather than as a showy refuge for men to discuss business and drink brandy. From the doorway, two walls of books ran the length of the room; at the far end was a long table with four plain chairs. Two skylights overhead admitted natural light. The smell of books and creaking floorboards underfoot lent the room an august sensibility.

"What kind of books are here?" I asked, looking around at the shelves.

"Mostly medicine and botany, but also some mathematics, philosophy, and astronomy. My great-great-grandfather started the library, so we have old manuscripts as well as printed books that my father and grandfather have added. See here, a commentary on Avicenna written by my great-great-grandfather. Almost everything here is in Latin, so I need to be expert in Latin."

I was drawn to a shelf with a few hymnals and Books of Hours, hand-written and decorated centuries ago on paper or vellum for Christians of wealth and nobility. Mother had several, but I was forbidden to touch them. I imagined the monks toiling in silent scriptoria of remote monasteries, creating page after page of meticulous calligraphy and rich illustrations. On occasion, they were moved to draw flourishes in the margins: intricate geometric and floral designs or fanciful creatures. In these marginalia the souls of those monks drew breath and sang, if only for a few stolen moments.

Andreas and I would return to his library to do schoolwork or play chess. He was a willing opponent, usually gracious in defeat, but hard on himself after a careless blunder. His game would always be limited by impulsivity.

In the Vesalius library one afternoon in our last year at the Brethren School, as Andreas labored over an algebra problem I climbed up the ladder to a high shelf looking for something amusing to read. I spotted a book propped up behind other books and pulled it out. I blew a cloud of dust off its cover, and opened to the title page. I gasped when I read the title: *On the Nature of Things*, by the Roman Titus Lucretius Carus. Written shortly before the birth of Christ, it had gone lost until it was rediscovered a century earlier in a German monastery. In school we were told it was filled with pagan heresies.

The title page bore the imprint "Thomas Ferrandus, Brescia, 1473," and was signed at the bottom by Everard van Wesele, Andreas' grandfather.

Was this book intentionally hidden? I was surprised to see that it was in verse, in the cadence favored by the great Roman poets. I paged through, landing on random passages, astounded at what I was reading.

Below me Andreas tossed his quill onto the table. "What are you doing up there, Scarecrow?"

"Be quiet. I'm coming down."

I climbed down and put the book next to my bag.

"What's that?" he asked, glancing at the book.

"An old geometry text," I lied.

"That figures. Now, quickly end my misery with this problem. You're lucky. You get the answers without even thinking. You'd be really stupid without that mind trick of yours."

I shrugged and examined his paper. "You're on the right track, but then you make careless errors. Be quick, Andreas, but don't hurry. You're much more deliberate in Latin, and it pays off."

"That's because Latin will serve me in my career. Algebra will not."

"You never know. Someday, mathematics may lend medicine a hand."

Andreas rolled his eyes. "Inconceivable. Let's get done with this problem and have a game of chess. I feel a victory coming on."

"Only if I play blindfolded."

I stayed on for dinner, and I caught up with Madam Vesalius as we rose from the table.

"Madam, there is a book in the library I'd like to borrow for a short while."

"Which one?"

"'On the Nature of Things'. By the Roman—"

"—Lucretius," she said. "I did not know we had a copy. It has an unsavory reputation. Your mother would be quite upset with me if I loaned it to you, let alone let you read it."

"I promise that I won't . . ."

"I must say no, Jan. I cannot betray what I know would be her wishes. You shall put it back where you found it."

That evening, with knots in my stomach, I went home with Lucretius' poem hidden in my bag. I went to my room, and behind my closed door I dipped my toe, then plunged, into the profane waters of *On the*

Nature of Things, carried along by currents of astonishment around every bend, yet looking back for fear that Mother would be in pursuit.

Lucretius believed that the universe is made up of tiny, immortal, and indivisible seeds—the term 'atoms' is also used—that move endlessly through an unbounded universe, colliding and combining unpredictably to form all living and nonliving things; Nature therefore proceeds with unending experimentation and change. Human existence is not a special creation, but merely a random outcome, and the continued existence of humanity is in no way guaranteed. When we die, our souls die with us, and there is no afterlife. Religions make cruel promises and advance foolish superstitions; the gods, whose existence he did not deny, do not require our ceremonial attention as they have no interest in human affairs.

Late at night, I put the book down and imagined myself in the presence of Lucretius himself, bearded and robed. I sensed I could speak to him, but that he would not answer.

"Across the centuries, Lucretius, you have shocked me with your atoms and our chance existence in an unthinking universe! If you had lived a century later, in the time of Christ, would you have dismissed Christian theology as readily as you did the Greco-Roman pantheon of gods? I say yes—you would have concluded that it was just as rife with its own set of superstitions and empty promises.

"In that case, Lucretius, would you find merit in the Protestant Reformation? Surely you would be offended, as was Luther, by the Catholic Church hierarchy with its excesses and hypocrisy. But would you have rejected his notion of eternal salvation, especially if, as Luther believed, it had nothing to do with good deeds in life, only blind faith in Jesus as Savior? Again I say yes."

On the Nature of Things gave voice to my own inner questioning of the religious teachings I was raised on. I was more and more skeptical of the various miracles ascribed to the life of Jesus—especially the central miracles of the Virgin Birth and the Resurrection. The ideas of Lucretius were disturbing when I first encountered them, but I was just as disturbed by the bloody image of Jesus on the cross, let alone the rite of the Eucharist—the eating of Christ's body and the drinking of his blood.

A few days later, before I could slip the book back into place, Andreas saw the title.

"A geometry text, eh? We have been warned about that book. I will tell your mother."

"Shut up, Runt. You will not."

"Did you read it?"

"I did. Your grandfather signed the title page."

"Really! What did you learn?"

I told Andreas about *On the Nature of Things*.

"Interesting, but I won't spend my time delving further into such views of God and Nature, just as I choose not to wrestle with problems of theology. I would just as soon consider them settled and move on."

I climbed the ladder and slipped the book back in place.

At university, however, I found in Antoine a schoolmate eager to examine and debate these ideas. I went through a period (to Antoine's dismay) of questioning the need to accept the existence of any god, as I could identify no tangible evidence for one. I could not, however, completely escape Antoine's argument that some entity was responsible for the creation of the universe. I could not return to Christianity, but I finally settled on the notion of an ill-defined Creator akin to Jehovah in the Old Testament, but indifferent to earthly history. This position was neither popular nor safe; only a few close friends were aware that I was a Christian in name only.

15 February 1565

Preparations for the journey were complete. We would leave for Leuven the next day by carriage. Marcus' younger brother Henk would look after the house while we were gone.

Marcus packed our new travel chests with clothes for a variety of conditions. We would each shoulder a bag with everyday things, including a small supply of smoked meat for times when food was unavailable or unsafe.

At town hall I confirmed that our passports were in good standing, though they often meant nothing to a border guard unaccompanied by a bribe. Across the square I purchased a letter of credit at the Fugger Bank. With it I could draw local coin from Fugger agents across the continent. One pays a premium for this service, but there are dozens of different monies to reckon with, and the agents redeemed unused coin on exchange. A letter of credit can be stolen, lost, or destroyed; as a precaution, I had Marcus sew six gold coins into the waistbands of our breeches.

Our plan was to travel by carriage as we could, but when roads became impassable—even the arrow-straight Roman roads might have sections of paving stones gutted for other uses—sooner or later we would have to rent horses. Some inns along the main roads were quite comfortable, but as a rule they were filthy, lice-infected places with vile food. When faced with a night in such a dreadful warren, we sought to pay a farmer for refuge in his barn, or we would sleep under the stars.

Besides my native tongue, I speak passably the French of Paris, the German of Basel, and the Italian of Padua, but these city dialects are of little value in the countryside where a man on one bank of a river may not be understood by a man on the other. Latin is spoken across Europe by the educated classes, but it is not in common use. I carry Garon's *Vocabulary* in my travel bag, which now covers eight languages, but in the deep countryside it may as well be used for kindling. It is said that there are over a hundred languages in France alone. Getting directions from a country peasant often ends up a comedy of hand signals and puzzled looks.

Whenever possible we would travel on policed roads, and if prudent, join with other travelers to hire an armed escort. On journeys I wear a saber as well as a dagger. Like all young gentleman I was trained in swordsmanship and became proficient enough to be our school champion. I dueled the way I played chess—I anticipated the opponent's moves and unleashed a swift and sure counterattack. I have never drawn a sword in anger or for defense, but I will use it if I must.

In the two centuries since the terrible Black Death swept across Europe, outbreaks of plague spring up at random. Travelers must be wary of passing through, or even near, areas where the plague is active.

I made my goodbyes to family and good friends, starting with my brother. I went to his office at the Van den Bossche Trading Company, a fine three-story building overlooking the harbor. I found him at his desk on the top floor, where my father once sat.

He looked up from his papers. "Sorry, we're not hiring now. Who let you in?"

We both laughed at the old family joke. "To what do I owe the pleasure?" he asked, pouring us both a brandy. Frans had gained weight and his breathing was labored. He had but a rim of hair left on his head. It struck me that my brother had become an old man, and that I was not far behind.

I told him about Zante. He smiled and shook his head.

"Why would I expect good sense from you at this point in your life? Mother will not receive this well. You may kill her yet, with all the worrying she does over you."

I let his comments pass; it was not the first time I heard them. "You will have to look after things at her house. Most of her friends are dead, and those still alive don't visit. She is lonely."

He nodded in resignation. But then he grasped my head with both hands and touched his forehead to mine. He had not done this since we were children. "Vesalius can summon you even in death. But know that I honor your friendship with him. Godspeed, brother. Get back before I die."

"There's no doubt of that. You will draw your last breath only when you have everyone else's money."

"Hmm. That would include your money." He smiled and went back to his desk. I turned to leave. At the door I said again, "See after her, Frans."

I paid calls to my nieces and nephews, and then steeled myself to see Mother. Despite the attentions of several suitors in years gone by, she never remarried. Now she was an elderly widow who had retreated into a house many times larger than she could manage, living out a charade of her past life at the apex of Brussels society. Her few remaining friends found her too tiresome for regular company; she would repeat herself or go silent because she could not follow the conversation. I suffered to see her this way. However imperfectly, she was my first and fiercest protector; now I was hers.

A few days before I left, I sat down next to her on the chaise longue in the sitting room. She had taken to rubbing her hands together as if washing them.

"How are you, Mother? Are those pains in your hands and feet any better?"

"Ha! They are worse. The doctor has been no help."

"I'm sorry to hear that, Mother. I'm sure he's doing the best he can."

"He's a thief, just like the rest of them."

I changed the subject.

"Mother, I am going on a trip to visit Andreas. I am leaving the day after tomorrow." It was convenient that she would not remember that he was dead.

Her expression darkened at the mention of his name. "Where is he this time? He will be the death of you with all these journeys. He has never been anything but trouble, that runt with the Devil's mark over his eye."

Mother had become rather less tactful as her faculties declined.

"He is in Ghent," I lied, "with the king."

"Which king?"

"Our king. King Philip of Spain."

"Spain? Then what is he doing in Ghent?"

"He is also king of the Low Countries." It had been two years since she could retain this fact, and I knew what she would say next.

"A king should stay in his own country," she said, her hand trembling as she wiped her nose with a handkerchief. "We should have our own king, not a greasy Spaniard."

"Someday we might, Mother. But now it's Philip, and he leaves Spain with his armies to fight with other kingdoms and nobles."

"All this fighting."

"Yes, Mother, mostly about land, but these days, there is also fighting over how the Church tends to its flock."

"That Martin Luther is the trouble. They should arrest him, that German scum."

"He is dead, Mother, but he has many followers, and they fight in his name."

"May they all burn in Hell! If Andreas puts himself in harm's way, that's his business. Why must you?" She furrowed her brow. "Which side is he on, Frans?"

"I am Jan, Mother. Andreas is a physician for King Philip, and the king is on the side of the Church. Andreas will not be in harm's way, and neither will I be."

"Well, that's good, at least."

She cried and begged me not to go. I promised to write, but that was a lie; there was no point in writing. For my entire life I struggled to shake free of her grip, but the tables had turned: old age, loneliness, and senility had made her fearful and dependent, and now it was painful to leave her. My heart ached for her, shrunken into her seat next to me, her damp eyes darting anxiously from within a wrinkled face with too much powder and rouge. I hugged her gently to me and I could feel her tremble.

"I will be back soon, Mother. You won't even notice I was gone."

"You will be careful crossing the streets."

"Of course, Mother."

The knots in my stomach tightened as the departure day neared, but beyond the usual apprehension I battled with my resolve to go at all.

The night before departure Andreas came to me. He sat at the foot of my bed, looking intently my way. Though I dared not, it seemed like I could feel his hand if I reached for it.

"What is the point of this loathsome journey," I said, "if I will be visiting a pile of dirt instead of you?"

Andreas cocked his head, but did not answer.

"What, you have no opinion on the matter? You were properly mourned in Brussels, after all. Anne saw to it that a mass was held for you at Saint Michael and Saint Gudula, complete with an Adrian Willaert requiem."

He shrugged.

"The turnout was better than for any of your dissections. It seems you are more popular dead than alive! There is talk of a statue in your honor, as befits a departed citizen of your stature—ho, the best puns are unintended—and if the pedestal is high enough, for once you will be taller than anyone."

Andreas allowed a smile at my provocation, but then his expression hardened.

"But you must not come, Jan," he said.

"I must not come? Why not?"

"You must not come," he repeated.

I found myself sitting up, staring at the empty space at the foot of my bed.

Marcus appeared at the bedroom door. "Were you dreaming, Master Jan? You were shouting."

"Yes, I was dreaming." My heart racing, I got back under the covers. Of course it was a dream.

16 February 1565

I got out of bed with my stomach clenched in a vise. Clutching my robe, I walked by candlelight through the cold house to say goodbye to it, a pre-journey ritual borne of fear that I might never see it again.

In the dining room I sat down across from two of my few extravagances—bequests from my father, to the irritation of my brother Frans: a sideboard with intricate geometric inlays, and hanging above it, a Pieter Coecke van Aelst tapestry recounting the myth of Vertumnus and Pomona. Pomona, a beautiful nymph-like maiden in a walled garden, shuns the advances of men. Vertumnus, the god of seasons, can assume multiple earthly forms, and befriends her in the guise of a kindly old woman. He then reveals himself to her and wins her love. Many are charmed by this tale; I am troubled by it. What sort of love is rooted in deception? Will the deceiver not deceive again?

I sat back and smiled as a memory sprang up in my mind. For a few years after my father died I stayed on at the family house with Mother. Andreas, sensing that Mother's grip on me was tightening, urged me to find a place of my own, which I did the summer before I went with him to Padua in 1537, almost thirty years earlier.

How disagreeable you were, Andreas, when I showed you this house! You were angry that I did not consult with you first.

"I'm glad you're finally coming out from behind your mother's skirts," you said, "but you can easily afford a much finer house than this sad little hut. There are hardly any grounds, just that pathetic little garden with barely enough room for a pea plant. Why don't you just go live in a cave?"

I stuck by my choice, but I was cut by your criticism; I wavered before going ahead with the purchase. Only my mother's disapproval could wound me more than yours. You never stopped insisting that I bought the house to spite you.

There is an element of truth to this.

Shaking myself back to the present, I remembered that I had one more goodbye to make. Before walking to Anne's house, I left Marcus with instructions for him and the driver to bring the loaded carriage there to get me; we would leave for Leuven directly from there. I took a last look at the front door of my house after I closed it behind me, hoping that months later I would walk through it again.

In the sitting room at Vesalius House, waiting for Anne and Anna to join me, I walked to the far end of the room to look at the hunting scene tapestry hanging there. Like mine, it was by Coecke. Andreas had purchased it, he told me matter-of-factly, for the very reason that it was larger than mine.

I heard the door open behind me, and turned to see Anne and Anna entering. I rushed ahead to greet them, and then fumbled in my pocket for the puzzles I had written down for Anna.

"I expect these all to be solved by the time I return," I said, in my best schoolmaster voice.

She smiled, but then took a handkerchief from her sleeve and pressed it into my hand.

"Would you leave this at Father's grave for me?"

"Of course. It will be my honor."

"I will say goodbye to you now, Uncle Jan. I cannot cry another tear. Come home safely to us." With that and an embrace, she left me with her mother. I took a seat across from Anne.

"Marcus will bring our carriage here to fetch me. We hear the road to Leuven is good, so it should be only a few hours."

"May all the roads treat you as well."

"I have never been that lucky, but there is always hope."

She managed a smile. "Where will you go after Leuven?"

"Paris; Ornans, to see Antoine; Basel, to see Andreas' publisher. Then over the Alps to Milan, Padua, and Venice."

"You chose a route laden with memories."

"Yes, I suppose I have. I may never be back to these places."

"But you will not go to Spain."

"Not even if the Pyrenées weren't in the way."

She nodded in agreement. "I pray I will never set foot in that country again. So, will you sail to this Greek island Zante from Venice?"

"Yes. Zante is controlled by Venice."

"You hate the sea more than you do the roads," she said, smiling again.

"Not true—I hate the sea *far* more than the roads. It took a few adventures on the North Sea with Andreas and university friends to learn that lesson."

On one junket I was very seasick, but you did not leave my side. We laughed about it after we made port, but I remember the worry on your face at sea.

Anne pulled a handkerchief from her sleeve, unfolded it and folded it again.

"Anna and I are touched that you are making this trip, Jan. We could never..."

"I know. I feel I am going for all of us."

"You have been a great comfort to us since we came home..." Anne took a breath as if to say more, but then seemed to think better of it.

I leaned forward in my chair, hesitating before I spoke.

"I'm sorry to be asking again, but is there anything else to say about the pilgrimage?"

She thought for a moment, then sighed. "No, except that as we prepared for the journey he took up with his *Fabrica* again."

"Hmm. He started working on a third edition five years ago, before you moved to Madrid."

"In Madrid he took it out from time to time, but the pilgrimage seemed to unleash him. He worked on the book steadily until we set off, and then every night in our lodgings—far into the night—through Spain and into France, right up to Perpignan."

Anne had resisted speaking of Perpignan, but I decided to press her again.

"Can you tell me what happened there? Why did you come home?"

She stood and walked across the room to a window; she tended to pace in a serious conversation. She gazed out the window while she spoke.

"At Perpignan he refused to pay some customs fee or other, and insisted on bringing his case to the local magistrate. We quarreled over this, but he was determined to see it through. One day amidst all this, a courier appeared with a letter for Andreas. Now that I think about it, there was something familiar about him—a burly fellow with a reddish beard—well, no matter. Andreas read it, then tossed it into the fire. He said it was a letter from his publisher in Basel—what was his name . . ."

"Oporinus."

"Yes, that's it. But he seemed shaken by the letter. That evening, he told me he was sending me and Anna back to Brussels. He would only say that the journey would be too hard for us."

She turned back to me, wiping tears from her eyes. "I can't deny that I was relieved to go home. He said he would join us in Brussels when he got back . . ."

"And that was the last either of us heard from him," I said.

"There is something else." She tucked her handkerchief back into her sleeve. "I told him Anna and I would never return to Madrid. I realized it would make an empty shell of our marriage, but I was dying a slow death there. The hostility toward him at court spilled onto me; I had few friends. The times he took us to Brussels when he traveled to the Low Countries with Philip were gifts—when we would see family and friends, most of all, you—but they only made me more homesick and spiteful."

I said nothing as Anne continued.

"Madrid was not the only problem. Andreas . . . was not easy to live with."

"He was unhappy with the Spanish court . . ."

"You don't understand. Even when we were still in Brussels, I dreaded his homecomings from Emperor Charles' military campaigns. He hated being a battlefield surgeon. Once home he preferred to be alone, except for you, and he barely tolerated me and Anna. You saw yourself how he jumped at a loud noise from the street or snapped at

Anna if she dropped a toy on the floor, but that was only the half of it. He had nightmares. There were days he would not get out of bed. A trifle could send him flying into a rage."

She stopped for a moment, gathering herself. "There were times when he threatened to strike me. In Brussels he kept his behavior under wraps, but in Madrid he got worse, and had no constraint."

I sat stunned at the thought of Andreas doing harm to Anne, but I had seen for myself what Andreas was like after a campaign.

"You are not yourself, Andreas," I said to you days after you returned from one of those campaigns. You responded irritably: "I'm just tired." Then you stood up and suggested that we go for a beer. Once again I bent to your will and let it go at that. I allowed you keep your darkness hidden.

"I am so sorry to hear of this."

Before I could think of anything else to say she turned back to the window and peeked around the curtain. "Your carriage is here. Make good use of the day."

She escorted me to the door. Looking up at me, her eyes shining with tears, she said, "You will write when you can."

"Of course."

"Come back to us safely."

We embraced, at first gently, but then our arms tightened until our bodies were firm against each other.

Several long moments passed; with her arms still around me, she leaned back far enough to see my face and whispered, "I will miss you." She pushed away from me and disappeared into the house.

I let myself out, glancing back for a last look at Andreas' door-knocker. Marcus was waiting beside the carriage.

"We are ready, Master Jan. Henk knows what to do. He will use my room until we return."

I stumbled into the carriage, under the same spell cast at Vilvoorde many years past. If there was a message in that embrace, it was laden with complications that did not exist then. Andreas, just a name to Anne twenty-two years ago, was now her newly-dead husband. To me he was a newly-dead friend, cherished more than any other, but with a disturbing part of his life that I had failed to notice.

As the carriage made for the city gate and the Leuven Road, we rode past the entrance to Montagne de la Potence.

By the time we were twelve, Andreas and I were roaming widely around Brussels. Mother, no longer in absolute control of my comings and goings, made us promise to avoid certain streets with unsavory reputations, and above all, the markets.

Andreas scoffed at her prohibitions. "You don't have to tell her where we go! Make something up if you have to." With his urging, I learned that I could safely lie to Mother because she thought it unimaginable that I would deceive her. Exploring with Andreas at first was tense but exciting, especially the crowded, noisy markets where we would buy a sack of nuts and wander among the stalls. I still feared being alone there, so I stuck to Andreas' side, but one time Andreas suddenly disappeared. I was overcome with panic; I rushed around searching for him to no avail. Finally, Andreas jumped out from behind a stand piled high with cabbage.

"Ha! I've been hiding from you."

"Don't do that again," I said, my voice shaking.

"All right. Well, I thought it would be fun."

Most often, we went to Montagne de la Potence. Really no more than a high hill, its footpaths climbed through grassy fields where sheep might graze, and up into woods carpeted by fallen leaves. I came to love these woods, but not without much coaxing from Andreas. To Mother, Nature was to be trusted only within the walls of our formal garden, under her control down to the last tulip. Beyond, the natural world was chaotic and dangerous; Montagne de la Potence was just such a place.

One time, we went all the way to the top instead of turning around where we usually did, at a statue of the Virgin set next to the path. Farther up the path ended at a gate. Andreas pushed it open.

"Let's go in," he said.

"The gate must be here for a reason."

"Oh, come on. Your mother isn't here."

We laughed as he grabbed my sleeve and pulled me through the gate. As we rounded a bend, Andreas let out a shout.

"It's the gallows! And there's someone hanging there!"

He dashed ahead for a closer look. A crow perched on the gallows cawed and flew off. Mother hated crows, with their blackness and ugly calls, making meals of dead flesh. She was sure they were satanic.

I stared in shock at the remains of a man suspended like a side of mutton at the market. Through tatters of clothing I could see light passing through his ribs. His arms and legs hung limp, with greyish muscle and sinew exposed where the skin had fallen away. A shriveled entrail sagged from a large gash in his abdomen. His head was cocked severely over the noose around his neck, exposing the top of his bare skull that still clung to a stubborn islet of hair. His eye sockets were hollow, his nose eaten down to bone, and I could see teeth where there were no longer lips to cover them.

Andreas motioned frantically. "Come here—you can see all the way through to his spine!"

The wind shifted, bringing the smell of rotting flesh.

"I'm not coming any closer. The smell is horrible and I want to leave. I'm going to vomit."

"Wait! There are so many muscles in this leg . . ."

I wanted to run, but that would mean going back through the woods alone. Trapped, I stood there with a handkerchief over my nose.

Andreas grabbed one of the legs by the ankle and pulled at it, first gingerly, and then harder, trying to get the corpse to turn. It jiggled like a puppet, then finally started to spin.

"What are you doing, Andreas? Don't . . ."

The leg suddenly gave way at the hip. "Yah!" he yelled, letting go of the ankle and running back to me, his face flushed with excitement.

"It came right off! I was not expecting that."

The dead man, with his leg now on the ground under him, was still spinning slowly enough to bring his contorted, eyeless face into view and out again.

I had had more than enough. "Please, let's get out of here!" I yanked Andreas' sleeve.

"All right, let's go."

We raced down the hill, one of us horrified, the other elated, and did not stop until we reached the streets. As we slowed to a walk, catching our breaths, Andreas squeezed my shoulder.

"Wasn't that the very best thing *ever*, Jan?"

I did not agree that it was the very best thing ever. But when Andreas bragged about our adventure at school, I could see in the eyes of my schoolmates that my status had risen.

A few days later, my mother received a note from Madam Vesalius. Andreas would not be going to school for a week because he had fallen in his room and broken his arm. The broken bone had been set by a fine physician and family friend, Nicholas Florenas, and in a week Andreas could return to school.

My mother sent a note back to Madame Vesalius, but did not permit me to go see him. "He should not be disturbed. He will heal well. Doctor Florenas cares for some of the best families in Brussels."

After a week Andreas appeared at my door for the walk to school, his right arm splinted and held in a sling under his cape. I was overjoyed to see him.

"Ho, Andreas! How is your arm?" I glanced apprehensively at his sling. "Does it hurt?"

"Not anymore. Well, just a little. I was going mad sitting around the house."

Mother came to the door. "You have been in my prayers, Andreas."

I doubted that this was true.

"Thank you, Madam," Andreas said. "I am quite fine, but I will have this splint for another six weeks."

"No rough games with Jan while you heal, Andreas."

"Yes, Madam. Thank you, Madam. My mother sends her thanks for your kind note."

We started down the street.

"So, you fell in your room?"

"I tripped on a shoe on the way to the chamber pot and fell hard to the floor."

I had seen Andreas fall hard many times at school, but he never did any damage beyond scraped skin.

"It hurt when Doctor Florenas set the bone, but he thinks it will be as good as new."

"Shall I carry your book bag?"

"Of course not. There's hardly anything in it anyway."

That day, we went to Andreas' library after school to catch him up in grammar. He suddenly closed his textbook.

"Enough of this. Come downstairs to the cellar with me."

I looked up, puzzled. "The cellar?"

"Just come on."

Andreas had me light candles for us both in the deserted kitchen, and then led me down to the cellar. Like all cellars, it was cold, dirty, and dark, and smelled of mold. Against the stone walls I could make out a few bins for root vegetables, some broken chairs, and a dusty wine rack.

"Is that all the wine your father has, Andreas? My father has a whole room full of wine."

"I know. Now come over here." He was at the other end of the cellar in front of a doorway. As I walked toward him, my nostrils flared.

"That smell . . ."

"Stop whining and come on."

Andreas lifted the door latch with his free hand, pulled it open, and waved me in. I stepped gingerly through the doorway into a fog of stench. In a panic I looked back at Andreas.

"Oh my God, I can't . . ."

"Yes you can. Go in."

With my handkerchief over my nose I squinted into a cramped room faintly lit by a row of small above-ground windows. In one corner was a washstand and two candelabras; in another was a hearth big enough for a cauldron suspended on a hook. Two tables took up the center space, the smaller of which was strewn with a collection of knives, saws, drills, scissors, hammers, needles, string, basins, pipettes, and rags.

On the larger table was a good-sized dog—or what was left of it—on its back, splayed open from neck to groin, its legs tied down with string. Even in the dim light I could see that whatever had been inside that dog had been taken out. Its head was shattered and lolled over the edge of the table, its protruding tongue pointing toward a bucket under the table that held its missing insides. Entrails caked with blood spilled over the edge of the bucket to the floor.

Blinking in disbelief and fighting off a wave of nausea, I thought of Mother bearing witness to this room. It was all I could do not to run.

"I do dissections here. I've been wanting to show you."

He looked my way, expecting me to speak, but I could say nothing.

"Two Easters ago, I was in the kitchen watching Agnes make soup. She sent me to the cellar to get some onions."

"Your cook sent you for onions? Our Greta would never . . ."

"The onions are not the point! Once I was down here, I got curious about this door. I tried it, but it was locked. 'Ask your father,' Agnes said when I asked her about it. I did and he showed me the room. Everything you see was here—the tables, the instruments, except the dog, of course—covered in dust. My father had not been to this room in many years. My grandfather Everard used this room to study anatomy, with those instruments, and he taught my father how to dissect small animals."

"But how did you start . . . doing this yourself?"

"I asked him to teach me. The next day he came home with a dead kitten in a bag. We dissected it here, on this table. I almost puked when he made the first cut! But he told me to think of it as opening a clock to see the workings. We did the kitten, a squirrel, and then a grown cat before he went off again with the emperor. He showed me how to use all these instruments. He said I was good enough to dissect on my own if I was careful with the sharp instruments, wore an apron, and washed my hands after."

"Is this not sinful?" I said through my handkerchief.

"Of course not—animals have no souls. But," he looked intently at me, "my father said this room must be kept secret."

"Why?"

"Because people might find it strange for a boy to be doing this. What would your mother say?"

I did not have to answer.

"So you must promise that you'll tell no one about this room."

"I promise. But how do you get the animals now?" I asked, glancing at the dog.

"There are dead animals everywhere, and you can trap small ones."

"Oh."

"Now I can do bigger animals on my own. This dog was run over by a wagon . . . you can see what happened to his head! After dark I went out and got him. I worked on him before I broke my arm, mostly after supper. There's not much left to do except his head, but it's too much of a mess."

He jostled the dog's head. I looked away.

"There is a method to it—an Italian named Mondino wrote a book two hundred years ago about how to dissect people, but it's the same idea for animals. You do the organs in the belly and chest first because they rot quickly. You see how they're arranged, and when you take them out you slice them open to see what's inside. Then you do the muscles to see where they start and end, and then how they move the bones. I try to draw pictures of what I see. They're terrible, but Mondino's book has no pictures at all."

"Why not?" I asked, glancing sideways at the dog.

"I don't know."

He shifted uneasily. "Well, what do you think, Jan? I wasn't sure about this at first—the blood, the cutting, the smell—but I love it. Let me show you a few things inside the dog. Say, if you are my astral twin, you should like this, too!"

"If you are my astral twin, you should like mathematics."

Our laughter could not hide the pleading in his eyes. For the first time in my memory he was seeking my approval. My throat tightened; to Mother this would be dark arts. But I could not refuse Andreas.

"All right, show me. But hurry."

I inched forward to confront the rotting, eviscerated shell of a dog, and gingerly leaned forward to peer into the cavity that until recently held the contents of the bucket underfoot. To my surprise, the dog's hollow interior was not horrifying; empty and wiped clean of blood, the surfaces had a dull sheen in the candlelight. Strings tied to rib tips and fastened to pegs at the edge of the table caused the chest to fan out in graceful arcs.

Andreas pointed out the stumps of the trachea and esophagus, the shriveled aorta and vena cava running along near the spine, and the space where the heart used to be. He showed me in the abdomen where one would find the liver, the kidneys, and the stomach, with the intestines winding around all over. I was surprised that he knew the names of these body parts. With a metal rod he called a "probe," he held up some of the large muscles at the hips and legs.

"Does your mother know about this?" I asked, stepping away to escape the stench and tamp down a wave of nausea. I noticed an open sketchbook on the table, and at the other end of the table, something covered with a sheet.

"She doesn't come down here, but she knows." With that he took up a corner of the sheet. "She doesn't know about this, though."

He lifted the sheet.

"My God, it's the leg!"

"Yes. I went back for it. I could not miss the chance to dissect something human."

"You have gone mad! What if someone saw you?"

"No one saw me. I snuck out of the house at night and went back."

"At night? Up there? How did you even see where you were going?"

"There was enough moonlight to see, but I suppose not quite enough. On the way back I tripped and fell. That's how I broke my arm."

"But your mother said . . ."

He cut me off. "I got myself back home and put the leg down here. I went upstairs, changed into my nightclothes, got down on the floor, and started yelling. My mother believed my story—and she must never hear the truth from you."

He furrowed his brow, as if reliving that night. "I cried from pain all the way home, but I got the leg. The sad part is that I only have one hand to work on it. I need you to help . . ."

"No."

"I'll give you an easy job. You can read to me out of Mondino's *Ana-thomia* so I know what I'm doing. You won't even have to look."

"No. Do not ask again. No."

"I need you to help, Jan. Otherwise I broke my arm for nothing."

"Get someone else to help."

"There is no one else."

"What about your brothers?"

"Nicholas refused, and Franciscus is too young."

"Get another friend to do it."

"I don't have any friends like you." He looked at me anxiously.

He was right. At school, he was known for his clowning and was a leader in games, but his sharp tongue and stubbornness did not win him friends. But as my confidence grew under his wing, I became his bridge to other boys. I pulled him away from fights about to start and tried to shut him up before he got himself into trouble in class. He knew I would be revolted by this bizarre secret pastime of his, but he trusted me enough to show me. If I agreed, I would have a secret of my own to keep—from Mother. If she knew, she would think me lost to the Devil. And maybe she'd be right. But Andreas was standing before me, making bare his need.

"All right, then, I'll do it."

I went to the cellar three times, reading to him from Mondino's section on the leg while he worked with his left hand. He coaxed me to hold a retracting hook when he needed his free hand to explore with his fingers a space between muscles.

"You don't have to look. Just hold it right here. No, here—and don't move."

Increasingly frustrated with the rotting leg, Andreas decided it was too far gone, and that his left-handed drawings were poor.

"Thanks for helping me, Jan," he said as we climbed the stairs. "Maybe I'll try to clean the bones." He shook his head. "I'll say this: it would have been easier with a picture to look at."

I barely endured those sessions, but I basked in Andreas' gratitude. The prospect of losing my soul to the Devil in the next life was out-weighed by helping Andreas in this one.

Six weeks later, the splint came off. His arm worked normally, but the healing was not perfect. Andreas let me feel the place in his right arm just above the elbow where the fracture was; the bone—the humerus, he said—was slightly bent and had a bump where the fracture was. It made me queasy to feel it, but he was proud of the deformity.

"No one has a right humerus quite like mine," he said. "You should have been there when the splint came off. My arm stank as bad as that rotting leg."

Andreas went back to his animal dissections, and from time to time I would go to the cellar with him. He discovered that dousing his specimens in vinegar would cut the smell. At school his attention wandered from subjects that did not interest him, but in the cellar he was capable of great concentration. His skill improved steadily; as he worked he muttered to himself: "You oaf, Andreas!" when he went too far with his scissors, or "Now that's a good job!" when he exposed a long segment of nerve and its branches with no damage. The cellar sessions were close to intolerable for me, but I became competent with a retracting hook and offered consolation or praise as needed, especially for his drawings, which he continued to make in a grease-stained notebook.

In years to come, standing beside a human cadaver and surrounded by hundreds of onlookers, he would use the skill he honed in his cellar to great effect.

Part Two

JOURNEY TO ZANTE

Leuven

17 February 1565

I was always happy to return to Leuven—the French know it as Louvain—the bustling little city where three decades earlier Andreas and I earned our baccalaureates. Marcus and I took lodgings at a fine inn near the Castle School of the university, a former château converted to classrooms and offices.

You never tired of telling me that your great-grandfather Johannes was a professor of medicine and mathematics here. His aptitude for mathematics did not pass to you.

For supper I took Marcus to the Café du Château. "The Château" had hardly changed since university days—grimy windows, tightly-packed tables, constant din, and air heavy with smoke, candle wax, and beer. Beer flowed freely, emboldening students to frisk a serving girl or pick a fight; more than once I had to drag Andreas away from a tense confrontation.

I had passed many happy hours there, joking, arguing, and playing chess. Some of our university friends went on to notable careers—like Granvelle, a Cardinal and diplomat, Gemma Frisius, a physician, mathematician and geographer who, with Gerardus Mercator, took maps and globes to new levels. Mercator was the only one in our circle who could defeat me at chess; when we played a crowd would gather around our table to wager on the outcome.

That evening with Marcus I sat like a ghost, long removed from the lively university scene; no one would know that I was the unnamed donor of the money for a new roof at Les Halles, the original university building downtown.

"You have fine memories of this place," Marcus said, looking around the room.

"Oh yes," I laughed, "but how did I put up with all this noise?"

"Aye, it's loud, but what a privilege to be part of it. The taverns by the docks are noisy, but there's no sense in the air of life opening up ahead, like here. The fates of men by the docks have already been settled."

He got up from his chair and started for the kitchen. "I'll go check on our meal."

For the first time I saw in Marcus the face of an entire class of people resigned to the life into which they were born, boxed in by a thousand years of imposed social division. It was true that change was in the air; old feudal ways were dying out, regional and international trade was burgeoning (with my family benefitting greatly), and educated people were needed to conduct the expanding business of government. But by and large, people were relegated to their place in life according to birth. It's true—these heirs of favorable birth carousing at the Château take their good fortune for granted, as did I in my time. Have we overlooked a Copernicus, a Vesalius, or a Leonardo pushing a plow through a field or casting nets into the North Sea, their talents never set free? What would you have done with your life, Marcus? Surely something other than traipsing around with me.

Marcus returned smiling. "The food is on the way," he said, "as well as more beer to wash it down. It's a battle scene in the kitchen."

"The greater the struggle, the better the meal. I've never gotten sick here."

Neither was true, but I was relieved to change the subject; I could think of nothing fitting to say about the atmosphere of privilege that surrounded Marcus here, with permission to visit but not to stay.

In the morning we walked to the center of town, Marcus to seek out carriage-men in the taverns for information on road conditions and military movements south to the French border; I would inspect from across the street the new slate roof I paid for on Les Halles. Then I wandered back in the direction of the Castle School.

My knees did not complain as I strolled past the Castle School through the west gate into the countryside. I soon realized that I was retracing the steps of an unforgettable adventure from Andreas' last year of medical school in Leuven.

Do you remember the execution of Ernst Bronck, in the fall of 1536, and what we did the very next day? Further evidence that I could never say no to you . . .

After our baccalaureates in 1533, Andreas enrolled in medical school at the University of Paris. I went along with him with no plan for myself. I took a few disappointing mathematics courses; after a year I returned to Brussels, but I traveled to Paris twice thereafter to visit. In 1536 Andreas was forced to return to Leuven for his final year of medical school. War was threatening between France and the Holy Roman Empire, and Paris became too dangerous for a Netherlander. Andreas was enraged over the situation; I would miss visiting him in Paris, but I would just as soon travel only a few hours to see him in Leuven.

In early Advent of 1536, I paid a visit to Andreas. We arranged to have dinner at the Château with our undergraduate friend Gemma Frisius, who had stayed on at the medical school.

Andreas and I had already downed a few mugs of beer when Gemma arrived clutching a broadsheet. His cheeks still flushed from the cold, he read it to us: "Hear ye, the Magistrate of Leuven, et cetera and so on . . . Ernst Bronck of Opvelpen having confessed to the theft of three pigs from the Hasse farm in Bierbeek, as well as other crimes, to wit . . . et cetera, et cetera . . ."

Gemma raised a finger and read on. ". . . Justice will be served by public hanging before man and God at the gallows outside the West Gate tomorrow at eleven o'clock."

Gemma looked up from the sheet. "I want to go."

"And I will join you," said Andreas, and then turned to me. He knew that I had never chosen to see an execution.

"And you, Jan?" he said, winking at Gemma. "It is your civic duty to see justice carried out."

Andreas and Gemma waited for my response. They both knew my

position on the barbarism of executions, but in addition I feared that seeing one would give me a long string of nightmares. That evening, though, the beer in my belly spoke for me.

"Very well. I shall not shirk my civic duty."

"Well said, Citizen van den Bossche!" Andreas boomed. Our mugs collided in a sloshing toast. Gemma motioned to a nearby serving girl. "Three more, if you please!"

The morning was sunny and not terribly cold. By the time we fell in with the stream of townspeople walking through the West Gate, the haze and headache from an evening of drink had cleared. Executions would reliably draw crowds from all levels of society, but the intermingling had limits; farmers and laborers walked to the gallows alongside elegant carriages that kept the curtains pulled closed.

My brave talk the night before did not at first carry over to the morning; my stomach churned as I walked along. Soon enough, though, I found some calm. Sunlight passed easily through the bare trees lining the road to warm us; the shuffling of feet kept time with a pleasant murmur of conversation. The smell of food was in the air, and in keeping with the good cheer of Advent, business was brisk for vendors of cakes, hot cider, roasted nuts, apples, and smoked meat. Street performers danced to bawdy songs for a few coins.

Gemma struck a note of caution. "Beware of your purses, gentlemen. The pickpockets will be out in force."

Presently we reached a clearing by the road, at the far end of which were the gallows—an elevated wooden platform with stone pillars rising on either end to support a thick crossbeam. The crossbeam had room for three or four victims, their bodies customarily left to rot or be savaged by jackdaws and wild dogs. But that day the gallows, in full view from the road, were empty.

"Must have been a while since the last hanging," Andreas observed.

We filed into the clearing and found a place amidst a crowd of perhaps five hundred men, women, and children—even babies swaddled in

The King's Anatomist

their mothers' arms. Although it was not the custom in Leuven, other cities collected entry fees, with children admitted free.

Gemma must have noticed that I was staring apprehensively at the gallows. He took my arm. "The pig thief is less of a draw than, say, a murderer or a witch," he whispered. "You'd have twice the crowd for them. And because he has already confessed, there'll be no torture."

"A touching gesture of mercy," I said.

Struggling to conceal my anxiety, I peered down at Andreas with my hands cupped over my eyes.

"Can you see anything from down there? Would you have a better view on my shoulders?"

"I swear I will kill you in your sleep, even if I have to hang next to the pig thief."

Gemma came to my defense. "He was just trying to be helpful."

"Now it will be a double killing—and good value. I hang only once for two murders."

More laughter. Standing in place with breaths misting, shoulders hunched, hands thrust into pockets, we awaited the arrival of the condemned man. People began to dip into the baskets of food that they brought along. A cheerful, gap-toothed woman with a boy clinging to her skirts offered us sweetcakes; we had already eaten from vendors on the road, but thinking it would be rude to refuse, I thanked her and ate one.

"Delicious, Madam. May I pay you for it?"

"Oh no, sir, I have plenty. Merry Christmas to you and your friends. At the university, are you?"

"Yes, Madam."

"Such a blessing to be book-learned. May your good fortune continue." At that moment the boy began to whimper, from boredom and cold, I suspected, and was silenced with a slap to his head. I acted as if I did not see the boy as he shrank back into the folds of her skirt, and wondered what good fortune awaited him.

There was no shortage of drink, as evidenced by rowdy gaggles of drunken men staggering through the crowd, stopping only to grope young women or vomit. Just behind us, one of them puked on the breeches of his comrade, prompting a fight, with the two of them ending up in a writing heap on the ground. They were cheered on until burly constables came and hustled them away.

The chatter of anticipation suddenly turned to cheers as a procession entered the gallows area from the road. A chevron of soldiers led, clearing a path for an open carriage carrying four black-robed city officials and the crier, and then a farm wagon in which Ernst Bronck knelt shivering in tattered clothes, hands lashed to the rails, his outstretched arms riddled with burns. His head drooped onto his chest and tears streamed down his bruised and swollen face. Bronck's confession clearly had not been given freely. Was he truly guilty? It no longer mattered.

The cheering that greeted his entry was followed by a pitiless hail of catcalls. Beside him in the wagon, a fat priest struggled to maintain his balance as he mumbled prayers in the general direction of the half-conscious prisoner. Stumbling behind the wagon were a woman and three boys—Bronck's family—their dazed faces streaked with dirt and tears, their terror and shame laid bare.

The sunny day and the camaraderie had lulled me into feeling that we were waiting for the curtain to rise on a Christmas pageant, not the cruel spectacle that was unfolding. I lowered my eyes, ashamed at taking part. I wanted to leave, but it was too late.

"Poor little beggars," I heard the sweetcake woman say to her husband. "They'll have no father, thieving bastard that he is." She cupped her hands to her mouth. "Thieving bastard!" she yelled as he passed. She turned to me. "Another sweetcake, sir?"

"You have already been too kind," I said.

Many in the crowd brought extra food, but not to eat. A salvo of rotten fruit and vegetables flew overhead and pelted the wagon as it rolled toward the gallows; some was directed at the wretched family trailing behind. A potato overshot Bronck and struck a little girl in the crowd sitting atop the shoulders of her father, opening up a gash on her forehead. The soldier driving the wagon, obviously a veteran of public hangings, wore his battle helmet and a heavy cloak. The priest had not dressed with the same forethought; to the great amusement of the spectators, after a cabbage exploded on his shoulder he slipped on some slimy leaves underfoot and tumbled off the rear of the wagon. His face red, he regained his feet and strode up to the lead carriage for a seat, but was not permitted on. He walked the rest of the way, cabbage leaves pasted to his cloak.

The procession came to a halt at the base of the gallows. The city officials mounted the platform. A cheer arose when a hooded figure appeared on the platform from a concealed stairway at the rear and stood in wait of his client beside a noose suspended from the beam overhead. Meanwhile, two soldiers climbed into the wagon and untied Bronck, lashed his hands behind him, and led him stumbling past his stunned wife and children. She reached for him, calling his name, but was shoved away by one of the soldiers. She fell backward at the feet of her children.

Bronck was dragged up to the platform where he would soon die. The crier held up his hand to quiet the crowd and recited Bronck's crimes while the cabbage-smeared priest read a last prayer into his ear. Once Bronck's soul was readied for Judgment, the soldiers lifted him onto a wooden stool under the noose. He wobbled unsteadily as the hangman fitted the noose snugly around his neck and adjusted the length of the rope. For the briefest of moments, Bronck lifted his head, but then let it fall back to his chest.

All was ready; the chief magistrate had only to give the signal. He stepped forward to give the order, but paused to be sure that Leuven's elites had exited their carriages and mounted high chairs secured by their footmen. When he was satisfied that everyone was settled, he nodded to the hangman.

Andreas came to my side. "You might want to look away, Jan."

The warning came too late. The hangman gave a hard tug to a rope that pulled the stool out from under Bronck's feet. His body dropped like a stone, then lurched to a stop in midair when the rope ran out of slack, crushing his trachea and breaking his neck with a sickening crack heard across the clearing. Men winced, women shrieked, and children cried out as his body twitched and spun under the taut rope. The executioner took hold of a leg to stop the swaying. For good measure, a soldier stepped forward and plunged his pike into his chest, bringing another round of cries and gasps from the crowd. Bronck's wife fell to the ground, her sons kneeling around her.

The spectacle was over. The city officials descended the platform, remounted the carriage and rode off, the family staggering behind. A few last vegetables were tossed in their direction, so as not to have to carry them home. Bronck would remain suspended in the gallows, in view of passersby, until decay and scavengers reduced him to bones.

If Lucretius had ridden beside Bronck instead of the hapless priest, he would have told him, "Fear not, you will find peace in unawareness, free of pain or worries, the same as it was before you were conceived. Your body's fate will be beyond your concern; but know that the substances of which it is made are immortal, and will find their places in the world you leave behind."

Justice having been done, the citizens of Leuven, momentarily chastened, shuffled back to the road. But soon pockets of chatter started up, the conversation having turned to Christmas preparations or the day's work ahead.

"I'm sorry, Jan," Andreas said. "That was not a pretty scene, but not nearly as gruesome as others."

"Good to know."

Andreas dropped back to walk with Gemma. I took little note of their excited whispers, so appalled was I at what I had just witnessed.

That evening in the Café du Château, Andreas leaned over to me and spoke in a low voice.

"Gemma and I are going to get the pig thief tomorrow night, and we need a lookout."

"You cannot be serious," I said, astonished. "The poor man . . ."

"Quietly, Jan," said Andreas, index finger to his mouth.

". . . the poor man's been dead a few hours," I said in an angry hush, "and already you're plotting to steal him and cut him to pieces."

"Exactly. His body is fresh, and in this weather his internal organs will be well preserved. Chances like this do not come along every day. And tell me—is it better for his remains to be eaten by jackdaws and wild dogs, or used to advance the medical sciences?"

"Fine, then. You and Gemma go and have your ghoulish fun. But count me out."

"We need you, Jan. We could ask one of the other students, but they may not keep the secret, and we want the cadaver to ourselves. You're the only one we can trust."

"I'm flattered."

"We can get a wagon and a horse from a farmer Gemma knows. All you have to do is wait by the road and signal us if there's any trouble. You know that the roads outside the city are not traveled or patrolled after dark . . ."

"Only by bandits and madmen like you."

". . . but of course, we will have to stay outside the gates until the next morning."

"Wait—my hearing must be bad. I thought I heard you say we'd have to stay outside the city until the next morning."

"You heard correctly. We will cut him down after dark. By then the city gates will be closed for the night. Gemma's farmer friend will let us stay the night in his barn. He will be paid well, and will ask no questions. The next morning we conceal the body in the wagon, ride it into town, and put the body in Gemma's cellar, which is perfect for dissection. The farmer will come for the wagon later in the day. That will be that."

"And Andreas and I will get right to work," Gemma said.

"There are laws against body-snatching. We will end up in prison, or in the gallows just where you cut him down."

"Not a chance," Andreas said. "The plan is foolproof, but a lookout is still a wise precaution. Come on, Jan. We need you."

I sighed in resignation. "I have lost my mind. I will come, but on one condition."

Andreas and Gemma listened to my terms.

"Not really!" they said in unison.

"Really. Either you agree or find someone else."

They looked at each other. "Agreed," Andreas said, holding up his mug. "To the proper study of anatomy."

The next afternoon we strolled through the city gates, leaving early enough to avoid suspicion. At dusk we went to the farmer's barn and rode the one-horse wagon on deserted roads to a shadowy edge of the gallows field. We waited there until dark, looking silently at the limp silhouette of Bronck as the sun set behind him. At nightfall, Andreas and Gemma lit a lamp and took the wagon to the base of the platform while I crouched at my post in a shallow ditch by the road.

Gemma carried a ladder up to the platform and climbed it to cut Ernst's corpse loose while Andreas held his legs. The body, suddenly released, fell on Andreas like a tree trunk and toppled him to the platform. Giggling like children stealing apples, they hauled the corpse down the stairs to the wagon. Gemma retrieved the ladder and got in the back to pull Ernst aboard with Andreas pushing the legs.

Our horse snorted and stamped his hooves as a group of ghostly figures darted into the clearing and quickly closed on the wagon.

"Dogs!" I yelled.

The snarling pack of four wild dogs were equally interested in Ernst Bronck, and they were ready to fight for him.

"Pull him in, Gemma!" Andreas yelled. He grabbed a shovel from the wagon and turned to face the dogs.

"Any closer and I'll split your heads open!"

The dogs sensed the fearlessness of their adversary, but were not scared off. They spread out, making testing moves at Andreas while Gemma wrestled with the corpse. One dog got close enough to nip at Andreas' boot, but paid for his attack with a shovel blow to the head. The dog staggered back and collapsed, but this seemed only to enrage the other three; they tightened their circle around Andreas.

Without thinking I picked up a rock and charged at the dogs, yelling at the top of my lungs. The startled dogs froze long enough for me to hurl the rock at one of them, hitting it squarely in the ribs. The dog yelped and retreated into the dark, as did the other two. Andreas and I pushed the cadaver into the wagon by his feet and jumped in before the dogs could regroup.

"Gemma, get us out of here!" Andreas shouted. Gemma took the reins and drove the horse across the field, turning sharply onto the road.

The corpse bounced to the edge of the wagon, but Andreas caught him under the arm and pulled him back. The dogs gave brief chase, but gave up. We watched them recede into the darkness.

"Well done, Jan!" Andreas exclaimed, clapping me on the shoulder. "That was a bit more of a fuss than I thought, but without you . . ."

I cut him off, my hands still shaking. "A fuss? Those dogs could have killed you!"

"They could have killed you, too."

"Don't you think I know that? So much for your foolproof plan. Don't ever ask me to do this again."

Gemma flicked the reins. "You know, mapmaking is looking like an appealing career right now."

Back at the barn, Andreas and Gemma brought the body inside for safe-keeping, and we shared a meal of cheese, apples, bread and beer. Andreas and Gemma giddily recounted the adventure, showering me with praise.

"Jan's charge was the turning point of the fight," Andreas said. "No doubt."

In spite of myself I began to feel better about the evening's events.

We laughed and joked into the night, forgetting that just a few feet away there was a corpse hidden under a blanket. Gemma faded and turned in. Finally, Andreas and I stretched out on piles of hay. In the darkness, I heard Andreas' voice.

"Scarecrow."

"What?"

"You are a magnificent friend. And braver than you thought."

"Someday I will learn to choose my friends more carefully."

In the morning, dressed as common farmers, we rode through the town gates with our load of hay and waved to the guards. In the alley behind Gemma's house, Andreas and Gemma carried the body down to the cellar and came upstairs to join me for breakfast. Not long after, the farmer came to the door and rode away with his wagon and a bonus to ensure his silence.

Andreas and Gemma immediately set to work to maximize the time before Bronck began to rot. Andreas insisted I stay for the first session.

Andreas had already laid out his instruments on a nearby table. He would never travel with his grandfather's instruments, and so had assembled a new set during the three years he was in Paris.

The two of them donned aprons, positioned the body supine on the table, and removed any remaining clothes. They washed the body of dirt and caked blood.

"Give me a little while, you two," Andreas said as he opened his notebook. "I always meant to sketch my instruments." We went upstairs and drank a beer; in a while he called us down. The sketch was finished:

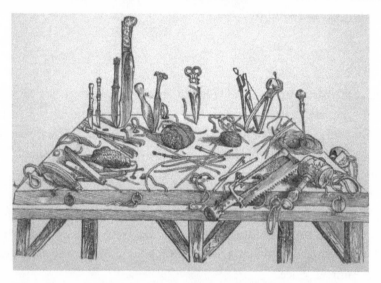

"That's very good," I said.

Andreas smiled. "Thanks. Now let's see what we can learn from this corpse."

I spoke up. "He has a name, remember? He is Ernst."

"All right," Andreas said. "Henceforth he shall be Ernst. Perhaps you would like to say a benediction."

"I would."

"I was joking."

"I was not. Gather round the table."

Andreas sighed. "I want to get started."

"You can spare a minute."

We stood around Ernst's naked body.

"Bow your heads." Andreas and Gemma shrugged and obeyed.

"Ernst Bronck, your crime on behalf of your family did not merit so savage a punishment. We ask you to receive the gratitude of these men, who humbly accept the gift of your remains in advancing their knowledge of the human body."

Gemma nodded. "Amen and well said."

Andreas clapped his hands and rubbed them together. "Well, we've had our ceremony. Let me have the razor, Gemma, and we will start—in humble thanks. We'll do the abdominal viscera now, because they will rot first."

He paused for a moment over the abdomen.

"He has several contusions from his . . . interrogation. Remember this one in the left upper quadrant."

He made a circular incision around the umbilicus, then an incision from the tip of the sternum to the umbilicus, and continued the incision from the umbilicus to the pubis. He then made two lateral incisions from the umbilicus to the crests of the hip bones.

"See, Gemma, how I have taken care not to go deeper than the skin. With the razor very little pressure is needed. Now we will separate the underlying fat from the skin. Ernst is thin, so we will have to be careful. Watch me do the first quadrant, and you will do the second. Keeping the skin flap taut, I make short, transverse cuts just under the skin. The first of us to make a hole in the skin is a donkey! The skin has two layers, the uppermost being the epidermis, which seems to have no function . . ."

Sometime later, after dissecting through the muscles of the abdomen and the peritoneal membrane beneath, the viscera were exposed. The large flap of omentum covering the intestines was carefully raised and folded up onto the chest.

"It's important," Andreas said, "to first observe the intestines as they are; knowing the course and location of the intestines will aid in making diagnoses. Now we'll follow the intestines back from the rectum to the colon, caecum, and to the parts of the slender intestine. In so doing we will see where they pass in relation to other organs. You do it, Gemma, I'll explain what to do. Reach down to the rectum with your right hand . . . that's it, make your way around to the caecum . . . there's the vermiform appendix."

A while later: "See the spleen, Gemma. It's lacerated, and it corresponds to the contusion we saw on the abdomen. Ernst was lucky this didn't kill him."

"He would have been better off," I said. "I've had enough. I'll be back later." Neither of them even looked up.

I came back with two roasted chickens and vegetable soup, which they devoured in the early evening before going back to Ernst. I heard them come to bed in the middle of the night, and when I arose in the morning they were already downstairs. I went down to check on them.

"We're making great progress," Andreas said to me, and turned back to Gemma. "Take the heart in your hands, and see where the various vessels arise from it . . . don't worry, you can move it around. See, the aorta arises behind the pulmonary artery and then arches back toward the spine . . ."

I stopped going down when I could no longer bear the smell. But I was struck by Andreas' deftness and enthusiasm as he proceeded, with patient explanations and instructions to a rapt Gemma, and by his intense concentration as he added notes and drawings to his notebook. Andreas had come a long way from the animals he dissected as a schoolboy, and beyond the rotting leg he stole from Montagne de la Potence.

Ernst's disappearance was not reported until days later, and by that time Andreas and Gemma had all but completed their work. I joined the bleary-eyed dissectors for a celebratory dinner of lamb stew, a loaf of bread, and a brandy cake.

We gathered around the table in Gemma's kitchen with a fire roaring in the hearth.

"Andreas has great skill and never tires," Gemma said to me. "I learned more anatomy in the past few days than I could ever learn at the medical school."

"Don't puff him up—he will be intolerable."

Andreas ignored my barb. "You did well, Gemma. Leave mapmaking to Mercator and stay with medicine."

I noticed that Andreas had brought up his notebook from the cellar. "Say, let me see your notebook."

"If you want." He pushed it across the table and turned back to the stew. The cover was stained with dried blood and grease.

"Ugh! How can you show this to anyone?"

"It's not for show."

Using only the corners, I leafed through it. The pages had been heavily worked with drawings and notes.

"You're getting better. Your lines are more confident, and look, you're even shading now."

"Now look who's puffing him up!" Gemma laughed between mouthfuls of stew. "But Andreas, you worked as hard with your pen as you did with your knife. Wasn't it enough to have Ernst in the flesh?"

"Ha! You sound just like Jacobus Sylvius, one of my teachers in Paris. To his credit he dissected with his own hands, but he rejected pictures as mere shadows. He believed only in seeing and touching."

"But you disobey your teacher."

"I admire Sylvius, but his view is too narrow. As a boy, I drew the insides of squirrels and dogs because it pleased me to try to copy what I saw. But as time went on, I found that the drawings sharpened my eye and my memory, and gave me a record of what I did. My pictures aided my notes, and vice versa."

Andreas took a swallow of wine. "Ernst is gone forever, but he lives on in this notebook, and when I open it next month, or next year, he will speak to me again."

"So, you're a necromancer as well!"

"That's the least of my powers, Frisius. Rub my ass and make a wish."

After the laughter died down, I said, "Andreas, remember when we were, what, twelve years old, when you stole the leg from the gallows . . ."

"Stole a leg from a gallows? At twelve?" Gemma said, his eyebrows raised. "That's a story I want to hear."

"You'll hear it someday, Gemma," I said. "But here's the point—once

Andreas had his prize, he tried to dissect it using Mondino's *Anathomia* as a guide. What a disaster that was."

"With no great help from you, Scarecrow, with your gagging and retching. The leg was very rotten, Gemma, and my right arm was in a splint."

"What's this?" Gemma exclaimed. "The story gets better! But I see your point: no edition of the *Anathomia,* in two centuries, has pictures, and our young one-armed thief would have had better luck with a picture to guide him."

"Exactly," I said, "but the picture must be helpful! For example, the *Margarita Philosophica . . .*"

Andreas groaned. "Must you always bring up that book?"

"Gregor Reisch's compendium of knowledge," Gemma said.

"Yes, published in 1503, as I recall . . ."

"What don't you recall?" Andreas said with a smirk.

"Stop interrupting me. It's a lovely and useful book with a competent section on mathematics, but the section on anatomy is poor."

Andreas shook his head. "The anatomy book that satisfies you has not been written."

"True, they're all tedious—but as you know, my problem with this one was with the picture."

"A petty complaint at best."

Gemma jumped up from his seat. "I have a copy in the next room. Let's see what Jan's talking about."

A moment later he put the book in front of me. With Andreas and Gemma peering over my shoulders, I found what I wanted.

"Never mind that the poor man has the face of a baboon, and arms like chicken wings. Even his penis is ridiculous, hanging over the edge of the drawing into nowhere."

Andreas chortled. "You wish yours was half that big."

"Be serious for a minute. You know as well as anyone that humans don't look anything like this inside. What purpose does this picture serve to any reader, expert or not?"

"The drawing is simplified, meant only for orientation and remembering terminology."

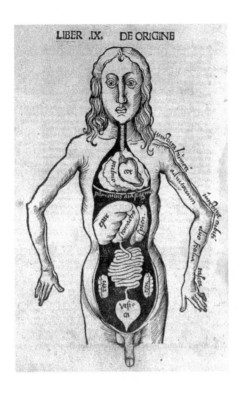

"Even if I grant you that, it is simplified *ad absurdum*. Are our abdominal organs flattened into a narrow plane, floating free in a dark hole? Is our heart a little pastry resting on a cloudy bed of lungs? Do our intestines wind around like sausage on display in the butcher's window, to empty into the urinary bladder? And where is the large intestine?"

"As I said . . ."

"Don't make excuses for this picture. Draftsmanship has made great advances, in particular with perspective—to show where things are located in space, and in relation to other things. Why not use those skills to picture the body? You are already a better draftsman than the oaf who drew this, and admirably, you strive to draw what you actually see. If Reisch's creature is the best we can do, then Sylvius is right! This picture is lazy and dishonest; it is neither precise nor beautiful."

Andreas shrugged. "But you have to concede that he's drawn an excellent penis."

We laughed and refilled our glasses.

Gemma was not ready to let the discussion drop. "Jan calls for precise pictures or none at all. But the notion of precision would apply to other sorts of pictures—maps, for example."

"But what if your map is not precise," Andreas said, "and lands your traveler in Rotterdam instead of Brussels? This is the contention of Sylvius about pictures of the body; they can lead you astray."

"A fair point," Gemma said. "The mapmaker will have to do better. But Jan, aside from precision, why do you speak of beauty in pictures of the body?"

"Do not encourage him, Gemma," Andreas said. "Precision is one thing, but beauty is the domain of architecture, paintings, and sculpture."

"Not so fast," I said, wagging my finger. "There is a philosophical matter to consider . . ."

At that moment there was a loud banging on the kitchen door.

"Open up, by order of the Constable! Open up now or we will use force!"

We looked at each other in shock. The only likely reason for a raid from the authorities was the missing corpse, now flayed and eviscerated in the cellar.

"The farmer!" Andreas said angrily. "He turned us in for a bounty."

"Hide that notebook and close the cellar door," Gemma whispered. "I'll try keep them up here."

My heart pounded. If caught, we would be in serious trouble. I closed my eyes to find some calm, but I saw only Mother's face.

Gemma opened the door and after a pause, shouted, "Wretch! I should let you freeze out there!"

Antoine de Granvelle charged into the room, followed by a blast of cold air.

"I guessed there'd be food!" he said, sniffing the air. "Lamb, isn't it? Here, I brought a bottle of Armagnac to keep us warm."

Antoine hung up his cloak and hat and turned to us. "Say, have you heard about the corpse that was stolen from the gallows a few days ago? I cannot imagine who would be interested in a fresh young cadaver."

Antoine had rightly divined Ernst's disappearance and saw his chance for another of his pranks.

"I can tell by your faces that I am on the right track! Don't worry, you thieving ghouls, your secret is safe with me, unless you haven't left me enough stew."

"Some divinity student you are!" Andreas said, shaking his head. "You are a sack of shit, Granvelle—but well played."

Antoine scooped a bowl of stew from the pot and took a seat at the table.

"If I have walked in on a dispute," he said, looking around at our faces, "count me in."

"It will be of no interest to you," Andreas said.

"If there is a dispute, I am interested."

Gemma showed Antoine the picture from Reisch. "Jan contends that because it is not a precise representation, it is without value. And ugly."

Antoine tilted his head as he examined the picture. "Well, precise or not, it's easier on the eyes than the real thing. I have been to one of your dissections, Vesalius, and I take no offense at being left out of this one." Turning back to the book, he tapped it with his spoon handle. "It's artless and crude all right, but at least it doesn't make me want to puke."

He leaned in for a closer look. "That's quite a cock on him, though."

"That, Granvelle, is not in dispute," Andreas said, "but irrelevant. Socrates, here," thumbing at me, "was about to expound on beauty."

Antoine looked scandalized. "Ha. What does a heathen like Jan know of beauty?"

"We shall see. Begin, Socrates, but I have the hemlock ready."

I stood at my place. "How timely that our theologian is here. Antoine, if mankind was created in God's image, would it not follow that our internal structures were created in God's image as well?"

Antoine sighed. "The scriptural meaning of our creation 'in His image' has been debated for centuries. I could give you a better answer if you asked a better question. Ask me this instead: 'Are our internal structures as well as external features designed by God?'"

"Consider yourself asked."

"Then I answer that that is the only possible conclusion."

"Would you say that all God's designs are perfect?"

"God's works are by definition perfect."

"And are all His designs beautiful?"

"It is not our place to judge His designs, but it would be hard to argue otherwise."

Andreas tapped his fingers impatiently on the table. "Is there a point to be made, Socrates?"

"Patience. I offer a syllogism: If our internal structures are of God's design, and if God's designs are perfect and beautiful, then our internal structures are perfect and beautiful. Antoine, is the syllogism sound?"

"It is."

"How better, then, to portray the body's perfection and beauty than precisely as it is seen? The more precise the drawing, the closer it is to God's design. Painters and sculptors celebrate the human form by careful attention to outward features. Our internal features should merit the same treatment."

I paused for dramatic effect. "I submit that in anatomy, precision and beauty are equivalent."

"Odd words from someone who is repulsed by our internal features," Andreas said.

"That is my failing, I would argue, not God's. Repulsion is learned, and can be unlearned. You are a prime example of this. And over time I have gotten . . . less repulsed."

Antoine sat back in his chair. "Really, Jan. Since when do you come to God's defense, when you don't believe that God is responsible for our existence?"

"That is not my belief, as you well know. I believe only that our Creator cares not a whit about what happens on Earth. I invoke God in deference to present company, but I arrive at the same end by substituting 'Nature' for 'God.' The only difference is that I'm not sure Nature has finished its work; on this I agree with Lucretius . . ."

"A heathen older than dirt," Antoine sniffed.

"Well, we can all agree, I think, that we look upon our bodies, and all living things, with a sense of wonder, whether it is God or Nature that keeps the ultimate secrets. One can also posit that God and Nature are one and the same."

Gemma clapped his hands. "Bravo, Socrates, I am persuaded! I say spare him!"

I turned to Andreas. "If my remarks are unworthy, I will drink the hemlock. Death in the service of wisdom is a noble death."

Andreas smiled. "Good speech! You may live, but stay a while and answer this: In anatomy, what is 'precision,' exactly?"

I stood to refill my bowl with stew. "That's a question hardly worth asking."

As I spoke those words, I realized that Andreas had sprung a trap.

"And to think I just spared you. You see 'precision' through the lens of mathematics, where everything takes place on clean sheets of paper. Two plus two is always four; $a^2 + b^2 = c^2$ is always true in right triangles. Gemma's maps would be precise in a similar way, assuming that they could be drawn to the last river, mountain, and coastline. Such a map will always be precise—unless, say, Iberia breaks off and floats away."

"God willing," Gemma said.

"Listen," Andreas said impatiently over the laughter. "The meaning of 'precision' in mathematics and cartography, for our purposes, is clear. But to teach and learn anatomy, we need to somehow transcend precision."

"Transcend precision? To what?" Gemma asked.

"To something like an ideal—a standard."

"But Andreas," Antoine said, "can we not agree that the precise and the ideal are one and the same?"

"Not in anatomy. In humans and in other animals, God has permitted variation in His designs. I have notebooks full of drawings—as precise as my skill allows—of different animals and an increasing number of humans, and I have picked through thousands of bones in the cemeteries of Paris . . ."

"I can testify to that," I said.

". . . and I will wager that no two creatures of the same kind are exactly alike. This is obvious in outward features—"

"—God in His wisdom did not have us all look like you," Antoine intoned, crossing himself.

"Stop interrupting. I was about to say that variation is also found in internal structures. Bones and organs vary in shape and size; blood vessels and nerves do not always follow the same paths. If we are to describe the structure of the human body, which skull, which heart, which vein, shall we choose to represent those parts?

"Galen himself instructs us about individual variation. He talks of a sculpture by the great Policleitus that is an ideal—a canon—of the human form. It follows that we need a canon of our inner structures—one that best represents our anatomy but leaves room for normal variations."

"Well, Vesalius," Gemma declared, "do you still defend Reisch's picture?"

"No. Jan is right—Reisch's picture is neither precise nor a canon. Such pictures can no longer be excused, even as aids to memory. It does more to deceive a student of anatomy than to enlighten."

I sighed. "Why didn't you just say so?"

"I wanted to hear your argument again, and have Gemma hear it as well. I have resisted it, but I confess I have been increasingly troubled by pictures such as this. Gemma, do you have your copy of Berengario's *Commentaria* here?"

With that, Gemma retrieved the thick volume and handed it to Andreas.

"Berengario's book," Andreas said as he searched through it, "published only fifteen years ago at Bologna, was the first to make a serious attempt at anatomic drawings. But here, look at this one . . ."

"This is meant to show the female organs of reproduction. It's a pleasing picture in its own way, but not as an anatomical drawing. It's a geometric fantasy."

"I know why you find it pleasing," Antoine said.

"Spoken like a Frenchman," Andreas said. "Berengario repeatedly insists that we rely on our own observations, but his pictures could not represent what he saw. The book is a valuable commentary on Mondino's *Anathomia*, but falls short in advancing our knowledge."

Gemma looked up from the book. "Let's accept that drawings can be wrong—but I remain puzzled by your notion of variation. If variation exists in human structures, how far from your 'canon' would a variation be before you would call it abnormal?"

"Good question. I'm not sure . . . but for now I would say that, excluding diseased and damaged parts, normal variations permit normal function, and abnormal variations don't. It's possible that some variations are more common, some rare. I will leave it to Antoine to explain why God's creatures are not always formed alike, and why sometimes they are monstrously and lethally imperfect."

"Only God knows the answer to that."

I could not resist challenging Antoine. "Our theologian offers the usual apology—it's another of God's mysteries, fodder for endless speculation."

"I wish you long life, heathen, because your next life may not be to your liking! But out of Christian charity I will let you have some Armagnac."

He poured us all a glass. "Merry Christmas, my dear friends. If my father knew I was sharing his precious Armagnac with the likes of you, he would disown me."

When the bottle of Armagnac was empty, we left Gemma's. Andreas and I parted ways with Antoine, whose rooms were in the other direction. Hunched against the cold and a light snowfall, we walked quietly until Andreas broke the silence.

"You know, Scarecrow, I value your thoughts on pictures, even as my own thoughts are not quite settled. But there is something else that's troubling me."

"What?"

"I did not make much of it with Gemma during the dissection, but I have a growing unease with Galen's grip on us over the centuries. Sylvius hates Berengario's book, not so much because of the pictures, but because Berengario on occasion took issue with Galen. To Sylvius, any questioning of Galen was heresy."

"What are you saying?"

"I am saying that Galen is not always right. For example, Galen teaches that the liver has five lobes; I can count only four. Galen teaches that the human jawbone is split at the chin; it is clearly not. These findings are in animals, not humans. He teaches that there are holes in the septum of the heart connecting the two ventricles; I cannot find them. This is so not just with Ernst, but with every dissection I have attended in Paris, public or private. Yet we defer to Galen as the final authority. Why don't others see what I see? Are they all blind?"

"Do you trust what you see?"

"I do. But that means that sometimes I will be at odds with Galen. The question is whether I will be public with my disagreements."

"You are not disposed to keep your disagreements to yourself. The profession you are about to enter will have to reckon with you."

Andreas and Gemma were not quite done with Ernst. After carefully scraping and boiling his bones clean, they constructed a complete skeleton and presented it to their friend Gisbertus Carbo in Leuven. The story Andreas told was that he had brought the skeleton with him from Paris. No one ever suspected that the skeleton was of a local and recent provenance.

Shortly after I returned to Brussels, a letter came from Gemma confirming that he and Andreas had met the condition of my participation in the theft of Ernst Bronck's body.

7 December 1536

Dear Jan,

I hereby report that Andreas and I met the conditions of our agreement yesterday on St. Nicholas Day.

In the town of Opvelpen, as I observed from a respectful distance, a diminutive but spirited Sinterklaas, with a white beard, red cap, and red cloak, rode up in a wagon to the door of a small farmhouse. He bowed and introduced himself to the woman who came to the door, and then to the three boys who edged into the doorway behind her. The woman covered her mouth with both hands in disbelief as he presented her with four roasted chickens, two loaves of bread, a dozen eggs, a bundle of carrots, and a sack of coins sufficient to keep the family in food and fuel until spring.

The widow, her face full of tears, took his hand and kissed it. Sinterklaas knelt and embraced each child, then waved goodbye to the stunned family and rode off around a bend to where I waited.

So it was that the thief who stole the body of their husband and father from the gallows, took it apart, and boiled his bones clean, was also the miracle-maker who brought sustenance and a measure of hope to that tormented family. Sinterklaas was aware of the irony, but was unprepared for the emotion of the moment.

Overcome, he made me take the reins, and did not speak all the way back to Leuven.

I pray that the widow and her children will keep hope alive in their hearts, just as I pray that we remember the lesson of compassion. Thanks to you, Jan, Ernst Bronck was a teacher in more ways than one.

Gemma

Gemma spent the rest of his life in Leuven at the university, and died in its service. In the graveyard of a small church I paid my respects to him.

I miss Gemma. He was a great friend and scholar, and unlike you, was content to settle in one place and could carry on a conversation about mathematics.

Despite the fine weather that followed us south from Leuven, the carriage ride was tense. In five days we reached Soissons; French Protestants in the region—known as Huguenots—were still furious three years after the massacre at Wassy by Catholic soldiers, and concessions granted by King Charles of France had done little to quell their anger. Vengeful Huguenot bands continued to raid Catholic villages in retaliation for the persecution they suffered, or even strike travelers at random. To our relief, we had no trouble.

In Soissons the coachman recommended a well-kept inn in the shadow of the basilica in the center of town. Marcus and I shared a dinner table with an English professor of languages who was northbound from Paris. He advised we continue on horseback. The Paris road, he said, was being patrolled by the king's soldiers, but their heavy military wagons had left stretches of road deeply rutted; travel by carriage was therefore a gamble. On horseback the main road was still passable.

"If I may," the Englishman asked, "what takes you to Paris?"

"We are looking for a friend," I said evasively.

"May you find him well and safe. Has your friend been in Paris long?"

"No, not long at all."

"Good, then. Paris has been free of plague for almost two years. I pray he was not caught up . . ."

"Thank you for asking, but he was not at risk."

I did not look forward to the backache and burning skin from a saddle, but I was glad for the protection of the patrols. In the three days it took to reach Paris, however, we saw for ourselves that peace was tenuous at best. More than once we saw royal patrols give chase to brazen young men who hurled stones at them and vanished into the woods.

I wonder if Brother Carel is alive to see this, Andreas! I don't think he'd be happy about it. Religious war seems upon us. Luther himself would be startled by what he has wrought. The Prince of Peace should find this an excellent time for the Second Coming . . . his flock needs urgent instruction in proper worship of Him.

Paris

27 February 1565

As we came over a rise, Marcus exclaimed, "I see spires. And look, the ramparts!"

The gates of Paris are just ahead. What will it be like without you? There is a part of me that does not want to find out.

Our horses' hooves echoed on the cobblestones under the massive archway of the Saint-Denis Gate, just as the skies darkened and snow began to fall. Emerging onto Rue Saint-Denis, we were met by the intense noise and activity of a city that by most accounts had become the most populous in Europe.

Europe's population had swelled in this century, and arable land had been taken up to its limits. The descendants of families that had worked the land for centuries had no choice but to abandon rural life to find work in cities. At our backs was the world they left behind: the hamlets, windmills, and copses scattered upon rolling fields of crops and livestock. Painters do not let us forget the countryside; their wistful, distant glimpses through city windows reminds us that the land is eternal, and waits patiently for our return.

Rue Saint-Denis was the principal thoroughfare leading south to the Seine. Teeming with people hunched against the weather, it was tightly lined with two- and three-story gabled houses of differing constructions. Many houses had shops on the street level. Stray dogs and children darted among the wagons and horses, and vendors with their wares in baskets balanced on their heads wove through the crowds and kept up their calls as the snow drove people to shelter. We stopped a vendor to buy cheese and bread, which we ate as we picked our way down the street. Paris drew people not only from France but from all over Europe, so different languages could be heard on the street. Churches had to post the languages spoken in the confession booths.

The gentle snowfall tossed bright accents onto the jutting surfaces of row houses on the cramped side streets and for a time would subdue the fetid smells that rose from the sewage trenches that ran down the streets, and disguise the slurry of mud and dung underfoot.

I smiled and shook my head as we passed a familiar landmark—the Fontaine des Innocents, built against the wall that enclosed the cemetery of the same name.

You would drag me along in the middle of the night to scavenge bones from the piles stacked along the walls. You would rummage like you were shopping for fruit. "If only your mother could see you now," you joked, while you stuffed the bones of fingers and toes into my pockets, and shoved femurs and ribs up your sleeves. Back home with your student friends, you would show them how you could recognize bones blindfolded, by touch alone. You would tell them how you broke your arm, and let them feel the bump it left on your humerus.

"You cannot not imagine what I did in this cemetery with Andreas," I said.

Marcus laughed. "Oh, yes I can."

As we neared the river we rode past the Church of Saint-Jacques de la Boucherie, just thirty years old, with its soaring tower.

"This church is the starting point for the pilgrimage to Santiago de Compostela. Paris butchers paid for its construction."

"A fine trade, butchery. Surely better than the fishing trade, by the looks of this church."

Wouldn't Santiago de Compostela have been a much more sensible pilgrimage for you? You would have ended up back in Spain. You would not have set foot on a boat. You could have convinced me to join you—not that I longed to cross the Pyrenées again.

Near the Seine we passed the grand houses of the wealthy bourgeoisie and nobility. Notre Dame Cathedral, with a frosting of snow on its towers and buttresses, was now in full view, looming over the Seine on the Île de la Cité like a huge warship at anchor. We crossed the river on the Pont de Notre Dame, itself lined with a hodgepodge of shops and houses, and stopped to admire the great cathedral.

"I have never seen anything more beautiful," Marcus said, transfixed.

"We'll get a better look while we're here, I promise. If we have sun, the Rose Windows will be quite a sight from the inside."

As we rode on to the south bank, Marcus asked, "Master Jan, do we know where we're going?"

"I would like to think so! We're going to a place I know well—if it's still there. It would be down this street. I am more than ready to get off this horse and out of the cold."

I stopped at a small street called Le Passé and peered down it toward the river.

You led me to a house on Le Passé after a big dinner and more wine than usual. You told me it was a salon that admitted women of learning and culture. Inside there were women, but not the sort to discuss issues of the day. They strolled about with trays of drink, or draped themselves over men whose hands were free to wander up a skirt or reach into a bodice.

I was not yet too drunk to realize that you had taken me to a brothel. Before I could leave you sat me down in a large armchair and left me with a pretty girl with coal-black eyes and ebony hair falling over her shoulders. I drank more wine. She breathed into my ear and shifted onto my lap. In another instant I was in a room with the coal-eyed girl. She undid the laces of her bodice and her dress slid to the floor.

All else was dark until you and one of your school friends, huffing and laughing, dropped me like a sack of grain on my own bed. Before the darkness reclaimed me there was a name, Ynez. I never told you but I went back a week later for Ynez. The proprietor told me she was gone. "Girls like that come and go. Sometimes they end up floating in the Seine." I turned and left.

I was startled by Marcus' voice. "What's down that way?"

"Just some houses on the river."

Le Passé opened into Place Maubert, and I was relieved to see a familiar sign. Le Pierwige was a brick-and-timber inn where I stayed for my year at the university and whenever I came back to Paris to see Andreas. It was beyond the reach of most university students, but I required its comforts. It was too costly even for Andreas, who, at any rate, wanted to live close by the medical school.

My knees were so stiff that Marcus had to help me off my horse. I paced a bit to loosen them, then entered the mid-afternoon quiet of the public room, spotlessly clean and warmed by a fire in a large central hearth. A bell rang as we opened the door, and a man rushed out of the kitchen to greet us, wiping his hands on a towel. I recognized him as the son of the owners, who was in his teens when I last saw him.

"*Salut*, it's Pierre, isn't it? Do you remember me after all these years?"

He stopped and studied my face. "Monsieur van den Bossche! *Quel plaisir! Ça fait longtemps!*"

We exchanged a warm handshake, and I introduced Marcus as my assistant. I asked after his parents, the original owners and hosts; he told me they both perished in the recent plague outbreak.

"I am so sorry, Pierre. I was very fond of your parents. They treated me like a son."

"Thank you for your kind words. And news has spread of the death of Doctor Vesalius. I am honored to have known him. I can still picture you two dining here. You laughed, argued, and played chess in equal parts."

"I will never forget those times, Pierre."

Our favorite table was over there, near the hearth. You would come often and allow me to buy you a meal.

"We have top-floor rooms facing the courtyard. You remember the chestnut tree there? It has grown since you were here last."

The two flights of stairs were worth the effort. The rooms were tidy and pleasant, not the dirty, Spartan cells of the roadside inns.

"These will be splendid, Pierre."

"I will see to your horses and have your chests brought up. May I assume you will be having dinner here? We are serving a *confit* of duck—a Gascon recipe of my mother's. I cannot equal hers, but I come close."

"My mouth waters at the memory of it. We would not think of dining anywhere else."

The snow gave way to clear skies by the time we had dinner and retired for the night. I stretched my legs out on the soft bed and pulled the down quilt up to my neck. As my knees quieted in gratitude, I watched the bare branches of the chestnut tree sway in the moonlight, each gust of wind sending jeweled curtains of snow to the courtyard below. Beyond the tree, curls of smoke rose from the rooftops to melt into the starry sky. Will we ever know how far away the stars are?

Paris feels hollow without you, but still I am happy to be here. If you had stayed at Leuven for medical school I would not have come to know this city. In the end you regretted coming here. In the end, I did not. I love Paris, but I feel certain I will never return.

I will do you one favor: I will look up your old teacher Guinter of Andernach. You had few kind words for him, but I remember him as a great scholar and a kindly man. Your shabby treatment of him has always disturbed me. He let you assist at dissections—you brought me to one—and he chose you to help him with his book. In gratitude you ridiculed him in print and revised his book without permission. I will ask his forgiveness on your behalf if I find him.

As for your other mentor, Jacobus Sylvius, he is, as you know, dead. What irony has come to pass with these two Galenists! Guinter, despite your disdainful treatment of him in the Fabrica, never retaliated; Sylvius, despite your kindness to him in the Fabrica, turned on you savagely.

28 February 1565

The morning sun was making short work of the snow, but left the streets muddy, and the city's stench crept back into the air. Marcus went off to repair one of our travel chests; I set out for Rue de la Bûcherie and the medical school.

As I walked through Place Maubert, I recalled an incident that took place right in front of Le Pierwige. In 1546, the brave scholar Étienne Dolet was burned at the stake as his books were tossed into the fire; his crime was speaking out against the Inquisition. I was not in Paris at the time, but if I were, I would have gotten myself to the other side of the Seine. His screams would have been heard at a great distance, even over the roar of the fire.

I strode into the office of the dean of the medical school and identified myself to the clerk as an old friend of Professor Guinter of Andernach.

"Four doors to the right," he said, without looking up from his desk.

I stopped at the fourth door and rapped on it softly; hearing nothing, I tried again.

"Come," said a voice from inside. I raised the latch and entered a stuffy office whose bookshelves were mostly bare, their contents emptied into crates on the floor. Behind a large desk, a man sat hunched over his writing. I could only see the top of his balding head; his nose was barely six inches from the paper. He did not speak or look up. I stood quietly before his desk, listening to the rapid scratching of his quill on the paper and the clinking of frequent dips into his inkwell.

I was not sure I was in the right office. "Professor Guinter?"

"Yes, yes." He continued to write.

Finally, he tossed the quill onto the desk and sat upright in his chair, removing the spectacles wedged on the bridge of his nose and squinting at me. He wore a crimson fur-trimmed robe over an embroidered black doublet. A lace collar peeked out from under a carefully-trimmed beard.

His face lit up. "What a relief! You are not one of my students. But forgive me for my rudeness. Ideas can escape my grasp so quickly these days."

"I am likewise afflicted, Professor."

He cocked his head. "You look familiar. Forgive me once more if we have met."

"We have, but thirty years ago, a long time to recall a meeting of no importance. I am Jan van den Bossche. I was a friend of Andreas Vesalius."

His eyes widened, and he bolted forward in his chair, his elbows landing on the desk as his hands cradled his head. He stared at me, unblinking. I glanced down at myself to confirm that I was buttoned up and free of breakfast crumbs.

"By the stars, well, I—yes, yes, of course I remember meeting you—the mathematician. You came to one of my dissections where Vesalius so ably assisted. He introduced us before we started. Do I recall correctly," he said, smiling, "that you did not seem pleased to attend?"

"Your memory serves you well. I have never developed a liking for them, not that it stopped Andreas from dragging me along. And it is only in a manner of speaking that I am a mathematician. You are too kind to say so."

"And you are too modest. Vesalius spoke proudly of you. Our faculty, he told me, had nothing to teach you after a year, and we lost you back to Brussels."

The faculty had nothing to teach me after a month. You begged me to stay, Andreas, and so I did.

"I enjoyed my time in Paris, Professor, but I was homesick."

My excuse was not quite contrived; at that time Mother's pull still rivaled Andreas'.

"Ah, but my rudeness continues. I pray you sit." He gestured to a chair opposite his desk.

He leaned back, his expression softening. "I was most saddened to learn of the passing of Doctor Vesalius. Some island in Greece, was it not?"

"Yes, the island of Zante. He was returning from a pilgrimage. I am on my way there to visit his grave."

"A fine and noble thing to do. You know, I have never had a student like him. I was but nine years his senior, yet I could never hope to match his energy and passion. He came to us uncommonly skilled with a scalpel and free of qualms about laying open a cadaver. Unlike many other students, he was untroubled by the smells and the handling of its parts . . ."

Would Guinter be surprised to learn that you were quite comfortable with entrails and stench by the age of twelve?

". . . and he was of great assistance to me in my own poor attempt at an anatomy text."

"Your *Institutiones anatomicae.*"

"Why, yes, the very one. During that time he made new discoveries before my eyes—my eyes such as they were. It was only later on that I overcame my vanity and got these," he said, patting the spectacles on his desk. "Perhaps that was why he found me so clumsy. Even with spectacles, my nose must almost touch the page to read or write."

"Mention of your book brings me to the reason for my visit—to offer an apology on Andreas' behalf."

"Really. How so?"

"Not two years after your *Institutiones* was published, Andreas published in Italy an edition he revised for teaching purposes, and did so, as you know, without your permission. He felt entitled to do this because of the work he did on the first edition. I did not think it was proper, and told him so, but he made no effort to square that with you."

"True, Vesalius could have extended me that courtesy. But upon reflection I took it as a compliment that it served as a foundation for his revisions. I left it at that. I have never seen his version, but I'd lay odds he improved upon mine."

"You are most gracious, but I have one more regret to express on his behalf. While you favored him with credit in the *Institutiones*, he did not return the favor in the *Fabrica.*"

With a tight-lipped smile, Guinter closed his eyes for a moment. "I was one of his 'croaking jackdaws.'"

I felt my face redden. Andreas had included a passage in the *Fabrica* memorable for its stinging rebuke of the teaching methods at the University of Paris. It was widely surmised that Guinter was the unnamed target of Andreas' scorn; apparently Guinter thought so as well. I saw the passage in my mind's eye:

"... that detestable procedure by which usually some conduct the dissections of the human body and others present the account of its parts, the latter like jackdaws aloft in their high chair, with egregious arrogance croaking things they have never investigated but merely committed to memory. The former are so ignorant that they are unable to explain their dissections to the spectators and muddle what ought to be displayed according to the instructions of the physician who haughtily governs the ship from a manual, since he has never applied his hand to the dissection of the body. Thus everything is wrongly taught in the schools, and days are wasted in ridiculous questions so that in such confusion less is presented to the spectators than a butcher in his stall could teach a physician."

"Alas, I know the passage," I said. "He was only pointing out ..."

Guinter held up his hand.

"What a loyal friend you are! Vesalius did not merely make a point; he thrust a dagger. To be sure, he could be an arrogant little snot, but any offense I took did not last long. We live in an age in which personal attacks are a currency of writings in the sciences. I have thrust more than a few daggers myself."

"But not at him."

"No, not at him."

He pressed his lips together, measuring his words before he continued.

"Tell me, do you believe that certain events are divinely fated? No matter; I do. And I believe that Fate has brought you here this morning."

He saw my puzzled look and continued.

"You may have deduced," he said, nodding at the crates, "that I am not long for the University of Paris. I have resigned my position to spend the rest of my days, God willing, in Strasbourg. In five days I will deliver my last lecture. I have struggled for weeks setting down even the first word, but just this morning, I tell you, a flood of words rushed from my hand to the paper. If you had walked through that door a week ago, these pages would be blank; a week from now, this chair would be empty. Will you do me the favor of hearing what I have written?"

"If it pleases you ... but I am not qualified to judge your lecture."

"In fact you are more qualified than most. I believe you are meant to hear it, and hear it first. Please, may I begin?" His voice was plaintive but insistent.

I had not bargained for this, Andreas! Well, it's the least I can do to repay him for your lack of respect. I will sit through his lecture though I doubt I will have anything useful to say.

"Of course. It would be an honor to hear it."

"Thank you. I am grateful." He donned his spectacles, took up his papers and stood.

"I will spare you the salutations, expressions of gratitude, devotions, *et cetera* ..." He cleared his throat and began to read with a raised finger.

"In this, my final lecture, I will venture a question: Shall we continue to worship at the altar of Galen?"

He looked up from the page. "Hearing this might keep some of them from napping."

"You certainly have my attention, Professor."

He continued, wandering from behind his desk into the room, his face buried in his papers.

"For thirteen centuries this question would be tantamount to heresy. But a young Fleming named Andreas Vesalius declared in his book *De humani corporis fabrica* that Galen is not only mortal but often fallible. Controversy has followed Vesalius ever since, even beyond his death this past year.

"But the beast has been loosed: the *Fabrica* is in a thousand hands, and Galen's authority is no longer unquestioned. Let me briefly review from whence we have come to set the stage for where we are going.

"Galen was part of a civilization we take to be higher than our own, privy to all possible knowledge and wisdom. To know medicine perfectly, we have believed, is to perfectly understand Galen.

"Whatever human dissection occurred in Galen's time, after him the practice all but vanished. Why? Aside from religious prohibitions, there was revulsion at exposing and touching internal parts. Many physicians held that anatomy was a subject for natural philosophy, but not medicine; I need not remind this audience that the physician makes diagnoses based on symptoms and external signs and effects treatment to balance the four humors—blood, yellow bile, black bile, and phlegm. Healing did not require looking below the skin, the only exception being those surgeries in which we have gained some competence.

"From the eighth to the thirteenth centuries, the great Moslem physicians took up Galen's banner and rendered his works into Arabic. But they did not always take him at his word. The eminent Rhazes, of whom Vesalius was a student, wrote:

Asked why modern scholars should attach critiques to the works of the ancients, I cite several reasons. Among these is that error is inherent in human beings ... Another is that the sciences continually grow and are refined as time passes.

"Europeans, wary of Arab scholarship and perhaps wishing to claim Galen's legacy as their own, translated the Arabic versions of Galen's work into Latin. I will leave it to others to judge whether the body of work from the Arabian era has been given its proper due.

"Thus we arrive in 1315 Bologna, where Mondino da Luzzi performed a public human dissection and then produced a manual, *Anathomia corporus humani.*

"Mondino, to his credit, restored the study of anatomy to the medical arts. But his descriptions mainly mimicked Galen's. Galen's standing as supreme authority only increased as scholars translated his recovered

Greek writings directly into Latin, cleansing Galen of the so-called 'Arabic corruptions.'"

He paused and smiled at me. "Here, I can say, 'I modestly refrain from reminding my colleagues that I am one of those scholars.'"

I laughed. "A clever jest if you choose to say it."

"I will consider it, but there are few audiences more disinclined to levity than the one I will face."

Guinter went back to his lecture.

"For two centuries after Mondino, a ritual took hold for public dissection throughout Europe. Ketham's *Fasciculus Medicinae* included Mondino's *Anathomia* as a section in his book. Colleagues, even if you had never before seen the title page of this section, you would know from your own experience what is depicted.

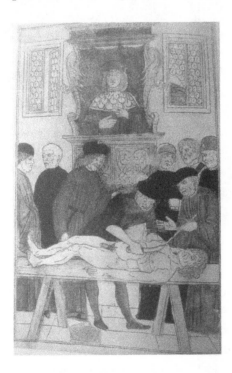

"A group of students and physicians listen as a professor sitting high aloft recites from Mondino while below, a barber surgeon does the cutting. Another professor demonstrates with a pointer.

"But then, in 1543, came Vesalius and his *Fabrica*. He wastes no time in issuing a bold, if not brazen, challenge to our pedagogy—right on the title page.

"He depicts a public dissection, but in revolutionary fashion. With a defiant glance out at us, Vesalius places himself beside the cadaver in the center of a theater surrounded by scores of onlookers. There is no professor on high, no barber surgeon, no demonstrator. There is only Vesalius, performing the dissection himself as he lectures.

"In his preface he levels unsparing criticism of our methods: the professor on his perch is detached from the goings-on; the barber surgeon wields his knife unskillfully; the demonstrator vainly tries to follow the recitation; those in attendance are more interested in the interpretation of the text than the specimen laid open before their eyes. In short, Vesalius asserts that public dissection has become a feckless ceremony at the altar of Galen.

"But Vesalius goes on to challenge Galen himself. An accomplished student of Galen, Vesalius took to heart two statements from Galen's own hand. The first: Galen's admission that in the main he studied animals, most notably the Barbary ape. The second: Galen's belief that seeing with one's own eyes and touching with one's own hands was essential to learning.

"This notion of direct observation, expressed by Moslem scholars and by Galen himself, has been largely absent from our current thinking—until Vesalius. In the *Fabrica*, he named no less than two hundred errors of Galen, and he attributed the errors to Galen's use of apes and lesser animals to represent human anatomy."

Guinter removed his spectacles and wiped his face with a handkerchief.

You have underestimated this man, Andreas. He has given the Fabrica a careful and honest reading.

"Have my remarks been fairly presented so far, Monsieur van den Bossche?"

"Absolutely so. But I am surprised that . . ."

". . . I find merit in your friend's work?"

"Well, yes. You are, after all, a Galenist scholar."

"So I am, so I am. With your permission I will keep going."

He secured his spectacles on his nose and resumed his travels around the room.

"My colleague Jacobus Sylvius, God rest his soul, was furious with Vesalius, borne of his fervent devotion to the Greek master. He called Vesalius 'a certain ridiculous madman.' To his dying day he insisted that Galen's work was derived from humans, and argued that if Vesalius had actually detected any true anatomic variations from Galen, it could only mean that those variations had occurred since Galen's time.

"I find this argument wanting. Unless God found fault with His own design, it follows that the human body has not changed since the Creation. It follows as well that the senses endowed to mankind by God would be no less acute now as then. Finally, let us say it: Galen, for all his greatness, was a man, and therefore fallible.

"Sylvius cannot have it both ways. If he concedes to Vesalius even one true variation from Galen, then he must choose between the word of Galen and the hand of God."

He looked up from his notes. "I may be hearing catcalls by now," he said, "but I will press on.

"Vesalius testifies to the greatness of Galen, but he declares that Galen needs correction and emendation."

He shuffled his papers. "Where was I . . .?"

You drew early praise from prominent physicians, but just as many attacks from Sylvius and others. So disturbed were you by this sustained onslaught that after you joined Charles V you burned all your papers in Brussels. Gemma was in Brussels at the time, but neither of us could dissuade you. You regretted it years later.

"Ah—here I am," Guinter said. "The findings of Vesalius may be disturbing, but his scholarship is sound; his detailed findings are taken directly from the human body; the illustrations are such as we have never seen. I ask, can we dismiss the work of Vesalius out of hand because he disagrees on some points with Galen?

"I prefer to think that across the centuries, Galen invited Vesalius to stand on his shoulders for a better view. And now behold Colombo and Fallopio, who in turn stand on the shoulders of Vesalius.

"It is time, dear colleagues, to acknowledge that we have been shackled by the authority we have conferred upon men long dead. Their findings must be subject to change by way of our own powers of reason and observation. Are there no mysteries left to be revealed? Should Copernicus not have shown us the structure of the heavens? Should Vesalius not have shown us the structure of the human body? Does God intend for us to close our own minds and cede the search for truth to the ancients? I submit that God thinks better of us."

My dumbstruck gaze followed him as he returned to his desk and sank into his chair.

In the Fabrica, you insulted this man. And yet, he has just mounted a powerful defense of your work.

He looked across his desk at me. "Well?"

"My reaction to your lecture, Professor, has moved well beyond surprise to admiration."

"I have struggled against these notions as one might struggle against committing a mortal sin. They have intruded my waking thoughts and roused me from sleep. But today they have broken free onto these pages."

"It took no small amount of courage to do so."

"Perhaps, but I must confess that I have omitted the most disruptive man of our century, Martin Luther. He has rejected the very structure of the Church and offers a different way to know God. But as we have seen, such challenges come with consequences."

"Yes. Andreas felt the pain of those consequences, and if Copernicus had not published his book from his deathbed, he would have felt it as well. Wars in the sciences are mostly fought with words, but not so of theology; Luther rejects the Church's dogma but insists on his own, and blood spills as a result. But you are under no obligation to mention Luther in a medical lecture."

"But I *am* obliged, if I am to be true to myself. Are we speaking in confidence?"

"Your words will not leave this room."

"There are rumors that I am a follower of Luther, and the rumors are true. It is increasingly uncomfortable for me in Paris. Luther was lucky to leave this world with his head; his followers have not always been so fortunate. I omit Luther because I wish to take leave of the city a free man, and alive."

"You have made an entirely practical decision. You will be in a friendly city in Strasbourg."

"One more confession: I fear that I will lack the courage to deliver this lecture. I don't need more controversy added to the rumors already circulating about me. I can safely take leave of Paris if I deliver a shop-worn Galenic recitation. No more is expected of a professor in his dotage. They will listen politely and see me off."

"I have every faith you will decide wisely. I only wish Andreas could have heard your lecture; he would make amends to you personally."

"But he did make amends to me. When he came to Paris, what, six years ago, in 1559."

"When he came here from Brussels for Henry II?"

"Just so. When the king, against all advice, went jousting to celebrate the marriage of his daughter to Philip of Spain, he took a shattered lance through his eye. Vesalius was rushed to Paris to tend to the king. I was admitted to the king's bed-chamber as an observer. He and the great Ambroise Paré did their best, but Henry was too grievously injured to be saved. Vesalius and I spoke during that time."

"Andreas never told me he saw you. How did he seem to you?"

"He was preoccupied, of course, but he greeted me cordially. He had great respect for Paré; apparently they had met before, as battlefield surgeons on opposite sides! But when the conversation turned to his service with Philip II, his mood darkened. As he spoke of his problems with the Spanish court and the prohibition on dissection, he was quite downcast. He may just have been exhausted from his attendance to the king, but I think he was not only frustrated but truly disconsolate."

To me you complained about Philip's court as one might grumble about the weather. But to Guinter, whom you had disparaged and not seen in years, you could not hide your despair. How is it that you opened your heart to Guinter and not to me?

"I am happy to say that we parted friends. After the king died he came to this very room and signed my copy of the *Fabrica*. I have to keep it out of sight!" he laughed. With that he unearthed it from a crate.

"He asked me what I thought of it; I told him only that I read it with interest. My own pride kept me from telling him that he had upended my comfortable little world."

He opened it to the title page. In the lower margin Andreas had written '8 July 1559. With gratitude, And. Vesalius.' Andreas had taken to using a signature with a shortened version of his first name.

I looked up from his signature. "It's fitting that it ended well between you."

"Yes, it was good fortune that we had that chance before . . . well, we have lost a great man. His name will be long remembered."

I stood and gestured to the door.

"I have taken enough of your time. Allow me to wish you farewell and good fortune in Strasbourg. I was honored to hear your lecture."

"The honor was mine. As for Strasbourg, I will pursue the quiet practice of medicine until my last days, God willing."

"May those days be far off."

1 March 1565

Paris

Dearest Anne,
Getting here from Leuven was no harder than usual, but there is tension in the air between Catholics and Huguenots.

If only Paris were a day's ride from Brussels! I think you would enjoy this city. It is Brussels writ large—more crowds, more dirt, and, I confess, a bit more dangerous. Save for the rich and noble-born, life is arduous. Yet there is a breeze of optimism in the air. There is enough work for food and a roof over one's head, and for those with a little money, for entertainments and taverns.

Paris is bursting at the seams, but handsome new buildings are rising above the hectic, dirty streets, and its university, though mired in its ways, attracts new thinkers that swirl around it like bees. I sense further greatness for Paris.

There are memories of Andreas everywhere I turn, bittersweet because he is gone. But I am haunted by not seeing whatever darkness was in him, and I cringe at the thought of how he treated you as a result. I met up with a former professor of Andreas', Guinter of Andernach, who remembers him as an outstanding student who has earned his fame. He recalls a reunion with Andreas when he came to Paris to attend Henry II.

I will show Marcus the city for a day or two, and we will leave for Ornans where Antoine awaits us. I will write you again from there.

To my dear and clever Anna: can you discover the secrets of this square?

16	3	2	13
5	10	11	8
9	6	7	12
4	15	14	1

You are in my thoughts every day. I carry you and Anna in my heart as I travel.

With devotion,
Jan

I sealed the letter without mentioning Guinter's sense of Andreas' despair, possibly because I was having trouble believing it myself. It was true that Anne was in my thoughts every day, but the passion those thoughts carried were hidden below the words. I struggled with my desire for her, what her skin would feel like against mine, the contours of her body in my hands, my mouth on hers. But Andreas' shadow always hung over the secret pleasure of those imaginings.

Marcus and I spent the next two days walking the city. Antoine's letter of passage earned us a private tour of Notre Dame, including the crypt and reliquary. Marcus was awed by the collection of religious relics, and wept at the sight of the Crown of Thorns.

"I will never forget this day," he said.

"Nor will I," I answered. I did not add that I was skeptical of the provenance of the bones and fingernails of saints, the severed limbs and bloody clothing of martyrs, and splintered fragments of the Crucifix, let alone the Crown of Thorns. Europe is infested with rogues selling questionable relics to the gullible rich. When I returned from a voyage years ago, Mother proudly showed me a new purchase—a lock of hair shorn from the head of Saint Gudula that she kept in a jeweled reliquary at her bedside.

"This will be yours someday," she said. She would not tell me what she spent for it.

When we left Paris, I embraced Pierre and paid him a double tariff, insisting that he take it as a down payment on my next visit.

I would never know which lecture Guinter delivered. Either way, I knew that Andreas had opened a renowned Galenist to an enlightened path to knowledge. I was filled with hope that the sciences would become free to go wherever observation and reason leads.

I took a long look back at the ramparts of Paris as we set out for Ornans.

Nine days from Paris we made Besançon entirely by carriage by way of Provins, Troyes, and Langres, thriving towns strung along a busy trade route connected by ancient but well-maintained Roman roads. The roads were patrolled, so I felt safe enough, but eventually I became queasy from the motion, and my back ached from the jarring ride. The towns had agreeable lodgings, but despite this I slept poorly; I cannot relax completely in strange beds, and more often than not I was awakened by drunken louts in the street below my window.

We reached Besançon in a cold rain. Above the spattering on the carriage roof, conversation among the passengers ventured gingerly toward the religious unrest that was sweeping through Europe. This region of France had become a hotbed for Huguenot persecution and Huguenot retaliation in kind.

That evening the clouds gave way to a brilliant starry sky. If the weather held, we would continue in the morning on horseback to Ornans, no more than a few hours farther.

Ornans

13 March 1565

Besançon was just stirring when we rode out on the Ornans road toward a rosy glow in the eastern sky. The air was fresh and clean, and Nature, waking to the season, had painted the hills with pale grass and dabs of purple and white crocus. Along with a distant herd of sheep being driven to grazing fields, we would make the gentle climb into the foothills of the Jura Mountains lying beyond Ornans. With luck we would be out of our saddles in a few hours.

If every day of travel could be like this, I thought, I would dare to see more of this world. My mood was further buoyed by the prospect of reuniting with Antoine. Marcus, a devout Catholic, was awestruck that he would be face to face with a Cardinal.

"I am not sure I will be able to speak."

"Don't worry. Antoine will be pleased to finally meet you. In private he is anything but formal, but you should call him 'Your Eminence.'"

Marcus smiled. "I did not become a Catholic yesterday."

Two hours into the ride, the road ahead disappeared over a gentle rise.

"We should see Ornans from there," I said.

Marcus urged his horse ahead with the pack horse in tow to get the first look, but when he reached the top he pulled up so suddenly that his horse reared.

"Careful, Marcus!" I called up to him. "Do you see Ornans?"

He settled his horse and turned to answer. His face, rosy-cheeked moments before, was ashen.

"I do, but . . ."

"But what?"

I put my heels into my horse's flanks, and when I joined him I saw why his mood had changed so quickly. Under the same brilliant morning sky that lifted my spirits, dead and dying men were scattered like stones across the downslope. A mile beyond sat Ornans, tidy and serene beside the River Loue, unruffled by the carnage on its doorstep.

We sat speechless, our horses stirring nervously under us.

"It will not take long to pass through the battlefield," Marcus said in a hush.

We rode into an eerie tableau that belied the mayhem that created it. The fighting must have been within a day's time; the corpses had not yet begun to bloat or smell. Besides our horses' hooves, the only sound was the jarring cries of crows, swooping down to feed on bodies that had already been laid open by sword or shot. People from nearby villages hastily picked through the gruesome leavings, some working in pairs stripping the dead men of their clothes. A few women wandered anxiously among the corpses, stopping here and there in dread of finding a missing husband or son. Men still clinging to life begged for help with arms outstretched.

The dead had assumed different positions where they fell: contorted grotesquely or stretched out in repose as if they had napped through the battle; collapsed upright on their knees or plunged forward, like sleeping babies, with their faces on the ground and their knees tucked under them.

The death blows varied in how they landed: a single, neat stab wound or a gaping slash; a severed leg or a slit throat; a smashed skull or a jagged crater dug by arquebus fire. A hail of canister shot could kill a solitary man or tear through a group, leaving them heaped lifeless upon one another. I was overcome with a voyeur's shame, unable to look away from these dead men as I rode by them, the very shame I felt watching Ernst Bronck hanged in front of his wife and children.

Halfway down the hill we passed a standard-bearer, barely in his teen years, terror frozen on his face and a hole in his chest the size of a dinner plate. Beside him was the banner that he carried to his death bearing the crest of the Huguenot prince Louis of Condé—a blue shield with three fleurs-de-lis below a golden crown. The dead soldiers following the boy's banner must have mounted an ill-conceived uphill charge into a fusillade of cannon. Most of the dead, like him, wore civilian clothes. The victors, judging from the few left on the field, bore the bright colors of the Swiss army.

What an appalling folly, to die that way in the name of Martin Luther or Pope Pius.

We finally rode past the last corpse. Thanks to Andreas I had seen enough to ride through this battlefield without puking.

This was but a skirmish compared to the battles you've seen. You wrote me how you could hear the battle cries from the field hospital, and smell the gunpowder. How you worked through the pandemonium, the ground underfoot sticky from blood, deciding whom you would try to save and whom you would leave to die. How you poured hot oil into artillery wounds and amputated stacks of limbs.

You longed for your cadavers, didn't you—who did not bleed, or scream in pain, or grab your sleeve and beg for a quick death. You wrote with a workaday attitude, but it was much worse than that, wasn't it?

Marcus and I rode silently to the gates of Ornans, where we were stopped and searched by a tense threesome of soldiers. It took Antoine's letter of passage to gain entry. We dismounted in front of Maison Granvelle, the place of Antoine's birth. The three-story stone château looked much as it did in 1537, when Andreas and I spent a few days there on our way to Basel and then to Padua. Two guards stationed at the front door advanced to us, hands on the hilts of their swords. I asked them to inform His Eminence that Jan van den Bossche had arrived. One guard kept an eye on us while the other went inside. Moments later the guard reemerged with Antoine right behind him, followed by two priests clutching documents.

"Finally you are here, and safely arrived," Antoine said, as he came forward to embrace me. "And this must be Marcus."

"Your Eminence," Marcus mumbled, and bent to kiss the ring on Antoine's hand.

Antoine stepped back and clasped his hands in front of him. He started to speak, but glanced angrily at the two priests who were whispering behind him. They stopped and lowered their heads.

"I regret that you had to see the aftermath of the battle that took place at dusk."

"Word of it had not reached Besançon. But I am glad to be with you again."

"If Marcus will see to your lodgings, we can take a walk in the garden before lunch. God has granted us a glorious day."

"Glorious for the living," I said.

"Yes, for the living," Antoine said, brushing off my curt remark. "We will not forget to pray for the souls of the dead."

One of the two priests, shifting impatiently in place, saw an opening and stepped forward.

"Eminence, if you please, your attention is needed."

"It can wait. Now go." They bowed their heads and retreated into the house.

Antoine led me through the entrance hallway to his study. In a shadowy corner of the hallway I spotted Titian's portrait of Antoine as a younger man, painted when he was Bishop of Arras and counselor to Charles V.

If Antoine were to sit for Titian now, his hair and beard would be grey and wispy instead of dark, his posture hunched instead of erect, his expression weary instead of vigorous. Antoine, three years younger than I, had aged beyond his years.

The study was once his father's, an imperial counselor in his own time. It was as I remembered it: spacious, book-lined, with an air of subdued elegance. A massive desk occupied the far end of the room in front of floor-to-ceiling windows. I motioned to a globe on an ornate stand.

"It's from Frisius, isn't it?"

"Yes, may he rest in peace. When he was here with you and Andreas. When was it—"

"Fifteen thirty-nine. You hosted a reunion."

"Yes. Gemma and I agreed to trade a painting for a globe, and when I was in Mechelen, we made the trade; I forget which painting I gave him. This globe is the most wonderful thing I own. If Copernicus is right, we're spinning around the sun instead of the other way around. I can't believe it, frankly, and he is refuted in Scripture. The Church has not taken a position on his theory; he has a few quiet supporters at the Vatican, and he was a good Catholic. Luther is more riled about Copernicus than the Church. He called him a fool who wants to turn astronomy upside down."

"His calculations are sound, Antoine, and show that our senses have been fooling us about the motion of the heavens."

"You and your numbers!" He gave the globe a gentle spin. "Don't you think we'd feel the Earth spinning like this? Still, I would love to know if our planet looks this beautiful from the heavens."

"You'll find out when you get there."

"There are no guarantees of entry, my friend."

I paused before a portrait of Antoine's dwarf Diego and his prized mastiff.

Diego was a gift to Antoine from King Philip. Dwarfs had for several centuries been fashionable in the courts of Europe. The Spanish court's coterie of dwarfs numbered in the dozens. Diego held a respected place in Antoine's household, as was clear in the portrait. Diego, with proud bearing and clothes befitting a nobleman, sports a fine sword and staff and rests his hand confidently on the back of the powerful mastiff. Their images seemed to jump off the canvas from a dark, featureless background that hides Diego's legs, masking his actual size.

Antoine came to my side. "They are both gone, I'm afraid."

"But in this painting they will live forever."

"Time will tell, but the painter—your countryman Antonis Mor—is making a name for himself. He has painted Mary Tudor of England." Antoine smiled. "I considered giving this painting to Andreas for his wedding."

"Because the subject is a dwarf?"

"Yes! But I thought better of it."

"So, even you have your limits. The Bosch painting was perfect."

"Then I did well. A sense of diplomacy is wise even among friends. Come—this way to the gardens."

He motioned to a door to the right of the windows. As we passed the desk, I noticed that it was awash in documents.

"I thought you were retired, Your Eminence."

"Alas, the Holy See can still find my desk and cover it with shit," he said with a rueful laugh. "But as it is shit from the Holy See, I must pretend it smells like fresh-baked bread."

He opened the door and turned to me. "How I miss speaking plainly with a friend! My face hurts from the mask I wear for the sour-faced clerics and nervous soldiers who infest my home. I miss Diego; that little bastard's wit had no equal and he gave me no quarter. And I miss being so close to you in Mechelen—though I am glad to be done with that Lutheran-infested piss-pot of a diocese. More and more I long for university life when we could drink beer and argue into the night about God and your Roman reprobate Lucretius. These days I bear my vestments like chains, and I have been tempted to throw this turd of a ring into the river."

He smiled. "You will keep all that to yourself. And don't worry, I will behave in front of Marcus; I want him to remember me as a proper Cardinal."

We went past two guards into his formal gardens, big enough to walk for a half-hour without retracing one's steps. Our footsteps crunched on gravel paths that fanned out through the garden, soon to spring to life. Still, I could not escape images of the carnage just a mile from this walled idyll.

"I saw Condé's banner on the battlefield. His side was slaughtered."

"Yes. But Condé himself wasn't there; he's roaming free somewhere. It was a mistake to release that son of a whore after he was captured at Dreux. He disregards truces and organizes raids on Catholic towns. This sorry bunch of peasants was caught by surprise and was no match for trained fighters."

We heard rapid footsteps behind us on the path; it was one of the two priests we saw at the front door.

"Eminence, the Swiss commander has been waiting . . ."

"He can wait some more, Brother Paul. Please leave us."

The priest ducked his head and after a few backward steps, scurried away. We continued to walk.

"There were a few dead Swiss on the battlefield. What were Swiss soldiers doing there?"

After a few paces, he turned to me. "They were mercenaries, fighting at my direction."

"What? How . . . ?"

"Hear me out, Jan. I can trust no one here, let alone these groveling priests who would take my confession and then share it with Rome. Will you take my confession—in confidence, as a sort of lay priest?"

"You puzzle me, but as you wish."

"As you gathered from my desk, King Philip and Pope Pius did not send me home to a life of leisure. They revile the Protestants, of course, and on this score they and the royal house of France find common ground. A Cardinal soon discovers that his duties are not always pastoral. The Swiss mercenaries are barbarians; even their commander has cow shit under his fingernails. But they will be well paid for their work on behalf of the Church, and they will spend it on wine and whores."

We reached a secluded corner of the garden where a small, ivy-covered chapel was built out from the wall.

"I did not wield a sword or fire an arquebus, but my hands are still covered in blood. I sent men to kill other men, and not for the first time. I cannot hide in my well-guarded house and pretend I am not equally culpable. 'Thou shalt not kill' indeed—perhaps God has instructed the Pope that killing Protestants is a righteous exception."

He shrugged. "Yet I cling fiercely—you might say desperately—to my faith. I cannot accept that our universe is without design or purpose, though there are times I envy your delusion of freedom from this perplexing God of ours."

"Just as I envy your delusion of an afterlife," I said.

"*Touché*," he said, smiling, and motioned to the chapel. "Will you pray with me, Jan? It would be a comfort to have a companion, even in the person of a miserable heretic. You may finally have your moment of revelation, and if not, it may be of some help at your Final Judgment."

"I will be honored to join you. If I ever face a Final Judgment, I would argue that I have lived at least as moral a life as the average Christian. And I would certainly point to these few minutes on my knees with a Prince of the Church. But would an omniscient God not know that I do so only to improve my odds for salvation?"

"As I said, we have a perplexing God."

The chapel interior was cool, dim, and musty, unadorned save for a simple wooden crucifix over the altar. I knelt next to Antoine and pressed my hands together at my heart as I had done so many times at Mother's side, waiting for God to make Himself known to me. It was an empty exercise but comforting nevertheless, in a wistful sort of way.

After a while Antoine crossed himself and rose, using my shoulder to brace himself.

"Thank you, Jan," he whispered, as he quickly dabbed tears from his eyes. "I put in a good word for you. Come, I have ordered up a feast for lunch."

In his private dining room, as we worked our way through snails in the Burgundian style, coq au vin with root vegetables, bread, cheese, and wine, we talked about my work in mathematics and of course, Andreas. We laughed over old university stories, and marveled at the success of the Fabrica despite the controversy it stirred.

"It is a *tour de force*," Antoine said. "Its importance can no longer be in doubt when learned men speak of "Vesalian" anatomy—but I am not equipped to judge the work. After the preface, it is highly technical, and our friend's Latin is rather prolix. To the layman, it is, quite frankly, a bore, and beyond the healing disciplines it may turn out to be the least-read of the great books. Nevertheless, the *Fabrica* is a splendid example of the bookmaking art, and the illustrations are masterful."

"No small thanks to you."

Antoine prevailed upon Titian to get you Stephan van Calcar, one of his best students. In 1538 he drew the three skeletons to go with your three drawings in your Tabulae anatomicae sex, *and then the* Fabrica *illustrations five years later.*

"Yes, Calcar. Do I not recall, Jan, that there was an incident related to that first manual of drawings, the . . . *Tabulae sex?*"

"Oh, yes. Andreas had drawn a diagram of the nerves for the *Tabulae*, but it disappeared. He had to substitute a drawing of the liver and reproductive organs. The nerve diagram soon turned up plagiarized in

Germany; he learned years later that it was stolen and sold by one of his students."

"It was not the last time he was plagiarized," Antoine said. "Well, about Calcar, Titian wrote me that he and Andreas drove each other mad."

"True in part. Back in 1541, Andreas asked me to come to Padua during the writing, for that very reason . . ."

Did I ever tell you that this was when Anne kissed me in Vilvoorde?

"And?" Antoine said.

". . . and I was witness more than once to harsh words between them. It often fell to me to settle them down. But their disputes were never personal; it was always about the book. For example, Andreas objected to Calcar's idea to put landscapes in the background of the muscle and skeleton drawings. Eventually, I got him to see that Calcar was right; they would make the illustrations as appealing to artists as they would be to physicians."

"*Bien joué.* You did well to convince him, and you are among the few who could."

"Sometimes, I would send Calcar to Venice to cool off. He would usually come back with a new idea."

Antoine smiled. "Titian wouldn't admit it, but I'll bet Calcar went to his mentor for inspiration. Later on, you know, Titian released Calcar—because he was too talented for Titian's comfort!"

I shook my head at the fragile sensibility of a great artist. "I passed a good deal of time with Calcar in Padua. I found him very companionable. I was surprised that Andreas did not credit Calcar in the *Fabrica*. I wonder now if Titian had anything to do with that."

A few moments passed in silence.

"Antoine, do you remember the name Guinter of Andernach?"

"Yes, one of Andreas' professors in Paris. Andreas dismissed him as a horse's ass."

"If he was a horse's ass, he is no longer. I met with him in Paris. He has come to admire the *Fabrica*."

"Aha, proof that there is virtue in reserving judgment."

"Yes, I had a good lesson that day. But I was surprised to hear from him that Guinter saw Andreas in Paris while he tended to King Henry, and I was disturbed by what he told me."

"I suspect that what disturbed you had nothing to do with that fool of a king. I want to hear this, but let's walk. I never eat this much food! It will take two able-bodied men to carry out my chamber-pot tomorrow."

"A pleasing image, Your Eminence."

"Ha! You sound just like Diego. I would have you take his place, but you are hopelessly tall."

As we walked along, Antoine listened without comment as I told him of Guinter's encounter with Andreas, and Anne's troubling account of life with Andreas in Spain. We stopped to sit on a bench under a bare apple tree. He crossed his legs at the ankles, put his arms into the sleeves of his vestment, and stared ahead while he spoke.

"It seems that behind a pretense of pious gratitude, Andreas convinced King Philip to grant him the pilgrimage. If we believe Anne Vesalius and the admirable Guinter, Andreas had been struggling with a profound unhappiness that he managed to hide from you. The pilgrimage, then, could simply have served as a respite from Spain—temporary at best, for Philip denied Andreas' request to retake his chair at Padua."

"But if Andreas was miserable in Spain, why did he keep it from me, his closest friend?"

"You grieve for him, yet grief is never unsullied. He has left you feeling hurt and angry. But are there other sides to your grief?"

"What do you mean?"

"I mean your own remorse at failing to see his pain, or your anger at his treatment of Anne."

I lowered my eyes. "It's true. I am haunted by the thought that I was blind to his misery when he needed me most. I should have seen through his breezy letters from Spain. His self-satisfied air when he came to the Low Countries with King Philip. And just last year, his grousing in Monzón. I was witness to quarreling between Andreas and Anne, but over small things. I was shocked to learn—or chose not to see for myself—that their quarrels were worse than that."

Antoine put his hand on my shoulder.

"But I daresay they chose not to show you. If there is one thing I have learned as a diplomat—and yes, infidel, as a priest—it is that one can never completely know another. There are always secrets kept hidden away, and therein lies a paradox in human relations: the secrets we conceal from those closest to us tend to be the darkest. I sense this is true not only for Andreas, but also for Anne.

"But that said, the deeper question turns on the motive for concealment—concealment to spare the other from worry or hurt, perhaps. Or concealment out of pride, or its inverse, shame. Or concealment of a betrayal. There are no bright lines of separation between them, and in the end such secrets may be borne of some alchemy of the three. This morning I allowed that God was perplexing. If so, He has certainly created us in His image."

The garden was enveloped in quiet as Antoine's voice trailed away. A breeze arose, and a few fallen leaves rolled across the path.

"You would think that God would prefer love to secrecy," I said.

"Love must make peace with secrecy. We of faith love God even as He conceals the workings of His plan for us. Likewise, our love for our dear ones is borne of faith—faith that they keep their secrets with just and loving intent. Out of love and faith we grant them unspoken forgiveness for secrets that we may never learn. And of the secrets we do come to learn, we must strive to forgive, even, as Jesus teaches us, the most abhorrent.

"Reason is a precious gift granted to mankind, but in human relations reason takes us only so far. In the end it is faith in each other—trust, if you prefer the term—and the capacity to forgive that allows love to take root and endure.

"The sacrament of penance provides a means to be absolved of our sins before God. Penance may also call us to make amends to other people; we cannot simply look past this life to the next."

"About this life we agree, Antoine. It's the matter of the next where we part ways."

"Which is why I prayed for you this morning, my friend. And you've had enough of my preaching for one day." He turned to me. "But use me as an example. I would have withheld from you my role in the slaughter you witnessed. Do you forgive me, Jan?"

"It is what Jesus would ask of me, isn't it? The burden of your duties is greater than I could ever know."

We sat for a while as a busy group of sparrows twittered in the hedges.

"How enviable to be a bird," Antoine said. "They conduct their business without care or remorse."

"And so it is for God, it seems."

"God in His perfection does not err, and therefore has no regrets. When He chooses to reveal His plan for us, in this generation, or the next, or in a hundred generations, our faith will be rewarded."

"What if He never does?"

"Then we will have not waited long enough."

We both laughed, but then Antoine's face softened.

"These have been difficult times for you, Jan. What else troubles you?"

"You have heard enough of my troubles for one day."

"I am not pressed for time," he said, and waited for me to speak.

"I am uneasy saying this . . ."

"Go on."

"All right. Even as I grieve for Andreas, I am angry that I let him take Anne from me."

"Surely this is not a new insight."

"Only in that I have allowed myself to feel it."

"You have drawn back a curtain on your friendship, my friend. What do you see?"

A while later, Antoine left me under the apple tree.

"You've unburdened yourself enough for one day. Stay a while and enjoy the breeze. I had better give some time to my two secretaries or they will piss themselves."

As I sat, a rosy-colored finch emerged from the depths of a hedge across the path and eyed me with a cocked head.

"Be thankful for your fine feathers and your straightforward life," I said to him.

Two nights later, unable to sleep, I sat at the writing desk in my room. After a long while staring at the blank paper before me, I picked up my quill.

15 March 1565

Château Granvelle, Ornans

Dearest Anne,
I hope this letter finds you and Anna bearing up.

Marcus and I are in Ornans with Antoine, free of his duties and back in the house where he was born. He remains crushed at the loss of Andreas, and sends his most sincere blessings to you and Anna.

The gods of travel have for the most part been merciful, but they grant no favors. Travel has not gotten any easier, and nowadays the religious uproar in France put a sharper edge to this leg of the journey. There have been reports of some fighting in the area.

You would enjoy some of the towns in France, like Troyes, that rebuilt its center with half-timbered buildings; the unanimity of style is quite striking. But my thoughts do not wander far from Andreas. In returning to Leuven, Paris, and now Ornans, I have relived many memories...

I tossed the quill on the desk. I had had enough of scribbling out another bland recital of travel news; I was even tired of writing about my grief over Andreas. I took up the quill once more.

. . . but Anne, even as the distance between us increases, I cannot help but feel closer to you through the memories we share.

I remember when we met almost twenty-four years ago. I could hardly look at you or speak, yet you befriended me.

I remember when you kissed me in Vilvoorde, a lightning bolt that left me dazed even two days later when I left for Padua to visit Andreas, still only a name to you. I tried to convince myself not to make much of that kiss. I had seen for myself the attentions you received from other men. I did not feel worthy of your serious notice, and my mother, who still had me in her grip, did not think you worthy of mine.

I remember that during that year away in Padua, I clung to the hope that the letters we exchanged—indeed, that you wrote to me at all—signified a deeper connection. I told Andreas about you but spoke of you only as a friend. Of course you were much more than that to me in my heart, but I was so uncertain of myself that I hid my feelings from him, and because I could not face the possibility of rejection, I hid them from you.

I remember introducing you to Andreas after we got his woodblocks to Basel and then came to Brussels. I made more than enough room for him to insert himself between us, and quietly stood by as he made you his wife.

I stopped writing, the quill suspended over the paper waiting for the next words until they finally came.

It is hard for me to stand up to Andreas; this comes as no surprise to you. It has been this way since our first day of school; I put my entire trust in him to lead me away from my mother's control. As a child, to challenge him was unthinkable—less so as a man, but I still lived under his spell. As I watched his interest in you grow I banished my feelings for you to a dark corner. When you married him, I resigned myself to be no more than a friend to you, and no more than "Uncle" to Anna when she came along.

My cowardice, dear Anne, was a great mistake. I will always love Andreas, but his death has left us in plain view of each other. Have you not felt what I felt, Anne, those times over the past year when we were pressed together in a crowded carriage; when I would take you by the waist to lift you over a muddy curb; when our hands would touch reaching for the same book; when our eyes would meet across a dinner table; when we huddled together in a doorway waiting for a sudden rain to let up?

I have loved you since the first day we met, as much for your wit, wisdom, and friendship as for your beauty. We have come to know each other deeply. Now I can dare to ask: could you have loved me in the beginning, before Andreas, if I had followed my heart? Is it not too late for you to love me now?

If you wish never to speak to me again, so be it. But I beg you to know that I intend no dishonor to you or to Andreas in revealing what my heart can no longer contain.

There would be no greater joy for me than to see to your happiness, and to Anna's, if you will have me. I would treasure sharing what remains of our lives. Would not Andreas want this for us?

With everlasting love and devotion,
Jan

I laid down the quill and slumped back in the chair, my head pounding. The fire in the hearth was ebbing, but despite the chill in the room my nightshirt was damp with sweat.

I'm sorry if you are angry with me, Andreas. I have loved her since before you even knew her. I know you knew that. But now, who better to safeguard her, and your daughter? I have no claim on her affections, but if she is willing to have me, can't I love her and still love you?

I watched the fire collapse into a bed of glowing coals. Instead of feeling the release of feelings long withheld, I was gripped by fear—fear of laying bare those feelings to Anne. I stood, letter in hand, and strode to the fire. I hesitated, then dropped the letter onto the coals. A black spot formed on the paper and spread until it burst into flame. The letter shriveled into a charred ball, then crumbled as embers rose from the ashes, glowing and then dying out.

The following evening, the eve of our departure, Antoine invited Marcus to dine with us. He coaxed Marcus to tell him of his family, and of the lives of North Sea fishermen. To honor our visit, he summoned a flask of wine sent to him from an abbey in Carcassonne.

"It is called 'Blanquette de Limoux', a pale wine with tiny bubbles that provide a novel experience of the wine in the mouth. The trick of it is to let the wine mature in the sealed flask."

I found it sharp and dry, and the bubbles went up my nose and made me sneeze.

"It's a clever innovation, Antoine, but I don't think it has much of a future."

"We'll see if it catches on," Antoine replied. "I find it festive."

As we rose from the table, Marcus asked Antoine if it would be possible to give confession to one of the priests on his staff.

"Of course you may, but I would be honored to be that priest."

Marcus swallowed, realizing he could not refuse.

The next morning we exchanged farewells in the courtyard. Antoine extended his ring to Marcus, and then took him by the shoulders.

"I am glad to know you, Marcus Schoop. May God protect you."

Marcus' eyes glistened. "Thank you, Your Eminence. I will never forget these past few days." Marcus went off to bring the horses.

After we embraced, I handed Antoine a letter to be posted; at daybreak I had written another letter to Anne. He glanced down to see the name on the letter and nodded, glancing over my shoulder to see Marcus coming with the horses.

"I'll see to it. Now get out of here before I have you detained."

"For what reason?"

"Reason? A Prince of the Church needs no reason, or if necessary, he simply invents one. But the reason is that I will miss you. Now leave before I change my mind. By the way, you will have no excuse not to stop here on the way back. Ornans is on the most direct route to Brussels after the Alps. I doubt you will be in any mood to wander around Europe by then."

He pointed at two men mounted nearby. "These papal guards will ride with you out of uniform so as not to draw attention; the uniform is a comfort to some, but a target to others. They will escort you as far as Montbéliard, and leave you at the Auberge des Juras. I have sent word to the innkeeper to expect two gentlemen with my guards. He will put you in his best rooms."

"But Antoine, it is not necessary . . ."

"I will decide what's necessary."

I looked again at our guards. One of them was burly, with a red beard.

"I have seen one of the guards before. He delivered the letter about Andreas."

"Yes. I entrust Émile with my most important tasks."

My eyes lingered on Émile's red hair and beard.

"Antoine, when Andreas and I passed through in 1537 on the way to Padua, do I not remember a red-haired child toddling around?"

He glanced his way, then back at me. "Oh, to have your memory. He has been in this household since infancy. We took him in as an orphan."

"How is that?"

Antoine looked down, then into my eyes.

"He is my half-brother. My father impregnated a servant, and she died in childbirth."

"I see."

"Émile is man of few words, but has proven to be uncommonly skilled and diligent."

~

Marcus recognized Émile as well. Émile largely kept his own counsel, but during the two-day ride Marcus was able to coax him into short conversations.

"An interesting fellow," Marcus told me when Émile was out of earshot.

An hour outside Montbéliard we were caught in a downpour, but when we reached the Auberge des Juras, the proprietor scurried to see to our comfort, showing us to our rooms and taking our wet clothes to dry. At dinner he sat us near the hearth and hovered over us as we ate.

"I will be sure to tell Cardinal de Granvelle how well we have been treated," I said to him.

"Most gracious of you, My Lord . . ."

"You have been addressing me as a nobleman, Monsieur. I assure you I have no title."

The proprietor furrowed his brow. "His Eminence wrote to expect the Count of Aarschot and his secretary."

I smiled and shook my head. "The Cardinal sometimes cannot resist a jest. There is no Count of Aarschot."

"But you arrived under escort," the proprietor said. "With respect, for me you will be the Count of Aarschot. I cannot question the word of His Eminence."

"I understand. For you I shall be the Count of Aarschot, in the company of my private secretary . . ." the name of a Brethren School classmate sprung into my head . . . "Jacob Taye." Jacob was a respected lawyer and politician in Brussels.

"Monsieur Taye," the proprietor said, nodding to Marcus.

By the time we arose the next morning, Émile and his partner had already left. We thanked our host, who again refused payment from me, and boarded a carriage that went farther northeast to Mulhouse to avoid a climb into the hills and then dipped south to Basel.

Basel

21 March 1565

For the first time in twenty-three years, I walked along the Nadelberg to Schönes Haus, the printing establishment of Johannes Oporinus. Once inside I was met by the oddly appealing sting of printer's ink in my nostrils and the creaking of working presses. Four typesetters on high stools bent over their letter cases near the large windows facing the street. I asked the nearest one for Oporinus, and when he looked up from his work, I smiled at him.

"Say, you're Fritz, aren't you? You set type for the *Fabrica*."

He peered at me through his spectacles. "My God—you're the friend from Brussels . . ."

"Right you are. Jan van den Bossche."

"I'll be damned. It's been more years than I care to admit!"

As we shook hands, his expression changed. "I was saddened at the news of Doctor Vesalius' death. In my mind his book is the greatest ever to leave this shop."

"The printing of the *Fabrica* was an exciting time."

"Exciting?" Fritz pulled off his spectacles. "Oporinus was difficult enough, but Vesalius hung around for months, sticking his nose into everything. I would have killed either of them for a copper penny, and the other for free."

I laughed.

I am sure you made a nuisance of yourself.

"I assure you that Andreas admired the work of everyone here."

"Aye, in spite of everything we knew that, and I confess he made that book even better. Well, welcome back! You'll find the old man beyond the presses," he said. "And tell him if he makes any more changes to this page, I will drown him in a vat of ink."

"I'll be sure to tell him." Apparently, Oporinus' obsessive attention to detail had not faded. It was a trait that made him a perfect match for Andreas.

I walked unnoticed through the busy printing floor. There were six presses now; when the *Fabrica* was printed, there were two.

I stopped at one of the newer presses as two men in ink-stained aprons bent to their work. One man inked a page of type set into a flat carriage, and the other swung a platform holding a sheet of paper into position just above the inked type. They slid the carriage under a heavy block of wood, which was lowered with a screw mechanism much like a wine press to bring the paper into contact with the inked type. After a few firm tugs, the carriage was brought back out and the freshly-printed page removed.

A typesetter would need several hours to compose a page of type, but after that, in the time it took for a scribe to copy that page by hand, the press could produce dozens of exact copies.

I found Oporinus hunched over a proof sheet. Pinned to a nearby wall in the same spot was a yellowed engraving from the days of the *Fabrica* printing:

"Johannes, it seems you are still driving your typesetters crazy."

Oporinus looked up, annoyed at the interruption, but then his face lit up.

"My word, you're here!"

He stood with difficulty and came around the table to shake my hand. He now had a full beard streaked with grey, but I could see that his cheeks were sunken and his hand was thin in my grip.

"I was heartbroken to get your letter about Andreas, but honored that you would visit here on your way to Greece."

"My voyage would not be complete without a visit to you. You brought his book to life."

"And his book brought this printing house to life."

"Business must be good, Johannes. I count six presses now."

He reached for the table to brace himself. "If by 'good' you mean turning out books, it is good indeed; seven hundred books have left this house with my imprint. If you mean profit, well, that's another story. My three stepsons find ways to dispose of my money as fast as I earn it, but I'm getting by. Let's go back to my office and have a brandy. I can close the door to the noise, but not, I'm afraid, to the smell of ink."

With a shuffling gait he led me to his cluttered office. He cleared a table of papers and poured us each a glass of brandy. His head bobbed slightly, and his hand trembled as he poured.

"I'm cursed by this shaking palsy. I can't set type anymore, and I write like a child. The doctor has given me a botanical but all it does is give me the shits."

He changed the subject by offering a toast to my visit; he used two hands to steady his glass. I took a polite sip, remembering that ink fumes do not mix well with the taste of brandy.

Oporinus leaned back in his chair. "It seems like yesterday that we printed the *Fabrica*. My God—I'll never forget the day you two showed up with the woodblocks. I expected them to arrive only with the shipping company, and I didn't expect to see Vesalius for months. And what a story you had to tell about the Alps!"

There was a knock at the door, and a head poked around.

"Sorry, Johannes, but Number Two is acting up. Carriage jam."

"Ach! Excuse me for a minute, Jan. I'm the only one the old girl will listen to." He left me alone in the office. I sat back and breathed deeply of the ink, searching for those lost times.

In the summer of 1542 we came here from Italy with the woodblocks. I had been in Padua for a year as you struggled to finish writing the Fabrica and feuded with Calcar.

With the text and woodblocks finally done, you hired a reputable Milanese firm to ship the woodblocks to Basel, but at the last minute you said, "I must go with the woodblocks. I will not sleep otherwise. We will go straight to Brussels after that, I promise." I dreaded the Alps crossing, but I wanted to go home. I didn't say so, but I yearned to see Anne.

The shipping company added a cargo of fabrics and provided an escort of four Swiss guards. It was a good thing, because we met up with a gang of peasant bandits in the Saint Gotthard Pass. Our guards, outnumbered but implacable, formed a line at the front of the caravan with drawn pistols and dared them to attack. The ragtag bandits had no stomach for a fight, and were about to retreat, but a wagon driver and I had to keep you from charging at them with a drawn sword. The leader of the guards upbraided you for your stupidity, but later on told me he admired your bravery.

"Those hunks of wood must mean a lot to him," he said.

"He would rather have died," I answered, "than to have his woodblocks used as firewood, and his book lost to history."

From Basel we went on to Brussels, where I introduced you to Anne.

Oporinus came back to the office. "Number Two printed most of the *Fabrica*," he said. "I should junk her, but I can't bring myself to do it. I love it like a blood relation."

He lowered himself into his chair. "So, after you two left for Brussels he came back in the winter. He drove us all mad until we went to press, but he still found the time to dissect an executed murderer and give the skeleton to the university."

"He wrote me about that. It was an unexpected pleasure for him."

"A pleasure for him, perhaps, but not for my typesetters—he made dozens of changes based on that dissection."

"His need for perfection was rivaled only by yours."

"Ha! Well, despite the chaos he would bring I hoped he would come for the 1555 edition, but he did not. And after he went to the Spanish Court he wrote only on occasion."

"It was not intentional," I said, not at all sure that this was true. "His court duties and his travels with the king kept him very busy. He had designs on a third edition; his wife told me he was writing comments in his 1555 copy. I fear it is lost."

"Maybe it will turn up. I must say I was surprised that he left Padua for imperial service before the ink was dry on the first edition. He was born for academia."

"Imperial service was a family tradition."

"Even so . . ." his voice trailed off; he sipped his brandy. "Scholarship aside, his teaching instincts were remarkable. As if the *Fabrica* weren't enough, he took on the extra effort and expense to produce that student edition, the *Epitome*."

"He believed that students needed a condensed introduction to anatomy."

A faraway look settled on his face. "You know, I was quite surprised that he wanted me to print the *Fabrica*—with the Aldine Press and other fine houses nearby in Venice."

"You're being modest—your shop had already built a fine reputation. When your old partner Robert Winter published Andreas' doctoral thesis five years earlier, you did a lot of the editing. He admired your scholarship in languages and your medical training. He saw something of himself in you."

"I was grateful for his trust in me, but the scope of the *Fabrica* was daunting—seven hundred large folio pages including two hundred woodblock illustrations. It would take two full-time typesetters upwards of six months to compose the pages. And he insisted on the finest paper. At the time, I was barely making ends meet."

He closed his eyes, as if reliving those times.

"My outlay for the printing could well have finished me off, even with Vesalius already paying for the woodblocks. I tried to get him to settle for less expensive paper—it was more than half the cost of the printing—but he would not budge. He said he would pay for the paper. I wondered how a young professor could afford the woodblocks *and* the paper."

"There was family money."

There was family money, all right—my family's. Calcar's art and the block cutter already cost you four hundred fifty florins. After you took on the cost of the paper, you came to me for five hundred florins.

Oporinus poured himself another brandy, winking at me. "He told me where he got the money."

I shrugged. "I was content to be a silent partner. And I'm still waiting for a payment."

"You might say he repaid you by putting you on the title page."

"What do you mean?"

"My goodness, you don't know?"

He fetched a copy of the *Fabrica* and turned to the famous title page with Andreas conducting a dissection surrounded by a mass of onlookers. I thought fleetingly of Guinter, wondering if he gave his lecture before leaving Paris. I followed Oporinus' trembling finger to one of the faces off to the right near the edge of the crowd.

A young man in a cap with a fair complexion and straight hair has his hand on his brow, looking down and away from Andreas and the cadaver. Is he repulsed by the scene, or caught up in thought, or both? But then my throat tightened.

"He never told me, and I never noticed."

"A fine likeness of you as a younger man, I'd say. He told me he always felt better when you were at his dissections, and so you would be with him on this page forever."

Calcar sketched me while I sat reading at your kitchen table in Padua. He said he was just passing time, but you had him do it, didn't you! I am deeply touched. But you still owe me five hundred florins, Runt.

Once again the door opened to the same worker.

"You need to speak firmly to Number Two. The carriage is jamming again."

Oporinus sighed. "Jan, I must go, but will you join me for dinner tonight at my house?"

"I would be delighted. May I bring along my assistant?"

"Of course. There's room enough at the table. If I could get my stepsons to move out, there would be even more."

He walked me as far as Number Two, which had drawn a small

crowd of workers. Oporinus shooed them away as he knelt beside the machine that had given birth to the *Fabrica*.

"Come on, get back to work. I don't pay you to stand around and gawk. Number Two and I need some privacy."

He looked up at me. "Do you remember where I live?" he asked.

"I do."

"Around sunset then," he said as he peered under the stalled machine. "What's troubling you, my dear lady?"

Marcus and I squeezed into an already crowded dinner table at the Oporinus residence. The lady of the house—Oporinus' third wife—was cordial but distant. Her three sons likewise had little to add to the dinner conversation; they made themselves scarce as soon as the meal was over. Oporinus, Marcus, and I remained at the table with glasses of brandy.

"So, it's over the Alps for you two. My chance to see Italy has passed me by—I'm too feeble to hazard that trip. The farthest I've been from Basel was to Strasbourg for my schooling, and then up to Colmar with Paracelsus after he was thrown out of Basel."

"You mean the physician Paracelsus?" Marcus asked. "My uncle heard him speak in Amsterdam."

"He has been all over, Marcus," Oporinus said, "and I knew him all too well. When he arrived in Basel—it was 1526—he had achieved some fame, and in Basel he treated noteworthy patients. By an odd turn of events he became the town physician, and he took me on as his secretary."

"I recall that his tenure in Basel was short-lived," I said.

"Short-lived and turbulent. His reputation was no match for his drunkenness and violent temperament. His position allowed him to lecture at the medical school, but the faculty saw him as a charlatan—he loudly rejected Galenic theory and practice in favor of his own. The students flocked to his lectures, in part because he went drinking with them afterwards.

"I will say this, however," he said, wagging his finger. "He was dedicated beyond measure to his calling, which was nothing less than a form of Christian love. In his lucid periods he was persuasive, even eloquent, both in writing and in speech."

"I heard stories of his cures," Marcus said.

"He did have impressive cures," Oporinus answered, "but just as many impressive failures."

He brushed some crumbs off the front of his shirt. "When he was finally chased out of the city, he went a few days north to Colmar. I followed him there with his books and his tools of alchemy: bellows, beakers, crucibles, flasks, and so on, and his agents: bottles of quicksilver, tectum argenti, and sulphur, ingots of antimony, ampoules of herbs, packets of barks and seeds, desiccated newts and toads, samples of feces from man and beast. I stayed with him in Colmar for two years—enough for a lifetime."

"Andreas was aware of your service with Paracelsus," I said. "He would have been interested to meet him."

"Oh, but they did meet—at this very table."

My eyes widened in surprise. "But how, if Paracelsus had been exiled from Basel?"

"I will explain." He looked down for a moment; he appeared to be calling up memories long undisturbed.

"In Colmar he wrote the *Paragranum*, his major opus, and then resumed his vagabond life. By then he had become more Christian mystic than physician. He was out of my life until the summer of . . . 1540 . . . yes, the year before he died. He snuck into Basel and came to my door in the dead of night. He was as filthy and disheveled as ever, but now bloated and tinged with jaundice. I put him up in my cellar. Now let me think—near the end of his stay with me was when Vesalius showed up, on his way back to Padua from Brussels; I believe he had gone home to visit his family . . ."

Your father had taken ill. It was a quick visit; you were writing the Fabrica and had teaching commitments. It was only the next year that I met Anne.

Oporinus' face brightened as his recollections cleared. "... yes, that's it. Well, the reputations of each had reached the other. Knowing them both, I was worried that this meeting could turn violent! Indeed, they argued into the night, but they took a liking to each other. In anatomy, they were both critical of Galen, but for different reasons. While Vesalius found Galen often in error, Paracelsus went further. He scoffed at the very idea of learning from a dead body, and readily confessed that he was almost completely ignorant of the subject. His notion of 'anatomy' was entirely different. He believed that the distribution of elements in our bodies corresponded to their distribution in nature—indeed, mankind was merely a replica writ small of the makeup of the stars and planets."

"There is a certain poetry," I said, "to the idea that we are the stuff of stars. But he thinks more like an alchemist than a physician."

"Vesalius said the same. But to that Paracelsus responded, 'Exactly! The two are inseparable; every single thing is composed of some proportion of mercury, sulphur, and salt, and in turn, these substances are found in the four elements that make up all things: earth, water, air, and fire. Alchemy is knowledge of experiments and making preparations using the four elements.'"

"Now the poetry descends to puffery and magic," I said.

"How did he come to his ideas?" Marcus asked.

"He would say that it was from his study of Nature and his unceasing experiments with alchemy. Throughout his wanderings, he sought out local healers to learn their ways."

"Johannes," I asked, "did you come to believe in him?"

"In the end I could not. But he drew no small number of followers."

"Did he and Andreas talk about medical treatments?"

"At great length. Vesalius may have broken with Galen on anatomy, but held to the Galenic theory that disease came from an imbalance of the four humors—black bile, yellow bile, blood, and phlegm. Paracelsus completely rejected humoral theory in favor of his own. Vesalius could make no sense of the old man's conceptions, and was especially skeptical of the idea that disease did not arise from within a person, but rather from external agents acting on the body. Diseases, Paracelsus claimed, could be countered by chemicals.

"To that Vesalius said, 'how can you believe that?' Paracelsus replied, 'I can believe it because I have used it to cure. I say you have killed more than you've saved with your bleeding, purging, and puking. I burned books of Galen's teachings with good reason.'

"Vesalius sat thinking, then toasted Paracelsus. 'It was a great privilege to meet you, sir,' he said. Vesalius left the next day, but stopped by to say goodbye. He hoped for some final words with Paracelsus, but the old man was still in a stupor from the night's drinking. Vesalius confessed that he was rather taken with the old man's peculiar genius. From the looks of him, he said, he did not think he would live long. Paracelsus slipped out of Basel a few days later. He died in Salzburg within the year."

"Andreas never spoke of this encounter," I said.

As I sipped my brandy I recalled a letter Andreas wrote me from a military camp in Cleves, shortly after he entered imperial service:

12 November 1543

Dear Scarecrow,

The newly-anointed Medicus Familiaris Ordinarius of Emperor Charles V greets you. Charles' forces are making quick work of the Duke of Cleves, but not without casualties, so I am kept busy.

Cold weather has imposed a lull in the fighting, and for amusement I am reading the Paragranum *by Paracelsus. Did you know that our Oporinus was once his secretary? Paracelsus is dead now, victim, I suspect, to his own chaotic life.*

Much of what he writes is utter drivel. He is ignorant of human anatomy, because he sees no need for it. Yet I admire his dedication to his methods in the healing arts and his stout defense of them. I found myself thinking of my apothecary father and his shelves of herbs; botanical study was part of my own medical education. How different are these remedies from those of an alchemist?

I will be back in Brussels after I deliver lectures in Padua and Pisa. I hope to find friendlier audiences than Charles' court physicians! My book has not been well-received by them. They are idiots, but their rejection stings nonetheless.

Fondest wishes,
Andreas

Oporinus had Marcus place another log in the hearth, and we re-treated into a comfortable silence.

So, you didn't read Paracelsus merely for amusement. You were attracted to him, if not to his medical theories then to his rebellious devotion to his calling. You saw something of yourself in him.

Marcus and I finally rose to go.

"Our deepest thanks to you and your good wife for a wonderful evening. I promise I will write to you when I have the chance."

I had a final question for Oporinus. "Speaking of letters, Andreas' wife told me of a letter he received from you when he was traveling through France on his pilgrimage. Had he contacted you about a third edition?"

"What letter, Jan? I didn't even know he had left Spain."

"She must have been mistaken," I said, and let it drop.

Milan

6 April 1565

I had not crossed the Alps in a quarter-century, but I was still overcome in equal measure with wonder and dread as we rode up toward the mountain passes. Once again I was awestruck by the snowy peaks, the proud legions of evergreens, the rolling expanses of meadow, and the shining lakes. The crisp air brings on a certain elation even as it seems there is less and less of it to breathe. But hidden within the magnificence of the Alps is a gauntlet of hardships no matter the season—bone-chilling winds; drenching rains; cruel snowstorms; washed-out trails; landslides; downed trees—not to mention the ever-present danger of bandits in those lawless reaches. Mountain inns provide little more than primitive shelter.

This time, to my relief, we had decent weather and trails with little winter damage. For the crossing we joined a group of Turin-bound merchants escorted by six French soldiers who, I guessed, were deserters pocketing some money while making for safe haven in Italy. My thighs and buttocks burned against the saddle with every step of my horse, but my spirits lifted when we descended to within view of Milan. We parted ways with the merchants and their escort as they headed southwest toward Turin.

"I cannot wait to get off this horse, Marcus. How far do you think we are from the gates?"

"At this pace we should arrive in two hours, perhaps less if you want to push the horses a little harder."

"I think not! Any more bouncing in this saddle and my ass will burst into flame."

Marcus laughed, patting his own behind. "My own ass thanks you. The city will wait."

Marcus sang a sea chanty in time with the footsteps of the horses; it took my mind off my sore body and allowed me to look forward to a reunion with Girolamo Cardano, a physician, mathematician, and astrologer. Andreas and I had stopped in Milan to meet Cardano in 1537 on our way to Padua, and I had passed through Milan to see him again in 1541 when I returned to Padua to be with Andreas. Over the years Cardano and I exchanged letters, mainly on mathematics.

Andreas' father knew Cardano back then, and had written ahead to him to expect us. Cardano had built a reputation in Milan as a physician, and his name was well-known in mathematical circles. But Andreas' father warned us that Cardano, while affable and brilliant, was known to keep ahead of his personal debts with gambling.

Marcus pulled me away from my thoughts. "We should stop by that stream and water the horses. We can finish our bread and cheese before we enter the city."

Marcus led the horses down for a drink while I leaned against a tree with my bread and cheese, listening to the rushing stream swollen by snow melt.

Just as a hard rain ended, we passed through those gates drenched and irritable. When we finally found Cardano's street, he came rushing out to greet us, a burly, ruddy-faced man who shook my hand vigorously.

"So," he bellowed, "this is the young mathematician. We must talk."

"Only if you wish to lull Andreas to sleep," I said.

"Then we shall send him to bed early." He turned to you. "You know, Vesalius, I promised your father a horoscope for you. It's time I did it."

"You may be interested to know," you answered, "that we are astral twins."

"All the more fascinating. I will set to work without delay."

It took Cardano ten years to produce that horoscope. The predictions it contained would be impressive were it not for the fact that you were already famous when he drew up the chart. I never received mine, but the visit itself was more than ample compensation.

Marcus tapped on my shoulder to get my attention and handed me a jug of water.

"Drink up, Master Jan. It will be a while before we have water from a mountain stream."

One of the few pleasures of mountain travel was to taste water as it was meant to be, not tainted by human activity and not disguised as the beer we drink in its place.

"Let's go," I said, after a long drink. "I wrote ahead to Doctor Cardano to say we were coming. Do you remember what I told you about him?"

"Of course. Outsized character, good chess player."

I found Cardano's house easily, but it looked in bad repair. I dismounted and rapped on the door several times with no answer.

Just then a man emerged from the home next door.

"The house is unoccupied, Signore," he said.

"This is Doctor Cardano's house, is it not?"

"It was. He has not been here for two years."

"What? I had no idea . . ."

The neighbor's face became pained. "Doctor Cardano had some family troubles."

"Please, can you tell me what has happened? I am an old friend from Brussels."

The neighbor hesitated. "Well, I wouldn't be telling you anything you couldn't hear elsewhere. Five years ago, Cardano's son Giovanni poisoned his wife after learning of infidelities, and for that he was beheaded."

I was speechless. An image came to me of two-year old Giovanni bouncing on Cardano's lap and pulling his beard.

"Alas, there is more bad news. His younger son Aldo took too well after his father as a gambler, and stole from him to cover his debts. There were threats from Aldo's creditors. One morning, Cardano was gone."

"Do you know where he went?"

"Bologna, it is rumored."

$\sim$

We took lodgings on the cathedral square. At dinner I told Marcus about how cordially Cardano received Andreas and me back then, and how Cardano and I talked about mathematics and played chess far into the night.

"We played with a finely carved set of ebony and ivory. He said it was from a local abbot. 'What a fine gift,' I said. He laughed and said it was not exactly a gift. 'The abbot is a learned man, but his passion for games of chance exceeds his skill.'"

"So Cardano won the set gambling with the abbot?"

"Yes . . . in games of chance, the laws of probability are more useful than prayers. But Cardano knew that the chance of winning on a roll of dice or the turning of a card is shadowed in every instance by the chance of losing—a lesson his son may not have learned."

After dinner I went for a walk alone, and ended up sitting on the steps of the cathedral. I had wistful recollections of that visit in 1537:

You were anxious to be on our way to Padua the next day, but Cardano would hear nothing of it . . .

"What would your father say," Cardano boomed, "if I sent you on your way with barely a look at this city?" He insisted that we join him on a walk to a nearby convent to see Leonardo da Vinci's *The Last Supper.*

The abbot of the Church of Santa Maria della Grazie—the former owner of Cardano's chess set—greeted Cardano warmly and showed us to the refectory. We entered at one end of a long room of generous proportions. The midday meal had just ended, and a few monks lingered silently at the long tables. Across the room, high on the wall over a doorway, was the monumental painting. It took up the wall's entire length, with its vertical dimension half that of the horizontal but still the equal of two grown men.

The giant tableau was so luminous that it seemed to float free of the wall.

"It is not technically a fresco," Cardano whispered. "With a fresco, the artist must work quickly, and mistakes are hard to fix. Leonardo painted on a dry wall so he could work carefully, but there was a price

to be paid; at forty years, it is already showing signs of damage, probably because it is on an exterior wall. Leonardo would be disappointed to see this, but he has only himself to blame."

Transfixed, we could only stand and stare.

"Go on, get closer," Cardano said.

We advanced on the painting, our eyes never leaving it, stumbling more than once on the benches under the tables. We finally stopped under it, craning our necks. It was like no other painting I had ever seen.

Leonardo set his last supper in a drab room, directing our attention to the colorfully-robed people at the table. Framed by a window behind him, a downcast Jesus sat at the center with the twelve disciples in two groups of three on either side of him. This could only have been the moment that Jesus revealed that one of them would betray him. The composition was masterful, the colors glorious, but it was the emotions on the faces of the disciples, so natural and genuine, that made the painting transcendent. It was a completely believable moment of human drama.

Andreas was stunned. "My God, Jan. Leonardo's people are natural. Their inner lives are revealed."

Cardano was pleased that we were so moved by the painting, but said nothing until we were back on the street.

"Come, let's go home and talk of Leonardo over some wine and a meal. I have arranged a surprise for you tomorrow."

"You granted us a rare favor in showing us *The Last Supper*," Andreas said, "but as you know we are anxious to get to Padua."

Andreas cast a glance at me, expecting support, but I merely shrugged. I had no objection to extending our stay in the comfort of Cardano's home. Once again, Cardano swept away Andreas' bid to take leave.

"I insist that you return the favor by remaining a short while longer. I promise that you will not regret it. Padua can wait a day or two. Make up an excuse if you must. In Italy, a lie with higher purpose is of equal value to the truth."

Andreas grinned. "I see that resistance is futile. We'll stay for your surprise."

"It's settled, then. We will be traveling a short distance from Milan in the direction of Padua, so pack all your things. I have made arrangements for fine accommodations for all of us for tomorrow night. I will send you on your way from there."

"Where are we going?" I asked.

"What surprise is revealed beforehand? You will see. We'll get an early start. No chess tonight, Jan. I'm tired of losing. You could make a good living playing chess in this city."

If seeing The Last Supper that day was remarkable, Andreas, the next was unforgettable.

My reverie was broken by my aching knees and the burning skin of my legs, bringing me back to present-day Milan. Night was descending on the cathedral square. I walked back to the inn and fell into bed.

In the morning I posted a letter to my brother with nothing more than a report of our progress. I wrote a similar letter to Anne, once again avoiding what I ached to write. Marcus and I rode out of Milan heading east, and I soon realized we would pass by Cardano's surprise destination those years ago.

We were beginning to wonder what Cardano was up to, getting us up at daybreak and leading us along farming roads . . .

"We have made excellent time," Cardano said as we trotted along, "and we'll be at our destination in time for lunch with our host."

"Our host?" Andreas asked.

"We're going to a villa in Vaprio d'Adda, just up the road. Our host will be Francesco Melzi, a Count like his father but also a painter of considerable skill."

He shifted his weight uncomfortably in the saddle and groaned. "I used to like riding, Where was I? Ah. Francesco. When he was fourteen, his father invited a certain artist to stay at the villa and tutor Francesco. The artist came to see him like a son. They . . . became very close. When the artist died, he entrusted his entire estate—all his works, notebooks, and papers—to Francesco."

"Would we know the artist?" Andreas asked.

"A man named Leonardo," Cardano said offhandedly. He urged his horse on ahead, leaving us staring at each other.

Presently we rode up to an imposing three-story monolith.

"This is not for repeating, but I think of Villa Melzi as a sarcophagus with windows," Cardano said. "But reserve judgment until you are inside."

A half-dozen servants rushed out to tend to our horses and carry our belongings inside, followed by the master of the house. Francesco Melzi was tall with fine features, his greying hair flowing freely from under a black velvet cap. Around his shoulders was a richly-embroidered purple cape.

"Girolamo, you are here!" He embraced Cardano, and then, to our surprise, embraced us as well.

"Welcome, distinguished young Netherlanders—I get so few visitors nowadays! Please come in . . . you must be hungry! Lunch is ready; it needs only to be set out. My staff will show you to your rooms, and you can refresh yourselves first."

"We are honored by your reception, my Lord . . ." Andreas began, but Melzi cut him off.

"Please, call me Francesco. And the honor is mine. You have come a long way. I shudder to ask about the Alps, but I shall ask despite myself."

He took us both by the arms. "We will have plenty of time to talk at lunch. Then, we will go to the library. Girolamo wants me to show you some things there that may interest you."

Villa Melzi's splendor was reserved for its interior. The passageway from the front door opened to an atrium whose walls rose to the third floor, with skylights casting generous light into the space. Huge tapestries hung along the walls of the marble staircase, and a life-size sculpture of a male nude, arm raised in greeting, stood by the base of the stairs. We were each assigned a room on the second floor with views of the river and hot water at the ready.

A waiting servant showed us to lunch. As we followed behind, Andreas whispered, "You could be living in a house like this if you were willing to part with some of your money."

"I would never find my way around," I whispered back.

The servant led us back downstairs through the atrium and into a dining room with a giant hearth and a table that could easily seat forty. A hallway at the far end of the room led to a shaded terrazza overlooking the gardens behind the house. Cardano and Melzi were waiting for us.

Melzi jumped to his feet. "Come, come! I hope you don't mind dining *al fresco*. I will be frank; I never use that dining room. I prefer small groups, like ours, for conversation, and today we can take advantage of lovely weather."

"You will hear no objections from us, Francesco," Andreas assured him.

Over a lunch of roasted capons, a chewy grain called *farro* flavored with the juice of oranges, and local wine, Melzi asked us about Brussels, our schooling, and our travels together. After a final course of pears with tangy cheese from the nearby village of Gorgonzola, Melzi produced a bottle of brandy.

"There is just enough in this bottle for the four of us," he said as he held the bottle up to the light. "This is from Cognac, the birthplace of François I. You may not think much of him, being subjects of the Holy Roman Empire, but he was a great friend of Leonardo's. The king was with him when he died in France."

He emptied the bottle into four glasses. "Don't fret about the empty bottle—I have more. A toast to my friends, old and new."

After we clinked glasses and took sips, Andreas leaned forward on his elbows.

"We are grateful for your hospitality, Francesco. Doctor Cardano kept this visit cloaked in mystery until we were close by, and it was only then that we learned of you and your friendship with Leonardo. Yesterday we were privileged to see *The Last Supper*, and we were staggered by it."

"*The Last Supper* speaks for itself," Melzi said. "Leonardo's artistic genius is established for all time, though he has left us only a small body of work in painting and sculpture. In my view only Michelangelo can be mentioned in the same breath. They were rivals, to be sure, but Leonardo wasted little energy on that crude and disagreeable fellow. His time was taken up with his many other passions."

"We know of his reputation as an engineer," I said, "but what else was there?"

"A fine moment, it seems, to see the library," Melzi answered. "But let's finish the Cognac first."

We walked upstairs to the library, directly over the main dining room. At the door, Melzi produced a key and unlocked it.

The library was splendid and capacious under a vaulted ceiling painted to resemble a blue sky with wispy white clouds. Bookshelves lined the walls of the main floor and a spiral staircase rose to a gallery of bookshelves and windows above them. The room was badly in need of dusting, and a haphazard array of tables piled with papers and notebooks took up much of the main floor.

As we entered, I noticed a painting tucked into a small alcove.

It depicted the legend of Vertumnus and Pomona, the same as portrayed by my tapestry at home. We walked over for a closer look with Melzi just behind. In the foreground, under a tree gently encircled by a vine, the reclusive, angelic Pomona is charmed by Vertumnus, disguised as an old woman. Pomona casts a welcoming gaze on the old woman's fingertips as they come to rest on her shoulder. The handsome palette, flowing composition, and beautifully-rendered figures clearly came from the hand of a master.

"It's beautiful," I said. "This can only be Leonardo's."

Melzi blushed. "The painting is mine."

"Francesco, forgive me . . ."

"Forgive you? I could be paid no higher compliment. Someday I'll find a better place for it, but first I must make some sense of *this*," he said, sweeping his arm across the room.

"You asked about the passions of Leonardo. They are to be found here, a torrent in pen and ink that rushed from his mind to these notebooks and papers. His art will secure his legacy, but it is here that you truly meet him. He was a kind and loving man, but his genius was terrifying. It was cruel of him to make me heir to it."

He looked around the room, forlorn. "There are thousands of pages of drawings here. I have been trying to sort them for some kind of catalogue. There are those that are purely artistic, but then, well, there is everything else."

"You've made good progress, Francesco," Cardano said, patting him on the back.

Melzi wrapped his arms tightly across his chest, and his voice quavered. "You are a good friend and a bad liar. I am overwhelmed. On the same page there could be a torso, a complex geometric figure, a horse's head, and one of his machines. How does one sort that?"

"How many times have I told you to get an assistant?"

"I cannot trust anyone else with these. You are among the few who have ever entered this room."

He turned to us. "And now you are counted among those few."

Melzi put a hand on Andreas' shoulder. "Girolamo tells me that you have a particular interest in anatomy. Leonardo was intensely interested in the surface features of the human form. But his interest did not stop there."

He motioned Andreas ahead to a table strewn with drawings. When Andreas reached the table, he gasped, turning his head slowly from one end of the table to the other. He finally dared to gingerly move a few of the drawings to see those lying below.

He wheeled around to face Melzi, astonished. "I cannot believe what I am seeing."

Melzi smiled. "You can start believing now."

I strode ahead to join Andreas. Before us on the table were hundreds of pen-and-ink drawings, perhaps two hand-widths by four, some bigger, some smaller, many crowded with notes.

"Jan," Andreas said, "These are anatomical drawings, from skin to bone."

From a corner of the table, Melzi pulled out a page of text.

"I came across this recently. Leonardo wrote it in Latin, but backwards, like all of his writings. He was left-handed, and reasoned that if right-handed people could write towards the side of their writing hand, why couldn't left-handed people? It's tricky to read even with a mirror; let me read it to you."

Melzi tilted his head, squinted, and read:

Dispel from your mind the thought that an understanding of the human body in every aspect of its structure can be given in words; for the more thoroughly you describe, the more you will confuse the mind of the reader and the more you will prevent him from a knowledge of the thing described; it is therefore necessary to draw as well as to describe.

Andreas and I exchanged glances. We were both thinking of that cold night in Gemma's kitchen after the dissection of Ernst Bronck. Andreas had reached the same conclusion as the great Leonardo about the power of drawings to explain.

"These drawings," Andreas said, "could be possible only if he did dissections."

"Indeed. He did more than a few—not that I went to any—and acquired as many bones as he could. He had an idea to produce a text with a young physician named Marcantonio della Torre, but it never got beyond talking, like so many of his projects. And sadly, the plague took della Torre."

He opened his arms. "Well. Feel free to examine them."

He and Cardano went off to look at some notebooks on another table.

I stood by Andreas while he picked up one page after another. "Look at this one," he said.

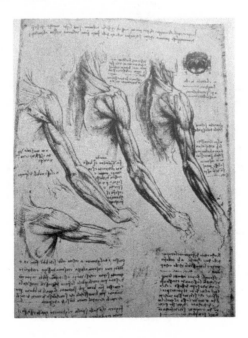

"It is exquisite."

Andreas shook his head in wonderment. "He is a keen observer and his draftsmanship is incomparable. Remember when you argued that night in Gemma's kitchen about the link between precision and beauty? With these drawings Leonardo has won your point. And see up in the corner? His mind wanders from the arm and shoulder to a view of the throat. His thinking can hardly be contained."

He picked up another page, dense with drawings and notes.

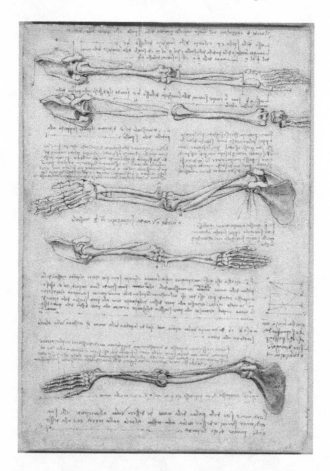

"In this one he draws the bones of the arm and shoulder from several points of view to show them fully and in relation to each other, a brilliant notion. The hands are exaggerated, and he glosses over the small bones of the wrist, but I suspect this was on purpose; his aim is to show the rotation of the forearm. And look, something you can appreciate—a geometric sketch in the margin. He was probably thinking about the forces involved in forearm or shoulder motion."

"Does it not seem to you, Andreas, that Leonardo looks past anatomy even as he studies it, that he wants to understand the body's workings?"

"Galen has provided us with those answers, Jan."

"But—"

Just then Cardano came back to us and looked over our shoulders at the drawings.

"They are magnificent, worthy of the artist who made them." He made sure that Melzi was out of earshot and lowered his voice. "But I am not sure how useful they are."

Cardano waited for Andreas to respond, but his eyes did not rise from the table.

Cardano shrugged. "Come, you two, and see some of his geometric drawings. He has also designed a flying machine."

"Thank you, but I'll stay here," Andreas said.

I went off with him, and came back to Andreas later on. He had hardly moved, and was so deep in concentration that I startled him.

"Oh! It's you, Scarecrow."

"He really did design a flying machine . . . and a cart that propels itself."

"Did he." Andreas was clearly indifferent to everything except what was on the table in front of him. "I've looked at dozens of drawings now, Jan. The world has never seen the likes of them. I feel like I'm dreaming. But see here . . ."

He lifted up one of the drawings.

"It's extraordinary," I said. "It approaches perfection."

"As a drawing, it is sublime—but as an *anatomical* drawing, perhaps too perfect. The strong natural sense in all his drawings seduces you into believing that they show the actual—and many do. But I doubt he drew this one with a female cadaver in front of him."

"How can you tell?"

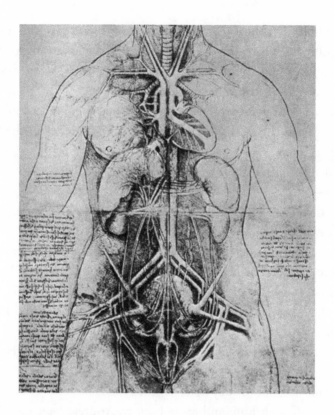

"It would escape your notice, but the heart and blood vessels are more like those of an ox than a human. The kidneys are too high in the abdomen. And do you see those thick structures, there, radiating from the uterus out to the flanks? They are pure fancy."

"Why would he would draw what is not there?"

"I wish I could ask him. Perhaps we are seeing the engineer in him conjuring the body as a machine, or the artist, arranging things in a way that pleases him.

"When he ventured beyond muscle and bone to the organs, he is less complete. For lack of cadavers he may have drawn from memory. Or he relied on animals—he still draws five-lobed livers. But yet, there are areas of intense study."

Andreas held up a page to me. "He appears to have done experiments on the flow of blood through the aortic valve of the heart. It's astounding that he even arrived at that question. Cardano may scoff at these drawings, but he overlooks Leonardo's triumph—to show that with sufficient skill, the structure of the human body is best captured through an alliance of words and pictures. Leonardo has opened a new road."

"Andreas, you are traveling the same road as he. Think of your notebooks."

"How can you compare my notebooks with his? I can never hope to approach him."

"I grant you are no Leonardo—but who is? The comparison I make is one of conception and intent. You could have written that passage that Melzi read to us. I will also point out that Leonardo is dead, and you are not."

I could see Villa Melzi in the distance as Marcus and I rode past. I thought for a moment about seeing if Melzi was there, but thought better of it; I did not want to delay our travels. But my final words to Andreas were still in my ears:

"Leonardo is dead, and you are not."

It was no coincidence, was it, that within a year of seeing Leonardo's drawings, you produced the Tabulae with its six drawings for your students, and conceived the Fabrica. The power of images was an idea already stirring within you, but Leonardo, from the grave, pushed you forward.

You said to me as we rode away from Villa Melzi, "From the looks of things, Leonardo's genius will stay hidden in jumbled piles in Melzi's library for a long time. And Leonardo knew that without written descriptions that rise to the level of his drawings, they will be beautiful to look at, but nothing more."

Legnago

Our carriage was within view of Verona when we were halted by a military patrol. The driver was ordered to head southeast to Legnago. The religious procession at the city's gates and the bonfires lining the road revealed the reason: Verona had fallen to the plague.

The carriage fell silent as we rode away from Verona; if we had ridden through its gates days earlier, we would have been swept up in the horrors unfolding there. For two centuries since the Black Death decimated Europe, the pestilence could strike a town or city at random and lay waste to the population with merciless efficiency, without regard to wealth or status. It was a rare European who was untouched by the plague.

I remembered when, in the summer of 1552, Andreas received word in Brussels that his younger brother Franciscus had been taken by the plague while himself tending to plague victims in Vienna. Franciscus had abandoned the law and followed Andreas into medicine. After his death, a rumor spread that the Doctor Vesalius who had succumbed in Vienna was Andreas.

The inns in Legnago were filled with displaced travelers, but we found a room at a price few would be willing to pay. We shared a dinner table with a handsome young Italian named Alfredo Contini, the son of a Florentine merchant who tired of his law studies at Padua and had gone off to Verona to write poems.

"I've been in Legnago two weeks," he said. "At the first news of suspicious deaths, I packed my things and left, but many stayed because the town physician declared that there was no plague. This pleased the town's merchants and innkeepers; nothing disrupts business like the plague."

"You were wise to leave," I said.

"More fearful than wise, Signore. As the pestilence spread, those with the means to do so fled until the city gates were sealed. Now, anyone caught leaving is executed on the spot and their body burned."

"Is there any news from within the city?" Marcus asked.

"Enough to confirm that it is the plague. Boccaccio's description in *The Decameron* holds after two centuries: a sudden fever with chills followed by *gavoccioli,* swellings the size of an apple in the groin or the armpits, Boccaccio's 'infallible token of approaching death.' They herald black and livid spots on the skin. The fingertips, toes, or lips turn black. Then comes death, only days after the first signs."

We were silent as the Italian continued.

"The stench of death is everywhere in Verona. Prisoners are freed if they agree to collect the corpses left on the curbs. A few priests have stayed to administer last rites; the doctors who remain have tried all manner of treatment, and all have failed. The people are easy prey for charlatans; one prescribes wearing arsenic in a pouch around the neck; another prescribes drinking urine."

Contini threw up his hands. "And what of the cause? The wrath of God? Malign conjunctions of the planets? Bad air? We know nothing more now than we did two centuries ago."

"To that list I add the Jews," Marcus said. "It is said that the Jews poison the wells to foul the water and release pestilence into the air."

Contini glared at Marcus. "Must the Jews be blamed for everything? Four popes have rejected the idea and still the persecution continues. Do Jews not drink from the same wells as Christians, and breathe the same air?"

Straightening up, he said, "I am a Jew. Would you have known if I had not told you so?"

Marcus flushed. "I meant no offense, Signore. I was simply repeating what is said."

"When the people of Europe cast about for blame, the Jews are always handy," Contini said dismissively. "Jews were massacred across Europe when the plague first struck two centuries ago, including in your own city of Brussels. Florence, the city of my birth, has expelled Jews several times. And now the Medicis, once our protectors, are turning against us for political gain. There is talk that Jews will be compelled to wear certain clothes and live in a ghetto."

"I regret hearing that," I said, but my sympathies went unheard.

Contini's eyes glistened as he spoke. "Christians have spent the last half-century persecuting each other. But Catholics and Protestants alike still keep a ready reserve of wrath for the Jews."

Contini caught himself, perhaps sensing the risk of speaking this way to strangers. "Forgive my outburst. I have no reason to burden you with my thoughts. I hope to finish our meal as it began, in fellowship."

"As do we, I assure you," I said. "Your points are well taken."

Marcus' comments, I knew, were not entirely innocent. The Church had for centuries sent mixed messages about the Jews. Marcus would single out Jewish shopkeepers for scorn, and at any news of a banking scandal in Brussels, he was sure that Jews were involved.

I had not even encountered a Jew until university, and those were only the chess players or mathematicians. I heard my father speak of doing business with Jewish traders and bankers, but they were never guests at our dinner table. Andreas had made mention in a letter from Basel during the *Fabrica* printing that the Jews were being expelled from the city. He did not elaborate, and I did not bother to ask why. As I recalled this, I felt ashamed at my own indifference to such cruelty.

Contini steered the conversation in a friendly direction. "May I ask what takes you to Padua?"

"We are on our way to Greece to visit the grave of a friend."

"I am so sorry. Your journey speaks well of your friendship. Forgive me, but was your friend in Greece to study the language? I dream of seeing the land of Homer."

"He was a physician, on his way back from a pilgrimage."

Contini furrowed his brow. "Such a story went round the university this winter past. Could it be that your friend is the great physician Andreas Vesalius?"

"Yes."

"His name is spoken with reverence in Padua. I would never choose to come near a cadaver, let alone one laid open. But when a friend showed me his book, I was awestruck. The drawings were beautiful, even lyrical. There was a certain liberation, even joy, in seeing what we look like under our skins, in seeing our humanness through and through."

Padua

14 April 1565

I had enough energy in the waning afternoon to visit the medical school, the only place in Padua I wished to see. In so doing we could leave for Venice the next morning.

Marcus asked to go with me. "I have never seen the inside of a university."

I recalled his wistfulness at the Café du Château in Leuven; I was thoughtless not to have asked him along then or in Paris.

"Come along, then. The winter dissection will be over, and the air will no longer smell."

I led Marcus through an archway into a courtyard of Hospitum Bovis, or "il Bò" by its nickname, the main building of the university. It was crowded with students chatting in groups or rushing to a class. Marcus looked around self-consciously as we were jostled by students brushing past us.

"Before the university took it over," I said, "it was a palace, and then an inn. When I came with Andreas in 1537, medical school classes were held in churches and houses around the city. It was not until 1542, the year before he left, that Andreas held his classes here."

"I would not know, but he seemed young to be a professor."

"He was not quite twenty-three. Andreas came here for his doctorate, but he did so well on his graduation exam that they made him a professor of surgery and anatomy the next day. It did not hurt that his reputation as a dissector preceded him."

You shrugged off my concerns about your rushing onto the faculty. "They think I am qualified," you said. I challenged you: "You will be the youngest faculty member by far. You're not the least bit anxious about that?"

"I am more than a little anxious. That's why you must stay for a while."

I continued with Andreas' story. "His first public dissection was in the courtyard of a friendly magistrate who built a temporary theater for the event. He started on December 6 and finished Christmas Eve; despite the cold weather the body finally rotted beyond use. He insisted that I come every day. By the end, he drew crowds in the hundreds."

You were a sensation, doing your own dissection while you lectured. Oporinus was right; you were born for academia.

The courtyard was emptying. "These days, dissections are held where we stand in a temporary theater. Someday, perhaps, they will build a permanent theater somewhere inside—but they'd better have plenty of windows."

Marcus peered up at the gallery of classrooms ringing the courtyard. "One of those classrooms was his," I said. "Let's go see it."

Up in the gallery, I pointed to a door where students were shuffling out, their voices echoing off the gallery's vaulted ceiling. "That's his."

We waited until the last student left and went in. The professor was still at the lectern, gathering his papers. He glanced up as we took seats in the back of the room.

"You two are rather late for today's class, and rather early for tomorrow's! Are you in this course?"

"No, Professor, excuse us," I said. "We are only visiting."

He looked us over. "What brings you here, then?"

"We are friends of a former professor."

"Ah—and who might that be? It's likely I know him."

I did not want to start a conversation, but I had already said too much. "Andreas Vesalius of Brussels."

The professor's eyes widened. He scooped up his papers and cloak and rushed up the aisle toward us. He looked young enough to be my son despite his beard and balding pate. When he reached us we stood to shake his extended hand.

"I am Girolamo Fabrizio. I have the honor of occupying the chair held by Doctor Vesalius, and most recently by Gabrielo Fallopio, God rest his soul. Please, please sit, but may I know your names?"

"I am Jan van den Bossche, and this is Marcus Schoop. We are passing through Padua."

"Did you come by way of Verona? There is word of the plague."

"We were barred from the city. The news from there is not good."

"I feared as much. God grant that Padua is spared."

He tossed his cloak on the back of a chair and sat. "After Fallopio died it was made known to Vesalius by the Venetian Senate—they have the power of appointment—that the chair was his to reclaim, but sadly it was not to be. It was not the way I would have chosen to advance my career."

"It's kind of you to say so. I know he considered it, but in any event King Philip did not release him from service."

"Really? All we heard here was that Vesalius sent strong signals of interest, and said he would explore the offer personally in Venice. But then, before he arrived, the Senate cooled on him; we never learned why. And Vesalius never met with the Senate; he continued on to the Holy Land. All very odd, the way it turned out."

You brushed off Philip's rejection in your birthday letter to me from Monzón, but you really wanted your chair back, didn't you? You and Venice seemed ready to defy King Philip, but then you and Venice lost the will to go forward. Why?

"And then, alas," Fabrizio continued, "the cruel fortune of his death. But he has left an enduring legacy. Here in Padua, Galen's anatomy is falling out of favor; Fallopio himself was a steadfast Vesalian, though he did publish a critique of his work."

"The *Observationes*," I said. "Andreas—Doctor Vesalius—wrote me from Spain about it. He admired it."

I saw the letter in my mind's eye:

8 September 1561

Madrid

Dear Scarecrow,
I have read a critique of my work, Observationes, *by Fallopio of Padua. It is well-researched and treats me fairly, though he takes issue with me in some areas. I will grant that in some cases he is right!*

I am writing a response, which I will call the Examen; *it has been a welcome diversion from the affairs of court. I find myself accepting of having my own errors brought to light. If Galen was fallible, how can I presume not to be? This is how our sciences advance, is it not? Or does it mean I'm getting too old for combat?*

When we saw Leonardo's drawings all those years ago, you mentioned that you saw in him a quest beyond anatomy, a search to understand how the body works. I told you that Galen had already answered those questions. Now I am not so sure. Dare I say it, he is wrong about the circulation of the blood. My Paris classmate Michael Servetus published theories on the pulmonary circulation; perhaps I will track it down. The zealot Calvin had poor Michael burned at the stake in Geneva some years ago, but for some religious heresy, not his medicine.

Autumn must be arriving in Brussels, and soon it will snow. My regrets. There will be snow in the mountains within view of Madrid, but only rarely in the city, and but a dusting at that.

Yours,
And.

Fabrizio's reply brought me back to the present. "The *Examen* was both gracious and scholarly. Sadly, it did not reach Fallopio before he died. It's a shame they never met."

I suspect that reading Fallopio's critique and writing your response made you long for your former academic life. Just a few years later, you had a golden chance to realize that longing, only to have it snuffed out by Philip.

Fabrizio bolted from his seat. "Good God, I am late for a faculty meeting—once again. I regret I must leave you, but stay as long as you want. It was an honor." He shook our hands and hurried off, leaving us alone in the quiet classroom.

Marcus ran his hands over the surface of the desk in front of him.

"Do you think Andreas would have preferred Padua to imperial service?"

"He never so much as said so."

Marcus patted me on the shoulder. "You stay a while. I will see to some provisions and meet you back at the inn."

"Fine—my knees could use the rest. Can you find your way out?"

"As well as any student," he said, and walked off. The door closed behind him, and his footsteps faded away.

The light from the west-facing windows cast long shadows across the chairs and desks.

I sat here thirty years ago while you taught. You stood on a box you kept behind the lectern! Many of your students were older than you, yet they hung on your every word.

The shadows crept to the wall opposite the windows. I went to stand, but my knees objected; I would sit a few more minutes.

Alone in the waning light, I was overcome with fatigue and dejection. I wanted to escape the classroom and its memories, get something to eat, and go to bed. I pushed myself to stand and started for the door, but instead I followed an impulse to go to the lectern. I managed a weary smile when I saw that Andreas' box was gone.

If you had returned, Runt, you would have needed a new box.

I looked up as a floorboard creaked. Did it come from the next room? At the same time the room darkened and cooled; the sun had likely dropped below a building. I squinted into the dim light and could make out a figure seated in the last row, almost at one with the shadows. I looked away and back again; the figure remained, and I spoke.

"Well, here we are once again in your classroom. Are you surprised I've come this far?"

I waited in vain for a response, feeling his presence against my better judgment.

"Your visit is timely, Andreas. You cannot deny that you disguised your unhappiness in Spain; that you used the pilgrimage to escape from Philip; that you intended to retake your chair in Padua. But why did you send Anne and Anna back to Brussels? Why didn't you abandon the pilgrimage in Italy and reclaim the life you missed so much? Answer me."

The room was now almost dark; the apparition was silent and even less visible. I dug my fingers into the edges of the lectern.

"Stay, Andreas! You have more to answer for. Do I beg you to forgive my blindness to the despair you hid from me, or do I rail at you for deceiving me? Does the depth of your unhappiness excuse your treatment of Anne?"

My demands were met with silence.

"If you won't speak, then just listen! Antoine has been persuasive about the contradictions in friendships, and you leave me no choice but to face alone the contradictions in ours. But you have left Anne widowed and alone. I think you know that I have loved her always. I think you know that it hurt me to the quick when you took her away from me. But I must relegate that to the past. If Anne can now see me as worthy of her love, will you smile upon our union, or deem it a betrayal? Your death cannot be undone, and you should have no say in my future or hers. But you do, damn you, Andreas, even in death."

I strained to peer into the deepening shadows.

"Will you not answer me?"

But the apparition vanished as the classroom went dark. I stepped down gingerly from the lectern and felt my way up the aisle toward a streak of light coming through a crack in the door. As I reached the chair where the apparition sat I could make out a bulky black cloak draped over it. It was Fabrizio's, left behind when he rushed away. I scoffed at my mind's own trickery, but I was still shaken by the experience. I did not share it with Marcus; he would have been sure it was Andreas. And I will never be sure it wasn't.

Venice

18 April 1565

The heavy overnight rains had ceased but the private carriage I hired for the day's ride to Venice became mired in a swollen stream, forcing us to wade out through cold, waist-high water, my boots sinking into the muddy bottom with every step. Perched on a fallen tree trunk, I watched Marcus put his shoulder to a pole wedged behind a wheel, with the driver cracking his whip above his straining team.

I wavered before setting out from Brussels, and now, at the other end of the continent, shivering and exhausted, I wavered once more.

> *Getting this far was hard enough. I am not sure I can face the sea, even for you. The times and places we shared are behind me (save Spain, where I would return only if I were dragged in chains). Beyond Venice there are no common memories, no one who knew you. All that remains is to stand over your grave.*

A final lunge from the horses brought the carriage onto shore, water pouring from the doors. At least our travel chests atop the carriage were secure and kept dry with thick coverings.

"Off we go, Signore," said the driver, unruffled by the delay; to him it was all in a day's work.

Hours later, still wet and mud-stained, we strode into the opulent greeting hall of Il Palazzo Piccolo, a luxurious inn within view of the Doge's palace.

"Forgive us," I said to the clerk. "We had some trouble on the road."

His condescending glare vanished when I produced Antoine's letter carrying the deputized seal of Philip II of Spain and laid a heavy sack of coins on the desk. We had made a stop at a Fugger Bank office on the way.

"We have fine rooms available, Signores, with excellent views." A lifetime of privilege had made me accustomed to his unctuous smile; I fully expected it.

"How fortunate for us," I replied. "We'll take your two best."

"Master Jan," Marcus whispered as I signed the guest-book, "this place is well beyond our needs."

"Beyond our needs, but well within my means. For all you have done to get us to Venice, you deserve to be coddled."

The coddling, I knew, would most benefit me, and further set my mind against a sea voyage.

Marcus laughed. "Very well—but I have one request. Tomorrow is Sunday. I wish for us to spend the Sabbath as God intended, as a day of rest. And I wish to attend mass to pray for a safe voyage."

"Agreed. Tomorrow we will attend mass at Saint Mark's Basilica."

Bathed and in our best clothes, we walked to the imposing basilica, a marriage of Gothic and Byzantine styles built as much to display the wealth and power of the Venetian Republic as it was to honor God. We took seats under the glittering mosaics that filled the huge dome high overhead.

During the mass, I felt Mother's presence beside me, and I remembered how desperately I loved her as a child even as I slipped further into her bondage. Without Andreas I might never have broken free. My mind wandered to the memorial mass for Andreas in Brussels, and how I wept at the thought of never seeing him again.

I am bone-weary and I long for home, but I have come this far, and I will go to Zante. Damn the sea—a farewell to you in the abstract will not do. I will keep my promise to Anne and Anna, and to myself.

We spent the afternoon admiring the basilica and the Doge's palace, both symbolic of the city's beauty and power. Yet, the little islands upon which it sat lent the city a certain fragility. The seas rise from time to time to flood Venice, and then they recede. But what if they didn't? All of Venice's wealth could not save it. I set the notion aside—only another Great Flood could cause such a rise of the seas, and the Great Flood is a fairy tale.

~~~~~~~

We presented ourselves at the admiralty with Antoine's letter of passage. The officer at the desk in the entrance hall begrudgingly unfolded the letter. His eyebrows raised as he read and asked us to wait while he took the letter with him down the hall, his heels echoing on the marble floor. He reappeared a few moments later and ushered us into the office of the commandant.

Commandant Corelli came around from behind his large desk to greet us. He had an easy manner despite his military bearing. His grey eyes were set deeply into a weathered face that spoke of many years at sea.

"As luck might have it, the galleon *Trieste* is set to depart to patrol the waters around Malta. I will instruct the captain to take you to Zante first."

"That is more than kind, Commandant, but I would not want to alter a mission."

"There is no urgency in getting the *Trieste* to Malta." He gestured to Antoine's letter. "It will be an honor to assist Cardinal de Granvelle. He writes that you will submit a report on the gravesite of Doctor Vesalius that will be read by His Majesty King Philip. It will be my honor to assist."

I thanked the commandant, amazed at Antoine's audacious use of leverage; the report to the king was a complete fabrication. He knew that at the highest military levels, diplomacy was as important a skill as warfare.

Corelli sent for the captain of the *Trieste*; in a short time Gerardo Leone strode through the door. He looked too young to have a command. Of average height and build, his dark, neatly-trimmed goatee offset his large forehead and close-cropped hair. His uniform was smartly tailored and trimmed with lace at the sleeves and collar.

Corelli issued his order and handed Leone our letter to read. He perused it and handed it back, making no effort to conceal his displeasure.

"But Commandant, Zante is well east of my intended course, and will delay my passage to Malta."

Corelli agreed that it would, but that nevertheless the order stood.

"Respectfully, am I commanding a warship or a ferryboat?"

I expected Corelli to upbraid Leone for his insolent remark, but he merely reaffirmed his orders. The young captain sighed irritably and turned to me.

"We depart at high tide on April 21. I will be pleased to welcome you and your servant aboard."

"Thank you, Captain, but a minor correction. Master Schoop is my assistant."

"Indeed." He turned to Corelli. "Am I dismissed, Commandant?"

"You are, Captain," Corelli answered. Leone bowed curtly and left.

The commandant stared at the door. I imagined that this was not the first time that Leone had tested his patience.

"I apologize for Captain Leone's behavior. He is a fine sailor and is eager to prove himself in battle. In confidence, his father sits on the Doge's Council, which can make his supervision . . . awkward. Sadly, the younger Leone has not inherited his father's tact."

"I understand, Commandant," noting to myself that the entitlements of privilege extended far beyond the Netherlands.

"There is a sixty-oar galley leaving port soon; galleys are fast, but sorely lack for comfort, and galley crews can be quite unsavory. A full-rigged galleon like the *Trieste* is much more suitable. If you prefer, you can wait for the next galleon departing for points that far south, but it may be weeks. Of course, there are pilgrimage boats, but I cannot recommend them. They are captained by men whose main concern is separating their passengers from their money, with little regard for their health and safety."

Leone's galleon certainly seemed a better option than a galley or an overcrowded boatful of religious zealots.

"The *Trieste* will suit us well. Captain Leone will find us agreeable passengers."

"I'm sure he will. God willing, you'll make Zante in less than two weeks."

The day before boarding I posted brief letters to my brother and Antoine to let them know that we had reached Venice. Our fawning desk clerk directed me to a shop specializing in lace from nearby Burano, where I had a bolt of their finest example sent to Anne. Burano lace had reached Brussels and become quite desirable. I enclosed a note:

20 April 1565

Dearest Anne and Anna,

We have reached Venice after the usual hardships of travel, and some unusual ones. Nevertheless we are bearing up well, and we set sail soon for Zante. My thoughts are with Andreas but never far from you, and they will sustain me.

I long to know how you are faring. You can post a letter to Il Palazzo Piccolo in Venice, where we will stay on our return from Zante, or to Château Granvelle in Ornans; we will see Antoine on the way back.

With devotion,
Jan

Part Three

ZANTE

20 May 1565

Twenty-nine days out of Venice the *Trieste* dropped anchor outside Zante harbor, having had none of the luck that Commandant Corelli had wished for us. Further, my optimism about winning over Captain Leone could not have been more wrong. It was not a good sign that Leone did not extend the courtesy of having us eat with the officers; Marcus and I ate with the crew.

Poor winds along the Dalmatian Coast sea lane got the *Trieste* only as far as Dubrovnik after eighteen days. Leone made an unplanned stop to re-provision, and when three sailors disappeared into the city and did not return to the ship, Leone took out his frustration on us. As we left Dubrovnik harbor, Leone appeared at my side.

"It is widely believed, Signore, that unwanted passengers at sea are a curse."

Leone was not joking; I had quickly learned that he was incapable of humor, and I was growing tired of keeping up airs of courtesy for none in return.

"It is likewise believed that sailors fall prey to superstition. Surely you don't think we cast spells to stifle the wind and make your sailors desert."

He stiffened and strode away without answering.

A day past Dubrovnik, welcome winds filled the galleon's sails and sent it on a brisk southeasterly reach. When Leone passed me on deck, I could not resist:

"Have you come to thank me for lifting the curse on the wind, Captain?"

He glowered as he walked past, and I realized I was foolish to provoke him. The man had absolute power over us while we were on his boat; let him just get us to Zante.

We finally entered the Ionian Sea. The ship lost sight of land and was alone on the open ocean, dependent on the vagaries of the wind and sea to reach land again. Even as the galleon cut resolutely through the water under sunny skies, I could not relax; I felt as helpless as a bug clinging to a leaf in a rushing stream. Every creak in the riggings, every shudder atop a swell, every flutter of a sail, came to me as omens of catastrophe.

Raised as a fisherman, Marcus had no trouble enduring the voyage, but I withered. I slept poorly in our small, airless cabin on a bed not much softer than a plank. When fresh food ran out, I could barely stomach the rations of salt pork, peas, and biscuits.

I spent much of the day on deck, watching the sailors in the riggings or looking out over the sea, dwelling on what lay ahead on Zante. I thought of how far I was from Brussels, and from Anne. Was she thinking of me as well?

Leone set a course toward the strait between Zante and the island of Cephalonia to its north, but as we neared the strait a squall drove us south past Zante. I had already had some bouts of seasickness, but the tossing of the ship drove me to new depths of misery. Marcus stayed by my side through the storm; men had been known to throw themselves overboard to bring an end to the suffering.

The storm had pushed the *Trieste* too far south to regain the strait; it had to round the southern coast of Zante against difficult currents to reach the island's only harbor on its east coast. Having finally prevailed, Leone paced the deck like a ferret as two skiffs were lowered; one would bring us ashore, and both would return to the ship carrying what provisions they could. He had lost enough time on Marcus and me, and would lose no more by fully re-provisioning. As our travel chests were lowered into the skiff, he sauntered up to us and looked me up and down; in truth, as sallow and stooped as I was, I could have passed for a stowaway just dragged out of the cargo hold.

"How the sea agrees with you, Signore!" Leone said with a smirk. "What a shame that you must leave us; I will sadly mark your departure in my log. A Venice-bound ship will make an official call here soon enough. I regret that it will not be the *Trieste*."

I had enough strength to match his sarcasm.

"You have been a most gracious host, Captain. May we have the good fortune of meeting you again. I will summon good winds for you. Goodbye."

We climbed into the skiff and did not look back as we set off.

The four sailors facing us bent to their oars; a fifth manned the rudder at the stern. I leaned back against a travel chest and stared blankly ahead at fishing boats bobbing in the harbor, and along the shore, at the plain, low-slung buildings facing the sea.

Heading away from the *Trieste* released me from the tension that had gripped me for the four weeks of the voyage. My eyes closed out of fatigue and relief; the rhythm of the oars lulled me into a quiet space with no reference to time or place. But then a spray of sea water broke the spell, and my attention snapped back to what awaited on Zante. As we neared the dock, I searched the buildings strung along the harbor, the few houses scattered in the surrounding hills, and the flags of a Venetian fortress near the top of a high hill. And then I found the object of my search: a grey stone church with a squat rectangular tower topped by an iron cross, visible over the rooftops at the north end of the harbor—the church of Santa Maria della Grazie, just as described to me by a *Trieste* officer familiar with the island.

"There's the church, Marcus."

"Yes, I see it."

Your pilgrimage ended here, and so will mine. The journey has been long and hard, but the last few footsteps will be the hardest. I had a dream in Brussels where you said, "But you must not come, Jan." Sorry, Runt, I am here.

Marcus put his arm around my shoulders as we neared the shore.

The sailors hastily unloaded us onto the dock and set off to provision. A grizzled villager saw the skiff unloading us and rushed up the dock with a pushcart to help us with our chests. He took us directly to the Customs House to present our documents, and when we reemerged, the sun was setting behind the hills. Our new friend took us to the only inn on the harbor. At the door, he motioned us away from our chests, insisting on bringing them inside himself. I paid him well for his services.

The inn being almost empty, we took a room for each of us. I intended to go back downstairs for a meal, but I was overtaken by exhaustion. While I stripped off my clothes I could see the *Trieste* still at anchor outside the harbor. I closed the shutters and fell into a heavy sleep as soon as I stretched out under the sheet.

21 May 1565

My eyelids were no match for the sunlight that knifed through the shutters; I awoke with a start, not sure where I was until I saw my travel chest at the foot of the bed. I laid back in bed until Marcus peeked into the room.

"I heard you stirring; you have slept like a stone. It's midday—you must be hungry. I think you will find the food more than acceptable— they flavor their dishes with local herbs and lemon."

"Midday, you say? Truly, I have not slept this well since we boarded that cursed boat. And yes, I'm quite ready to eat."

I swung my legs over the side of the bed and stood, only to feel the room sway. I sank back down on the edge of the bed.

Marcus laughed. "You'll feel like you're at sea for a few days yet, a parting gift from the *Trieste*. And you have to regain some strength."

I tried again to stand, this time with success, and walked slowly to the window. I pulled the shutters open to dazzling sunlight and the smell of the sea. I squinted until my vision cleared, and looked out beyond the gently rocking masts of Zante Harbor, taking note that the *Trieste* was gone. The sea was of a blue unknown to the Low Countries, under a dome of paler blue sky that settled upon the sea at the horizon; somewhere beyond was the mainland of Greece. Below me, a cobblestone frontage street traced the curve of the harbor. Jade-colored coastal hills swept away from the harbor in both directions, descending to narrow beaches at the water's edge.

In the harbor, while turnbuckles slapped against the rocking masts, men and women chatted as they tended to their nets and sails; ashore, others cleaned the morning catch on wooden tables and tossed the entrails to hovering gulls. A few dogs sniffing at the catch were shooed away, only to return for another chance to grab a fish. A pair of soldiers casually shouldering muskets strolled along the frontage.

I became aware of an uncomfortable fullness in my lower abdomen. "Marcus, I need to piss, but I doubt I will ever shit again."

"Ha! The chamber pot's over there, and on the subject of your bowels I have good news. These Greeks cook with more olive oil than the Italians. No one on this island can be bound up for long. I'll get you dressed and downstairs."

Marcus saw the smile leave my face and understood why.

"This morning while you slept I found the way to the church. It's but a few minutes' walk. The graveyard's behind the church."

I looked up at him, my throat tightening. "Did you . . .?"

"No. It is for you to see it first."

I devoured freshly-caught grilled fish flavored with herbs I had never before tasted and served with bread and wine. After a while Marcus declared the meal over, waving away the innkeeper and his bottomless pitcher. I lingered at the table, steeling myself for the moment when I would at last confront the inescapable reality of Andreas' death.

"We should go while there is plenty of light, Master Jan."

Only a few townspeople were out in the afternoon heat. The wine and the lingering effects of the sea voyage made me a little unsteady, so Marcus stayed close by. He led me north along the harbor and turned up a street at the edge of town. Shortly we stood before the weathered portals of the church I had spied from the skiff the day before. A wooden sign mounted on its plain stone façade announced its name—Santa Maria della Grazie—the same as the convent in Milan that housed Leonardo's *The Last Supper*. The cornerstone was inscribed "1488."

Marcus saw that I spotted a rusted iron gate to the left of the church.

"Through that gate is a path that leads to the graveyard."

My stomach knotted. "I can't go just yet."

"Then let's first go inside the church," he said.

We entered and blinked into the gloomy church interior, lighted only by muted shafts of light fighting through grimy western windows. The air smelled of mold, dust, and incense, and was cool enough to make me shiver. Beyond a stone font and an alms box were rows of austere pews in poor repair divided by a central aisle leading to a simple altar. Above it was a wooden crucifix from which hung a crudely-rendered Jesus. In addition to the usual stigmata, the Lord's left big toe was missing, and His left thigh was rent from the knee to the hip where the grain had split open. A large, dingy painting of the Madonna and Child in the solemn Byzantine style teetered at an angle on the east wall over a votive table. It was hard to imagine a more dismal house of worship.

We walked part way up the aisle on the gritty stone floor, and seeing no reason to go farther, turned to go.

"*Buongiorno*, gentlemen."

Emerging from the shadows behind us and striding our way was a tall, brown-robed friar, a man of thirty years if that, arms tucked into his sleeves. He bore a friendly expression on his lightly bearded face. He bowed his head in greeting when he reached us.

"I am Fra Pietro. Welcome to our sanctuary. We are unused to visitors at this hour, though vespers will be at dusk. I hope you will come, though you must endure my chanting. Our priest, Father Gregorio, died this past fall of a sudden illness, after twenty years' service on Zante." He crossed himself. "The archdiocese, I have been informed, has no plans to replace him, so the duties of Santa Maria della Grazie have fallen to me. How may I be of service?"

After introductions, I collected myself before proceeding. "We have traveled here from Brussels . . ."

I paused; he studied my face and sensed my difficulty. "Perhaps we should sit," he said, gesturing to the pews.

After Marcus and I took seats in a pew, Fra Pietro knelt child-like to face us from the pew in front of us. He folded his hands on the back of the pew and waited for me to continue. I was surprised and comforted by his engaging informality.

"I believe that a dear friend of mine has within the year been laid to rest in your graveyard."

He furrowed his brow, and then met my eyes. "If you speak of the Flemish physician Andreas Vesalius, then yes, he is here."

I lowered my head.

"Your friendship," he continued, "must have been profound for you to have come this far. I am told he was a great scholar and a physician to royalty. His pilgrimage attests to his piety, and he is surely at peace in the Kingdom of Heaven. By your leave I will take you to the gravesite."

He led us through a passage to the right of the altar to another door. The young friar shouldered it open to blinding afternoon sun that fought with the cool, dark church interior. Marcus went first, and turned to wait for me. I stood fast in the doorway, squinting, stomach churning, my legs once again refusing to move.

Fra Pietro came to my side and put his arm around my shoulders. "Come, we will go together," he said softly.

We made our way along an uneven stone path past rows of gravestones, Marcus catching me a few times when I stumbled. Fra Pietro led us down one of the last rows and stopped in front of a gravestone standing by itself in the shade of a gnarled olive tree. The journey halfway across the world had ended at last, and I had given no thought to what I would do upon reaching this moment.

Such moments, it turns out, impose their own plan.

I regarded the gravestone, a plain waist-high monolith dappled with light streaming through the leaves of the olive tree.

The plain reality before my eyes put to rest the frightful conjurings I had carried with me across the continent, and my dread fell away as a cloak might drop from one's shoulders. I calmly read to myself the inscription on the gravestone:

ANDREAE VESALII BRUXELLENSIS TUMULUS
QUI OBIIT IDIB. OCTOBR MDLXIV AETATIS SUAE
LVIII. QUUM JEROSOLYMIS REDIISSET.

I read the inscription aloud for Marcus: "Tomb of Andreas Vesalius of Brussels, who died on the 15th of October 1564, age 58, as he returned from Jerusalem."

Will this be your epitaph, Andreas? Is this how you will be known here, shorn of your fame and reduced to a few bare circumstances?

As tears fell from my eyes I heard myself speak.

"Well, Runt, Marcus and I have come to say goodbye—but I don't mind telling you it was very inconvenient getting here." I jutted my chin at the gravestone. "And I see that your math is as poor as ever. You were forty-nine when you took up residence here, not fifty-eight."

Beside me, Marcus choked back laughs through his own tears. Marcus was used to hearing us tease each other, and would sometimes join in.

Marcus' laughter provoked laughter from me, which only made him laugh louder. Fra Pietro looked back and forth at us and was himself drawn in. The laughter finally faded, leaving the three of us wiping tears from our faces and letting a few straggling guffaws escape.

"Forgive us," I managed to say. "You must think we have gone mad."

The friar, his eyes shining, shook his head.

"No, far from it," he said. "There could not have been a more beautiful sanctification of your friendship. Light-heartedness, it is clear, was your way with each other in life; why should it not be now? God, ever-present, sees the genuine love you have for the man who lies here. The soul of your dear friend delights in your laughter."

"We are grateful for your understanding," I said. "I can only hope that Andreas had the benefit of your presence at his burial."

"Alas, I arrived here a week later. That duty fell to Father Gregorio, may he rest in peace. Sadly, he himself fell ill and died only days after I arrived."

He straightened up. "But I have overlooked my own clerical duty. May I offer a few moments of silent prayer?"

Marcus bowed his head, and I followed suit.

It was good that I came, Andreas—out of love and sentiment to say goodbye to you, and to bring this place out from the shadows and chase the mystery that would have followed me forever.

I would have thought it more likely to have wept in anguish than to make jokes at your expense. I suppose I would expect the same were the situation reversed. Let Marcus and Fra Pietro pray for your soul; I will settle for my memories of you—unless you send your apparition around again, but I would rather you didn't.

Fra Pietro raised his head. "May the Lord keep you, Andreas Vesalius."

I touched the friar's elbow. "We are grateful for your presence with us this morning."

The young friar smiled. "I was unhappy at the Vatican—or rather, the Vatican was unhappy with me—and I was sent here. But Zante has turned out to be my Promised Land. The Church has all but forgotten Zante; I minister guided by my training, but also as I see fit. I believe this was God's plan for me."

In Fra Pietro I saw the embodiment of Brother Carel, our beloved first schoolmaster in Brussels, if not in appearance, then in his manner—warm, informal, and of independent mind. I was happy that Fra Pietro would be nearby.

I looked slowly around the graveyard. It struck me that Andreas' gravesite had been receiving more attention than most. The patch of ground in front of his stone was covered with neatly-edged creeping thyme, unnaturally green for the climate, and the gravestone was free of dust and lichen.

"Fra Pietro, do I have you to thank for the fine condition of the gravesite?"

"Oh no. I was raised in the heart of Rome, and I know nothing about plants. The credit belongs to a navy physician stationed here who treated your friend when he came ashore. He attends lauds once weekly, and then tends this gravesite. It was he who told me of the renown of Doctor Vesalius."

"He treated Andreas? I would very much like to meet this man. What is his name?"

"He goes by his Latinate name: Vitus Tritonius. I expect him tomorrow."

I sensed that I had heard the name before.

"But why does he do this?"

"I assume it is out of respect for a great man of his profession, but if you come here not too long after sunrise you can ask him yourself. Of course you are welcome to attend lauds . . ."

Marcus and I returned to the inn without saying a word to each other. Once at the inn I was overcome with the desire to sleep. I took a light meal and was in bed before dark, leaving instructions with Marcus to wake me at dawn.

22 May 1565

I was already out of bed when Marcus came to wake me. I told him I would go to the graveyard alone.

"Are you sure you don't want me along?"

"I'll be fine."

"You're still wobbly from the sea voyage."

"I'm steady enough to get there and back. Go and learn something about this town."

He nodded and left me.

Leaning on the doorway of the inn, I shaded my eyes from the low-hanging sun. An undulating forest of shadows from the masts of the boats moored along the harbor crossed the frontage street and rose up the walls of the buildings. I walked slowly on the cobblestones that seemed to be floating under my feet until I reached the flat dirt road that led to the church. As I approached, a handful of people were coming out; I gathered that lauds was over.

I lingered across the road, halted by the same apprehension of seeing Andreas' grave I felt on this spot the day before. Rather than enter the church I went through the side gate and followed the path until it joined the walkway that led to Andreas' row. As I walked my anxiety faded, no longer in dread of the graveyard I could only imagine before.

As Fra Pietro predicted, a man in shirtsleeves knelt at the gravesite, clippers in hand. Nearby were two buckets of water, explaining why the planting looked so healthy. I was only a few paces away when he heard my footsteps and looked up.

"*Buongiorno*," he said. "I usually have no company at this hour."

"And *buongiorno* to you. Fra Pietro told me you would be here today, Doctor Tritonius."

He searched my face. "Do I know you?"

"Good Doctor, I am Jan van den Bossche of Brussels. Doctor Vesalius was my dearest friend."

Tritonius scrambled to his feet. He was of medium stature and olive complexion with close-cropped hair and a neatly trimmed beard. His bearing was youthful but the lines on his face and the grey wisps in his beard gave clues to his age.

"He said you would never come," he said, barely above a whisper, as if speaking to himself.

He dropped the clippers by his feet and wiped his hands with a rag he took from his back pocket, staring at me with alarm.

I held up my palms as a sign of reassurance. "I did not mean to startle you. I traveled from Brussels to pay respects at Andreas' final resting place, and when I came here yesterday I learned from Fra Pietro that you were the one tending so admirably to his grave."

Tritonius could only glance away and back; I filled the awkward silence.

"You seem to know who I am, Doctor," I said. "Forgive me if I am confused."

He finally found his voice. "It is I who must be forgiven. When Doctor Vesalius was near death he spoke fondly of you. He . . . hoped that you would not take the risk of such an arduous voyage."

He gestured to the gravesite. "I tend it in honor of my esteemed teacher."

It was my turn to be surprised. "You were his student?"

"I had just entered medical school at Padua when he was appointed to the faculty. I attended his first public dissection that winter—it was Advent."

I nodded and smiled. "In 1537 I traveled with him to Padua and witnessed that dissection. The daily sessions went for over two weeks."

"Then we were in the same audience. Word quickly spread of his brilliance and skill, and by the end, on Christmas Eve, he drew large crowds. I became an admirer, and I daresay a friend. I was privy to several private dissections at his home. He let his students perform parts of the dissection under his eye."

"Well, I left Padua for home shortly after that public dissection ended. I visited him again a few years later, but I'm afraid I don't recall meeting you—yet your name is somehow familiar to me. Perhaps he mentioned you . . ."

"Perhaps," he said, glancing away again. "He left Padua in 1543 as soon as the *Fabrica* was published, the year I graduated. Then I entered the military."

Another awkward silence until I spoke.

"I understand that you treated him when he came ashore."

"Yes—and I will forever rue my failure to save him."

Tritonius stood before me with anxiety carved into his features. I had not expected this meeting to be as uneasy as it was, and I wanted to put an end to it—for his sake more than mine—yet I wanted to hear more from this man who attended Andreas' last days.

Tritonius clasped his hands together at his chest. "This must be a most difficult time for you."

"It is, but I very much value what you have already shared. And how fitting that one of his students was here to be with him at the end. I would most appreciate speaking with you further."

"There is not much to tell . . . it is not easy to speak of it."

"I'm sure you can understand that would be a comfort to me, and to his widow, to have a fuller picture."

Tritonius weighed my request and then nodded.

"Of course. You have come a long way. Please come to my house this evening for dinner. My housekeeper will prepare an excellent dinner for us, and I have some wine that needs to be enjoyed before the heat kills it. I assume you are at the inn on the harbor; walk south from the inn and turn up the last street. You will see a whitewashed house a short way up the hill on the left. You will have no problem if you come before sunset."

"That's most kind. I gladly accept, and I will leave you to your work."

I glanced at the gravestone and sighed. "I could never have imagined this, and I daresay neither could you."

He looked down, avoiding my eyes. "No, never."

I took a few steps toward the stone, and let a wave of sadness pass through me. This spot would be my last earthly connection to Andreas.

"It's a small thing," I finally said, "but his age is wrong. He wasn't fifty-eight—"

"—I know . . . the stonecutter—"

"—anyway, if Andreas knew he would probably laugh at the error," I said, trying to lighten the mood, but the anxious expression on

Tritonius' face remained unchanged.

"I look forward to seeing you this evening," he said. We shook hands. He bent to pick up his clippers and stood again to watch me off. It was an odd thing to notice right then, but his pupils, even in the early morning shade of the olive tree, were noticeably constricted.

Marcus was nowhere to be seen when I returned to the inn. I tried to rest, but my awkward meeting with Tritonius tugged at me. What did he mean by, 'He said you would never come?' The 'he' could only be Andreas, and Andreas knew me well enough to guess that I wouldn't make this trip. I could understand why Tritonius would be surprised to see me, but I would think he would be more welcoming than unnerved.

I decided to go for a walk to clear my thoughts.

After stopping at the inn for a heel of bread and a boiled egg, I wandered along a back street and came to the start of a well-maintained road winding into the hills. I took it, thinking it would lead to the fortress I spied from the *Trieste* skiff.

Two shirtless, sun-darkened boys found me interesting enough to follow, and a harbor dog, eyeing my food, ambled along with me as the road climbed past walled hillside pastures and stands of olive trees. The boys entertained themselves by throwing rocks at the dog, but they soon turned back to town with good reason; the steepening road called for more effort than they were willing to put into it, especially as the morning went from pleasant to hot. Even my canine companion abandoned me in favor of a shady spot under a cart. Two soldiers on horseback cast puzzled glances as they rode downhill past me.

I pressed on, at last spotting the Lion of St. Mark flag flying above the battlements of the fortress. I crossed the stone courtyard to its gates breathless and thirsty, my shirt soaked in sweat, my knees complaining loudly. Panting, I hailed two guards stationed on the wall above the gate.

"Good morning. May I enter and rest a while?"

"Do you have business in the *fortezza*, Signore?"

"No, but . . ."

"Then I am afraid we cannot admit you."

"I see ... but the walk up the hill was more than I bargained for. I did not think of bringing water."

The guards exchanged smiles and shook their heads. "With respect, Signore," said one, "that was ill-advised. And you would do well to wear a hat with a brim!" The second guard beckoned me to wait. "I will bring you a jug of water. If you collapse up here, we'd have to write a stinking report!" They both laughed loudly.

The guard reappeared at the gate with the jug and handed it through.

"This is clean spring water. Drink it all, but slowly."

He produced a small sack from inside his tunic.

"Take this, too. These are currants that grow on the island. Rest on that bench over there under the olive tree and enjoy the view."

The guard above the gate called out to me.

"Signore, if I may, from where do you hail?"

"The Netherlands."

"The Netherlands! No wonder." He pointed to the sky. "You see that shiny ball up there? It is the sun. Do you ever see it where you live?" The two guards once again burst out laughing.

"I was wondering what that was," I said, and laughed with them.

"Are you a pilgrim, Signore?" asked the guard at the gate.

"You might say, soldier."

I sank onto the bench not three paces from the edge of the hill, which fell steeply away to the town below. The leaves of the olive trees covering the hill sparkled in the breeze. Beyond the rooftops along the harbor the great expanse of sea deepened in color from turquoise to a dark, rich blue as it met the pale blue sky at the serene, unblemished horizon.

The fortress was built there not just for the view; enemy vessels could be spotted at great distances, and withering artillery fire would rain down on them if they dared come within range. Venice had clearly decided that Zante was worth defending.

In the shade of the olive tree, with a scented breeze ambling by, my breath quieted and my limbs became pleasantly heavy. As I drank from the jug and dipped into the sack of currants, I followed a boat leaving the harbor, its sail luffing and then snapping taut as it found the wind. I wondered if the people of Zante knew that they lived in as fair a place as could be found on Earth.

From my vantage point I found the squat tower of Santa Maria della Grazie, and could even glimpse the graveyard through the trees.

How remarkable that your student Tritonius was stationed here, and now serves as your gardener. I put him quite on edge this morning, and by his words, you doubted I would come here. Of course you were not far wrong; I wavered before starting out, I nearly turned back in Venice, and if I knew in advance what the sea voyage would be like, I very well may have. But in the end I'm grateful to have made it here; your resting place is no longer a mystery to me. I will never return, Andreas, except in my memory— much more often, I think, than if you were buried in Brussels a carriage ride away.

I will have dinner with Tritonius tonight. Tell me, why is his name familiar?

I sat for a while in a state of calm, held in the present moment by the soft breeze and the sunlight shimmering on the surface of the sea. Such rare moments of enveloping peace and wonder are all the more sublime because they often arrive without notice. One might find God's hand in moments like these—or the deepest expression of human awe before Nature.

I stood to go, and waved to the guards as I placed the jug and sack by the gate.

"God be with you, Netherlander," yelled one of them. "Keep to the shade on the way down!"

By the time Marcus got back to the inn, I was half asleep in my room. His eyebrows raised when I told him of my climb to the fortress.

"It was too hot for a walk like that! And I'll wager you didn't bring water."

"Right on both counts, but I am the wiser for it. And how was your morning?"

"Along the harbor I struck up a conversation in broken Italian with some fishermen. They were amazed to meet a fisherman from the Low Countries, and asked me along on an overnight sail."

"You can't be serious!" I said. "Haven't you had quite enough of the sea for a while?"

"I feel a bond with them; like my people, they make a living from the sea. I want to see how they go about it. There might be a thing or two we can show each other."

Over the years, Marcus could not resist occasional fishing runs with his cousins. I did not deny him then, and he knew I would not deny him now.

"Go ahead. If you don't drown, at worst you'll come back stinking of fish."

He smiled. "Sailing conditions look to be excellent. I'm sorry to be leaving you alone this evening."

"But I won't be alone. I am invited to the house of Doctor Tritonius for dinner."

He furrowed his brow. "The man tending the grave?"

"Yes. When I met him there this morning he acted like he'd seen a ghost. Incredibly, he was a student of Andreas'. Andreas died in his care, and during that time he came to know my name. There is something odd about the man, but I want to know more about Andreas' last days."

"If I may, his devotion to tending the grave seems odd."

"Agreed. But Fra Pietro's theory is the most likely—a disciple's devotion to his teacher."

Marcus shrugged. "It's as good a theory as any. Until tomorrow, then, Master Jan," he said, "but I have some news. I stopped in at the Customs House this morning. A Venetian galleon is expected to make port within days and then sail to Venice a day or two after that. The customs officer said we'd be wise to be on it. No other ship is due here for weeks."

After Marcus left, I considered walking back to the graveyard; I still had Anna's handkerchief to leave there. But my knees throbbed and I needed rest; it could wait until tomorrow.

The sun had set behind the hills when I turned up Tritonius' street. I could see him pacing at his front door, and when he saw me, he rushed to the road to greet me.

"Ah, here you are," he said, taking me by the arm. "Please come in."

He led me into a house built in the classic Roman style, a design well-suited to the climate. The entrance hall led to a stone-paved atrium open to the sky, from which all the rooms of the house could be reached. Perhaps ten paces across, the atrium was fragrant from flowering vines that clung to one of the walls. On the wall opposite the entrance hall, water poured from the mouth of a lion's head and splashed gently into a scalloped font.

"It is fed by a stream that comes down the hill," Tritonius said, anticipating my question. "I am lucky to have it."

He motioned to a table near the fountain. "If it pleases you I thought we would dine out here."

"It very much pleases me," I said, gazing around as we sat. "A house like this in Venice would be highly prized. And the island itself has many charms. I regret that Andreas did not live to enjoy it."

Tritonius looked away. "I, too. May we use our first names? It is Jan, correct?"

"Yes, and by all means, Vitus."

An open bottle of wine was at the ready. Tritonius called out, "Selene!" A young woman hurried to the table from the kitchen doorway. Vitus watched his dark-haired housekeeper stretching up on one foot to light the candelabra near the table, her blouse riding up to expose the skin of her waist.

"Bring the meal when it is ready, Selene."

His eyes followed her as she disappeared through the kitchen door. I suspected that Selene's domestic services extended beyond cooking and cleaning.

He poured us both a glass of red wine. "It's from the town of Montalcino in Tuscany. God surely gave us this wine to drink with lamb. Or perhaps the other way around."

Selene's skill was borne out with savory grilled lamb and vegetables brightened with the same currants given to me by the soldiers at the fortress.

In the dim candlelight, I noticed again that his pupils were unusually small, and at one point in the meal when there was a lull in conversation his head briefly sank onto his chest. Vitus made sure my wine glass was never empty, and insisted on opening a second bottle near the end of the meal to make toasts to Andreas.

"Thank you for having me, Vitus. I dreaded coming here, but I am making my peace with his death. It's an extra comfort to be leaving him with one of his students."

Vitus pressed his lips together. "It is my honor."

I gazed up at the stars for a few moments to clear my head as Selene cleared the table.

"A naval vessel bound for Venice is expected to reach port soon. If I may, I want to ask about Andreas' last days—not only for myself but for his widow who awaits news in Brussels."

He took a gulp of wine, using his sleeve to catch a few drops dribbling down his chin.

"As I said, there's not much to tell." He offered me more wine, but I put my hand over my glass.

"Please," I said, leaning forward in my chair. "Whatever details you can provide ... I cannot imagine making this voyage again, nor can I imagine his family coming here. They are relying on me."

He drew back, perhaps realizing that I would not let the matter drop.

"Of course," he said, as he fidgeted with his wine glass. "Mid-October last, a pilgrim ship sent a sick passenger ashore with the first mate. I was called to the harbor to see him. I had to look twice to believe my eyes—I had not seen him in years, but it was Andreas."

He took a swallow of wine. "The ship had been driven off course by storms west of Crete, and they were running out of food and water. Vesalius had taken sick a week before they dropped anchor here, and he begged to be sent ashore."

"Was Andreas the only one taken ill?"

"The only one ill enough to be sent ashore."

"And what of his illness?"

"He was barely conscious. I judged it dangerous to transport him up to the hospital at the fortress so I treated him here, in my house. I sent Selene away, and had her leave food and supplies at the front door. After I got him settled, he recognized me."

"So, he was able to speak."

"Well, yes, for a short while . . . he cried out from pain in his limbs. He was weak and feverish, with swollen, bloody gums, and he had already lost a few teeth. The skin on his legs had areas of black putrefaction."

I winced. "What was your diagnosis?"

"Sea scurvy—quite advanced."

"I have heard of sea scurvy. Is there no treatment?"

Tritonius took another draft of wine. "None that has been known to succeed. He talked fondly of you, and of his wife and daughter . . ."

Tritonius says you were gravely ill and barely conscious, yet you could recognize him after twenty years and speak of your family and friends.

". . . In a day's time he was near death. I eased his pain with a medicine used by Paracelsus himself."

"Laudanum."

"You are familiar with it?"

"Andreas spoke of it years ago."

"It is the opium—a substance from certain kinds of poppies—that is the most important component. A German trader who stops at Zante sells me opium in powder form that I make into a tincture."

"If it eased his suffering, I'm glad you had it."

"It was all I could do."

We both sat silently, Tritonius twirling his wine glass until it slipped away from him and spun across the table. I grabbed it and set it upright.

"Vitus, I spent enough time with Andreas to know that maladies reach a point beyond help."

"Thank you, Jan. Your understanding brings me some solace."

A gibbous moon had risen into the sky over the courtyard; I was tiring, and once again I felt uncomfortable in his presence, especially as he was drunk.

"I'm sorry to have made you recall those difficult days, but it is a comfort to know what happened. The hour is late, and I should be getting on. Thank you for having me."

He offered to walk with me back to the inn, but I was in better condition for walking than he, and I insisted I could find my way back. We started toward the door, but he took my arm.

"Before you go, let me show you something."

He stumbled into the house and returned with a book I recognized as the *Fabrica*, as well as a worn notebook. He swept the table with his sleeve before setting them down.

"I bought it when it first came out in 1543. It was costly, but I had to have it."

He opened the book to the title page. In the lower margin was an inscription—"To my good friend, Vitus Tritonius. And. Vesalius."

I looked up at him and back to the signature. "Hmm. When did he sign this?"

"I took it to him for his signature right after I bought it."

He closed the *Fabrica*, steadied himself, and handed me the notebook.

"Remember that dissection in Padua in 1537, the one we both attended unknown to each other? Well, this notebook holds my notes from that dissection. Twenty pages worth. It is ... a treasure to me."

I thumbed through his notes, feigning interest in his slurring commentary. My clearest memory of the dissection was the stench, and I had no interest in seeing his notebook. But I stopped turning pages at a rough sketch entitled "Description of the third pair of nerves."

He took notice of my pause. "Clearly, I am no draftsman. See here . . ." He reached over my shoulder to turn the page.

I hurried through the rest of the notes. "Thank you, Vitus. I really must be on my way."

At the door, he grasped my hand as he weaved in place. "I trust I will see you again before you depart."

"By all means. Good night, and thank you again."

I made my way carefully down the road; I had consumed much less wine than Tritonius, but enough to heed my steps. I looked over my shoulder; he was still in the doorway. I waved and he turned away, holding onto the doorframe as he went inside.

On any other night the solitary walk would have been welcome. The sunset breeze had died away, leaving the dark surface of the sea as smooth as smoky glass. A strip of moonlight glowed upon the waters, setting in relief the masts of the boats moored in the harbor. It was a tranquil yet haunting scene, worthy of a painting, but could not distract me from the feeling that things on this island were not fitting into place.

My first encounter with Tritonius at the gravesite was awkward, but we were passing a pleasant evening despite the talk of Andreas' last days. Yet I grappled with his retelling of it, drunken though it was. By his own account Andreas seemed much too sick to recognize a former student or hold a conversation. And then, the inscription in the *Fabrica*, and finally, the sketch of the nerves in his student notebook and his tense reaction to it.

As I turned on to the frontage street, it came to me in a sudden jolt why his name had teased my memory. Back in my room, I lay awake for a long time before sleep came.

23 May 1565

Thanks to a wine-filled evening and its unsettling conclusion, I awoke with a headache and a knot in my stomach. I was not sure when Marcus would return from his fishing expedition. I took myself downstairs for a bit of breakfast and a glum walk along the harbor. As I passed the customs office, I stopped short, wondering what Zante's official records contained about Andreas.

The one-room office was empty save for a lone official behind the counter writing in a ledger, with a row of ledgers on the shelves behind him. The air was dusty and still, and the clerk had beads of sweat on his expansive forehead. He looked up as I approached.

"Ah, *buongiorno*, Signore vendena-booshi. You are looking much refreshed since your arrival the other day. How may I be of service?"

It was some consolation to hear that I looked better than I felt, and I rather enjoyed the Italianate version of my name.

"And *buongiorno* to you, Signore . . .?"

"Penzi. Sergente Penzi, Customs and Administration."

Men like Penzi, who thanklessly shoulder the quotidian duties of state, are disposed to flattery; I thought it prudent to dispense some.

"Of course, Sergente Penzi. I well remember your courtesy and efficiency. I am impressed that you recall my name."

Penzi's expression brightened. "You are most gracious, but it is my duty to know Zante's comings and goings. Your man inquired yesterday about the next naval vessel bound for Venice. I trust he relayed that information to you; in fact it is within sight of the harbor now. I will see to it that they know you intend to sail with them."

"Zante is fortunate to have your service, and I will make it my business to commend you to your superiors when I return to Venice."

"Please, Signore, do not trouble yourself . . . unless it is convenient to do so."

"It will be no inconvenience at all. Now, let me state my business and not take you from your work. As you recall, I am on Zante to pay my respects to an old friend who died here."

"Of course—Doctor Vesalius. My colleague recorded his arrival. I regret the sad circumstance that occasions your visit."

"Thank you. But I am here as well on behalf of his widow who could not undertake this trip. There is her fatherless daughter to consider."

He nodded sympathetically. "We are a long way from Brussels."

"I can attest to that, Sergente. But upon my departure, Signora Vesalius begged that I bring back as much information as possible about her husband's last days. May I confirm with you the date of his arrival?"

"It will be no trouble." He closed the ledger in front of him, slid it to the side, and turned to the row of ledgers at his back. His fingers ran along the bindings until he found the one he wanted and transferred it to the counter with a thud and a puff of dust.

"Let me see . . ." he said to himself, as he opened it and turned the pages. "Ah, here we are. Monday, 12 October, 1564. Disembarkation from the pilgrim ship *Blessed Family*, Andreas Vesalius of Brussels, occupation physician, age forty-nine, ill."

"Your colleague met him, then?"

"It is not likely. With pilgrimage vessels there is always fear of contagion. The first mate would bring the credentials of ill passengers into the office while such passengers remain on the dock until examined by a naval physician. The priest is also summoned in case last rites are needed. Sadly, it is often the case."

"I understand. And finally, I assume there is an entry for his date of death."

"The date of death would not be in these customs records, Signore. These records are a civil function, and document only arrivals and departures. Births and deaths are recorded elsewhere."

"Ah. Can you direct me to that office?"

"You are already in that office, Signore." He looked over his left shoulder to another shelf of ledgers against the wall. "The information you seek is kept in those ledgers, under military jurisdiction."

"With respect, Sergente, one wonders why this information isn't completely civil or completely military."

Penzi's patient expression told me that I was not the first to wonder.

"I can only say that it has always been this way. But let me retrieve that information for you."

He went to the shelf with the military ledgers, pulled one out, and thumbed through the pages.

"Ah—here we are. 15 October, 1564, pronounced dead by Doctor V. Tritonius. Burial at Santa Maria della Grazie."

"Thank you, Sergente. Is there any other information in your ledgers that might be of value to the family?"

"I am afraid not. The ledgers record only the bare facts. You might speak with Dr. Tritonius."

"We have met."

Penzi replaced the ledger and returned to the counter.

"I wish I could be of more help."

"But you have been more than helpful."

"It was my honor. Have a pleasant day, Signore vendena-booshi."

I was almost out the door when Penzi called out to me.

"Signore, would you perhaps be interested in information about the other pilgrim who came ashore that day?"

I stopped and turned around. "The other pilgrim?"

"Yes." Penzi reopened the first ledger. "Disembarkation from the pilgrim ship *Blessed Family*, Georg Boucher of Nuremberg, occupation goldsmith, age fifty-eight, ill."

"Fifty-eight?" I walked back to the counter.

"Yes, and by God's grace he survived."

"How do you know?"

"Because," he said, consulting the ledger, "he left the island on 27 October aboard the *Principessa della Urbino*, a merchant vessel bound for Venice. Without a travel document issued from this office, foreigners cannot board an outgoing vessel. In fact I was the one to issue his document. It occurred to me that Signore Boucher may have been a traveling companion of the doctor's, and therefore a mutual acquaintance of yours. His family filed an official inquiry as he had not returned home. Our office confirmed his departure, and Venice customs confirmed his arrival in Venice on 15 November, where he made a sizeable withdrawal against his letter of credit. Other than that, investigators could find no mention of his name at inns or travel depots. He seems to have disappeared."

I managed to maintain my composure. "I do not know the name. Can you describe him? I can make inquiries when I return."

"It was a while ago, of course, but I recall that he was of less than average height, dark hair, perhaps a bit grey, clean-shaven . . . and—in this I could be wrong—there was a birthmark somewhere on his face. But I could be confusing him with someone else."

I managed a thank you and left the office. The sun's heat struck my face, but not as hard as the blow from the unwitting Sergente Penzi.

Marcus was not yet back from his overnight sail, leaving me to wrestle alone with the unnerving surprises from the customs office atop those from dinner with Tritonius the night before. Standing in the doorway of the inn, I thrust my hands into my pockets and found Anna's handkerchief, meant for her father's grave.

Before long, I was walking around the side of the church and down the graveyard path. I sat back against the olive tree next to the gravestone, facing its unmarked back. I stared at the blank stone, absently folding and unfolding Anna's handkerchief, turning over and over in my mind the unexpected revelations of Zante. Finally I stood to go.

> *You and Tritonius have made things more difficult in ways I could not have imagined. How can I ignore what I have learned here? Is it possible, what I'm thinking, or is it madness?*

I took a long look around the deserted graveyard.

> *I will never be here again. I have no choice but to try.*

I walked out of the graveyard, taking Anna's handkerchief with me.

Marcus was effusive when he returned that afternoon. "They are good sailors and good fishermen. The boat is seaworthy, with clever, watertight joints, but with too much beam for these calm waters. A sleeker design would serve them well . . ."

He stopped talking and eyed me with concern. "You look troubled. I should not have left you alone."

"I am troubled, but your fishing trip has nothing to do with it." I told him of my evening with Tritonius, and what I learned quite by chance at the customs office. When I told him what I wanted to do, his face drained of color.

He studied my face. "You are serious about this."

"I am."

He crossed himself. I was tempted to do the same.

In a quiet corner of the inn's public room we weighed my intention to dig up Andreas' grave.

"This borders on lunacy," I said, "but if I leave Zante forever with these doubts hanging over me, I will have no peace. There are legal channels to pursue, but it would take months, even years, for the case to work its way through the Venetian bureaucracy. Even if the grave were opened tomorrow, seven months have passed since the burial. Andreas told me once that a corpse buried underground will not decay as fast as a corpse left hanging on a gibbet, but then other conditions come into play—moisture, heat, depth, burial in a coffin or a shroud. I can't see waiting here for permission that we may not get. By then, there would be more decay, and it will not help that Tritonius will be hostile."

I leaned closer to Marcus. "I can't do this alone, yet I can't compel you to help. If we are discovered the authorities on Zante will not be merciful, and not even Antoine could keep us out of a dungeon. And I fear worse could follow. I will bear no ill will if you want no part of it. I almost wish you'll bring me to my senses."

"You've laid it out plainly," Marcus said, "and by your leave, so will I."

"Go ahead."

"Risk-taking is not in your nature. That you are willing to risk this shows how important this is to you." He took a sip of beer. "You're right—you cannot do this alone. If I decline, I condemn you to a life-time of unanswered questions about Andreas. And in declining, I condemn myself to the same fate. I, too, want to know the truth. So count me in, and with some luck, we can pull it off."

Then he smiled. "Besides, we're just going in for a look—we wouldn't be grave-robbing, because we're not taking anything with us."

I laughed. "You would have made a fine lawyer. But I'm afraid that distinction will be lost on the local authorities. Are you sure you want to do this? I'm terrified enough at the thought of opening that grave, and I can't even begin to think about what it would mean if . . ."

"But that's why I'm sure." He took a swallow of beer and set down his mug. "If we're to act, we must be quick. That navy ship will not stay more than a few days, and we must do our work in time to be on it."

Marcus was right about acting quickly, but I had no idea what to do. While Andreas had dragged me along on several grave-robbings in years gone by, he and his acolytes did all the work; my job was to be a lookout, alone with my own fear and revulsion.

Marcus leaned toward me. "If I may put a plan to you . . ."

"Please do. I have no plan of my own to counter it."

"We'll need a day to prepare, so we'll do it tomorrow. By night, of course. The street behind the inn," pointing his thumb over his shoulder, "runs to the edge of town just like the frontage street, and ends up squarely at the church. This is the best way to the graveyard, for our purposes."

"Why not the usual way?"

"The moon's almost full," he said, "rising in the east over the water. On the frontage, we'd be lit up like moths. The back street will be still be in shadows. Also, the street's unpaved, so our footsteps will be quiet."

He paused to see if I was still with him. "Go on," I said.

"We'll wear two layers of clothing, normal clothes on top, work clothes underneath. The digging will be dirty work. We'll set our clothes aside for the work and change back into them when we're done. We'll have clean clothes to wear back to the inn so we don't look like the grave-diggers we will be by then."

Marcus' cunning surprised me. "I would never have thought of that."

"We'll make our move as midnight approaches. The town will be still as a tomb by then. We should have enough time for the work, if we work steadily . . ."

"Still as a tomb." You would have seen the humor in that.

". . . and we will have to avoid the two soldiers patrolling the frontage together. Tonight I'll get a sense of their routines, but I'm pretty sure they stay on the frontage. When it's safe, we'll slip out of the inn and go around to the back street."

"Well-reasoned, Marcus. Tomorrow night, we will take your route to the graveyard. But we will need tools."

"Indeed. We'll be needing two shovels, an iron crow, and a lantern."

"Very well, purchase them in the morning."

"I won't be purchasing them."

"What will you do, steal them?" I snickered.

Marcus did not reply, and when he saw my puzzled look, he continued.

"How would it look if a foreigner went into a shop to buy shovels and an iron crow, of all things, and if our little job behind the church is found out?"

"I see . . . but how . . . ?"

"I will steal the tools."

"What? I can't let you take that risk."

"Yes you will. There are things I have not told you about myself, and you may as well hear them now."

"All right, go on. But you are making me uneasy."

"When Cardinal de Granvelle took my confession in Ornans, it was a great honor for me, but also a great trial because he is your friend."

"I don't understand."

He took a deep breath. "You knew me as a fishmonger, but for a few years before my other business was thievery. I never robbed from the higher classes; I'd have ended up hanging from the end of a rope, and then maybe under the knife of Master Vesalius in his cellar. I was a petty thief, robbing from my own kind, people who had nothing of value except what I stole from them. The constables who chased like hounds the thief of a rich man's house wouldn't even sniff at robberies of common folk. Why waste time on a few coins stolen from a honeypot or a granny's battered silver bowl?"

He shook his head, as if recalling his thefts and the people he stole from.

"I had a decent return with low risk, but I got to hating myself and gave it up. Fishmongering was an honest living, but truth be told I did not feature spending my days gutting herring and haggling over the price of a cod. What I would truly love would be to build boats, but I could never raise the money to start such a business. An old comrade from my thieving life tempted me to come back to it for higher stakes. But then you came along."

He looked at me, his eyes shining.

"You treat me far better than I deserve. I don't remember all the people I've thieved from, but for those I do, I find a way to leave them some money where they'll find it. To them it will be one bit of good luck against all the rotten luck in their lives."

I was never in doubt of Marcus' character, but for the first time I saw the depth of it. After a few moments passed I reached across the table and grasped his forearm.

"Can you tell me what Antoine said to your confession?"

"He said I had already done my penance in leaving money for those I stole from."

"His Eminence was wise to leave it at that."

Marcus smiled. "There was more. He also granted me an indulgence for the hardships of traveling with you."

I laughed. "That indulgence is wasted on you. You will spend no time in Purgatory, and Hell has no use for the likes of you."

24 May 1565

I could not drive my thoughts from what was in store that night. I dug out my notebook to follow some threads of ideas I scribbled down along the journey about defining the end of an infinite series, but I could not think beyond the bizarre shape Anne drew in that dirt path years ago. I went for a walk along the harbor to calm myself, but to no avail; all that was left was to wait and worry.

Marcus, meanwhile, had been busy much of the night and into the morning. He monitored the harbor patrols and then acquired the tools we needed from the unlocked sheds of sleeping townspeople. He finished preparations in time to join me for lunch.

"These people cannot have much experience with thievery," he said between bites. "I hid the tools in a corner of the graveyard. We wouldn't want to be seen tonight walking along with digging tools and a lantern."

For the first time, I noticed a few flecks of grey in his curly hair and wispy goatee, and a few creases radiating from the corners of his eyes. As I listened to him, I laughed to myself. Learning of his former life did nothing to shake my trust in him; in fact, I was grateful that he had the skills and courage for the task we faced, as I had neither. With Andreas, I preferred being led; so it was here with Marcus.

"Let's try to get some rest, Marcus. We have a full evening ahead of us."

The harbor was still and the moon was halfway up the eastern sky. At my window in our double layers of clothes, we waited for the patrol.

"They should be passing by any time now, heading away from the church," Marcus said.

Sure enough, they came into view, stippled by the moon-shadows of the masts, talking quietly as they ambled along. Once the soldiers were well down the street, we crept down the stairs, slipped out the door, and walked up the alleyway beside the inn to the next street.

Marcus stopped me before we went around the corner.

"I saw no patrol on this street last night," he whispered. "Walk at a normal pace. If we're stopped, you say you couldn't sleep and woke me to walk with you. And we're on this street to avoid the bright moonlight."

"Those are the two truest things we can say."

We walked quietly alongside the buildings and emerged from the shadows opposite the church, pale grey in the moonlight. As far as we could tell we were not seen. We crossed the street and followed the path along the church wall and into the graveyard. Shielded by the church, we would be concealed from the street, and the town had yet to expand beyond the graveyard wall. The moon, our adversary on the way to the graveyard, now became our ally, lighting our way and our work; we hoped to minimize the use of the lantern, whose light would arouse the suspicion of some late-night stroller or a sentry in the fortress high overhead.

As we neared the grave, I was flooded with images of the gruesome work just ahead of us, and I felt my will wavering. Marcus must have sensed this, for he grabbed my arm and issued orders.

"Take off your outer clothes. Give them to me and wait here—I'll get the tools. I'll hide our clothes where the tools are." With that he disappeared into the dark.

I stood alone until Marcus came out of the shadows in his work clothes, carrying the stolen tools. Marcus laid the shovels, the iron crow, and the lantern on the ground beside the grave. I peered down at the tools and then at the dark outline of the gravestone. My breathing became heavy, a sign of the struggle within me between will and fear.

"But you must not come, Jan," you told me in a dream. Was I dreaming?

Marcus picked up the shovels and handed me one.

"When you put yours to work, so will I mine."

I looked at Marcus in astonishment. He waited with his right forearm resting on the top of his shovel, gesturing to the gravesite with his left hand, unknowingly striking the very pose of one of the skeletons in the *Fabrica*. Calcar spoke of the illustration as a classic death motif: *"He gestures to a grave in need of digging."*

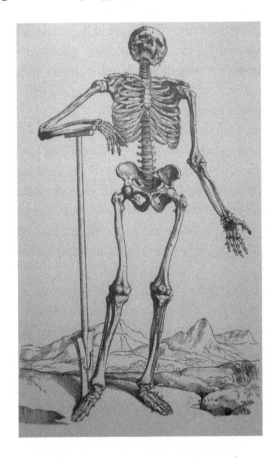

Like Calcar's skeleton, Marcus beckoned for action; it was up to me to strike the first blow.

I thrust my shovel into the dirt at the edge of the creeping thyme that Tritonius had planted and tended.

"The die is cast; I have crossed the Rubicon," I whispered.

Marcus looked at me quizzically, then with the blade of his shovel divided the thyme into six sections. We then undermined each one with our shovels deep enough to preserve the roots and set them carefully aside. When we refilled the grave, we would put them back in place. The thyme would stay green at least until after we were gone. Tritonius was not due back for many days.

The grave surface was now laid bare, the dirt moist and dark thanks to Tritonius' regular watering. We began to dig, Marcus taking the end nearest the headstone, I taking the foot. Marcus worked with the steady rhythm of the laborers I used to watch in the streets of Brussels. Taking care not to disturb the stone, he piled dirt along the lengthwise edges of the hole so it could be easily swept back in.

Marcus tossed two shovelfuls of dirt for every one of mine. I strained to keep pace, trying to clear my mind of everything but the feel of the shovel handle, the chunking sound of the shovel piercing the earth, the weight of the dirt as I hefted it up—but my mind insisted on bringing up images of those nights long past when Andreas and his students dug like excited dogs for a freshly-buried cadaver, and how I winced as they struggled to lift it out of the grave, head and limbs flailing, and into a cart.

As I dug, it occurred to me that I had never used a shovel—what could there be to it? But within minutes I was breathing heavily and my lower back was stabbed with pain each time I lifted a shovelful of dirt. Marcus glanced over and saw my problem.

"Slide your lower hand further down the handle."

Of course—a simple matter of lever and fulcrum, a principle any laborer applied to their work without a second thought. I dug with more skill, but soon blisters formed on my hands.

After a time we had to step into the deepening hole to continue digging, working back to back with shortened strokes. Dirt started to slide back into the hole, so I had to heave the dirt farther up the mound to keep it out.

> You preferred taking bodies from graveyards known for shallow graves, and with good reason. How ironic that I would never agree to dig while you were alive.

The moonlight served us well until we were chest-high in the hole. "Marcus," I whispered, between heavy breaths, "we will... need the lantern ... can't see much now." The next stab of my shovel blade met resistance. As I lifted the blade, I saw, even in the darkened hole, that I had unearthed dirty cloth.

"Marcus, come look."

He made his way to my end and squatted down. Gently brushing away dirt with his hands, he found an edge and followed it about two feet toward the gravestone.

"We won't be needing to open a coffin," he said. "This looks to be a shroud, and I've found the same at the head. The rest of our work should be by hand. When we've done as much as we can without the lantern, I'll light it, and we'll bring it down here."

He reached up to the edge of the hole and produced a jug of water. I drank slowly, only able to swallow small amounts between labored breaths.

"Ready?" he asked, after taking a drink himself.

My heart pounding, I nodded.

Marcus returned to the head end and brushed away dirt with his hands. Numbly, I did the same at my end, tense, aching, and breathing hard. Bit by bit we uncovered a form, unmistakably human, wrapped in a stained shroud of similar make as the bed-sheets at the inn. The shroud's top fold overlaid the body in its length. The remaining work to expose the corpse would be quick and quiet with no coffin to unseal, but the amount of decomposition would be greater.

With difficulty I straightened up and took stock of the moment: I was shoulder-deep in a grave behind a church on a Greek island, astride a shrouded corpse that could be Andreas.

I must be dreaming. Do I want this to be you?

There were four possible outcomes: the first, now eliminated, that the grave would be empty; the second, that we would find Andreas in the shroud; the third, that we would find someone else; or the fourth and by far the worst, that the corpse could not be identified one way or another.

Marcus touched my arm. "We have only a few hours until sunrise."

I calmed myself; it was now only a matter of unfolding the shroud. "Right. You take the feet. I need to see the face."

"I'll light the lantern now," Marcus said. I shuffled up to the head as he vaulted to the surface to get the lantern. It held two candles. From his pocket he produced a flint, a steel, and dry tinder wrapped in a cloth. He laid the tinder on his lap in the center of the cloth and put the wick of one candle next to the tinder. With a few deft strokes of the flint against the steel, sparks flew and ignited the tinder, which in turn lit the wick. With that candle he lit the other one.

Eerie light filled the grave. Handing the lantern to me, he said, "You'll need only one hand to move the shroud."

I straddled the corpse, facing Marcus at the feet. With the lantern in my right hand, I took hold of the corner of the shroud with my left. It would open right to left.

"Ready, Marcus—on the count of three . . ."

The shroud was damaged and crumbly—moisture had reached it from above—but it held together as we peeled it back. Under the top fold was another, folded the opposite way, with indistinct stains at the face, shoulders, waist, knees and feet. The so-called shroud of Christ in the chapel at Chambéry came to mind.

I switched the lantern to my left hand and reached with my right for the corner of the shroud, which would unfold from left to right. My hand was shaking, and I withdrew it.

Marcus raised his head and fixed his gaze on me. "I am ready for the next fold."

I grimaced and grasped the corner. "On the count of three, then, before I lose my nerve. One. Two." I swallowed. "Three."

Marcus' lower end came away with little difficulty. "I can say that the body is unclothed," he said, "and male."

At the head it was a different matter; the shroud lifted easily off the left shoulder, but it was stuck hard to the face. I gave the shroud a gentle tug; it tore away from the upper body, leaving exposed a decaying right shoulder and a patch of rib cage. But the shroud covering the face clung stubbornly to it while the surrounding fabric gave way. I picked at the edges, hoping I could expose the face, but it held fast.

I groaned in disbelief. I was counting on a good view of the face—especially if enough detail was preserved to see a birthmark over the right eyebrow. The top of the skull was exposed; was the hair curly like Andreas'? But the head was shaved.

Marcus by now was peering over my shoulder. "Perhaps some water will loosen it off the face."

He handed me the jug. I poured water slowly over the face and watched as it soaked in. I waited, and then took a free edge and lifted it. The shroud yielded at first but then held fast. I gave the lantern to Marcus and unsheathed my dagger. Under the free edge, I probed for a separation under the shroud with the dagger's tip.

Suddenly, I lost my balance and fell backwards. Marcus caught me, but I kept my grip on the edge of the shroud. In my hand was the entire facial fragment of shroud, as if I had peeled an orange. I scrambled back to the head, hoping that I had exposed the face, but except for smears of muscle and fat still adhering to the facial bones, what remained of the face was now stuck fast to the remnant of shroud I held in my hand. The frontal bone of the skull was exposed over the right eye socket where Andreas' birthmark would have been; the tissue was gone, stuck fast to the grisly fragment.

"Oh no!" I cried out, but Marcus quickly silenced me. I slumped against the side of the pit and put the fragment on my lap. In the lantern's light the underside was splattered with strands of withered muscle and lumps of fat with bare spots of shroud showing through. Desperately, I tried again with my dagger to find a place for separation, but the fragment crumbled to pieces in my hands.

In near panic, I stared down at the shards of a human face, perhaps that of Andreas. I crawled back to the skull, staring at me through its empty eye sockets, and set down the remains of its face next to it. A resentful Andreas took shape over the facial bones. I squeezed my eyes shut and tried to think.

From the chaos inside my head sprung the recollection that Andreas had described in the *Fabrica* the eruption of his hindmost tooth, his thirty-second and last; he had written me about it.

I turned to Marcus, waiting alongside me. "I need to see the teeth."

I knew only that a quarter-century ago, Andreas had thirty-two teeth, and that several years later, on one of his military campaigns, he had had a molar extracted—but he did not say which.

I hooked a finger under the tip of the mandible, grimacing as I pushed up through decaying tissue to the lower incisors, and holding the skull steady with my other hand on the forehead, pulled down on the mandible. Held in place only by strands of dried muscle at the angles of the jaw, it gave way with a sickening crack. I gathered myself, and as Marcus repositioned the lantern, I peered into the gaping mouth. All eight incisors—four upper and four lower—were present, but of those to the rear, several upper and lower teeth were missing.

Examining the teeth, I realized, was a waste of time. I had no detailed knowledge of Andreas' teeth, and it was a rare European a half-century old who had not lost teeth for one reason or another. If this man died of sea scurvy, he could have lost teeth shortly before death. I was not certain of anything, and I needed nothing less than certainty.

I fought for calm as I inspected the rest of the corpse. Some ribs were exposed, as well as some of the small bones of the hands and feet. The body had been buried with no clothes or jewelry. Some skin and fat had come off on the shroud, but the degree of deterioration of the remaining skin was enough to eradicate any surface details. I knelt over the corpse and hung my head. The worst had come to pass. I would never know whether or not we had unearthed Andreas. What a foolish, gruesome gamble this was!

Marcus put his arms around my shoulders. "You have done as well as anyone could, and you must never regret the attempt. But now we need to finish our work quickly and quietly. Everything must go back as close as possible to how we found it."

As I struggled to stand, my knees crying out, my eyes fell upon the exposed areas of the right shoulder, scapula, and clavicle with dried remnants of muscles, ligaments, nerves, and blood vessels clinging to them. The bone of the upper arm, the humerus, was still in its place in the shoulder, covered by parchment-like skin as it extended down towards the elbow.

"Wait, Marcus. Bring the lantern near. There's one more thing I have to do."

Marcus pursed his lips. "As you wish, but we must be quick." He held the lantern over my head as I once again unsheathed my dagger, this time neither squeamish nor hesitant.

I learned a thing or two in your basement, and I daresay I'm one of the few who has read your tedious book from cover to cover. In my mind's eye I see one of your muscle-men at mid-dissection, with the right pectoralis major muscle freed from the sternum and reflected away from the chest to expose the two biceps tendons of the right arm.

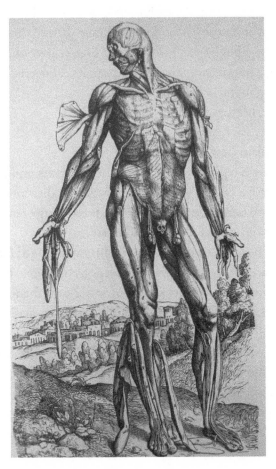

I lifted the right arm by the elbow and turned it outward—*you would say "externally rotate," Andreas*—and held it fast on my knee. The arm stayed in its joint. I located the shaft of the humerus between the biceps and triceps muscles with my fingertips and stabbed down to the bone through that space near the shoulder. I then carried a deep incision down along the length of the bone to the elbow.

The decaying skin and much of the underlying fat fell away like moldy paper, but the muscles were still recognizable.

In the interest of time, I reflected back the pectoralis muscle the opposite way by cutting it near its insertion on the upper humerus to expose the biceps tendons, and then, where they emerged from under the edge of the deltoid muscle, I cut them and pulled them down and away toward the forearm. Beneath the biceps was the brachialis muscle; I scaled it away from the bone. Now the lower shaft of the humerus was exposed to the elbow. I carefully ran my fingers over and around the bone, forcing a finger under the triceps muscles. I lingered over the arm for several long moments and then stood up.

"I'm done, Marcus. Let's get out of here."

"But what . . ?"

"I will explain later."

In silence we replaced the disrupted body parts and refolded the shroud as best we could. With Marcus sweeping dirt into the grave, I smoothed it and tamped it down with whatever energy remained in me, my bleeding hands smeared with dead tissue.

When we had refilled the grave with dirt, we changed into our clean clothes. We carefully repositioned the sections of thyme, tamped them down, and poured the remainder of our water over them. We shuffled our feet around the site and sprinkled olive leaves to mask any signs of tampering.

Marcus took a last look and was satisfied. He took the tools and work clothes and hid them in thick brush on the other side of the graveyard wall. If someday they're found, it wouldn't matter.

We did not speak until we got back to our rooms, when I told Marcus what I had learned.

It was no small relief to wash the blood and dirt from my body and stretch out on my back; lying still quieted the jarring pain that came with movement. I closed my eyes against images of the night's grisly work, scarcely believing what had happened.

25 May 1565

By the time I reached the fortress, the afternoon sun had dipped behind it and cast the bench and the olive tree in shadows. The fitful naps I took over the day eased my exhaustion from the work of the night before, but not my anger.

I arrived in enough time to regain my breath, drink from my jug of water, and wait until Tritonius came through the gate. I did not want this encounter to be in a public place; if there was an open conflict between us, it would arouse suspicion.

The gate opened, and Tritonius rode through on horseback.

"Vitus!"

He turned in the direction of my voice and smiled broadly.

"What a surprise to see you up here!" he said, dismounting and taking a seat with me on the bench.

"You're wise enough to ride up and down," I said. "I walked up here quite by chance the day I met you. It's no easy stroll, but the view is magnificent, and I wanted to see it again. And you can see the church from here—even the graveyard."

"So you can," he said, peering down the hill. "As often as I have passed by this bench, I have never sat here."

I pointed at the harbor. "That galleon there—the *San Lorenzo*—is on its way back to Venice, and will set off in a day or two. Marcus and I will be on it. I wanted to be sure to say goodbye to you and express my thanks for your dedication to Andreas' memory. You will always be in my thoughts."

"Likewise. I will tend the grave as long as I am stationed here."

"That is a comfort. But before I depart, Vitus, may I trouble you with a few more questions? I want to be sure I'm clear about a few things."

Tritonius shifted in his seat. "Of course. But there is little else to add."

"Well, when Fra Pietro told us about you, I was anxious to express my gratitude. But you were more than surprised to meet me—alarmed, it seemed."

He furrowed his brow. "You yourself noted how your sudden appearance might startle me."

"I must say I was struck by your dedication to tending his grave, even nine months later."

"Vesalius was my teacher and a great man. I tend his grave out of respect."

"Yes, of course. Oh—I don't want to overlook thanking you again for dinner at your home the other night, and for the details you provided on Andreas' illness. I was amazed that as he lay delirious and on death's door he could recognize you and speak coherently about me and his family."

Tritonius looked at me quizzically, his pupils constricted even in the shadow of the tree. "He did have lucid moments, during which I came to learn about you. I told you this."

"I'm also wondering how a man near death was able to sign your *Fabrica* with such a steady hand."

"But I told you he signed it when it was first published."

"That's the thing—I have seen his signature his whole life, and it's only in recent years that he took to signing his first name 'And.' instead of 'Andreas.'"

He sat upright. "I'm not sure what you're getting at."

"And then there is the matter of your notebook. That's how I finally came to remember how I knew your name. A certain drawing in your notebook caught my attention: 'Description of the third pair of nerves.' Do you remember it?"

His expression clouded over. "There are many sketches in that notebook."

"But I think you know why that particular drawing caught my attention."

"I'm afraid I don't."

"Well, among Andreas' first assignments at Padua was to deliver a series of surgical lectures. Andreas was quite a competent draftsman; for the lectures, and the dissection that followed, he prepared a large illustration of the veins that was so well-received that he was asked to prepare illustrations of the arteries and nerves as well. He decided to publish these three drawings with three illustrations of the skeleton drawn by the artist Calcar. This became, of course, the *Tabulae anatomicae* of 1538."

"None of this is news to me."

"Then it will be no news to you that the drawing of the nerves did not appear in the *Tabulae* as intended, but was replaced by one of the liver and the organs of generation. Andreas' drawing of the nerves that you so crudely copied in your notebook was stolen before he could send it for cutting the woodblocks."

"I do recall that. It was regrettable."

"Before the drawing went to the engraver, Andreas showed it to a few friends. One of those friends, Vitus, was you."

"What of it?"

"Just this. The year after the *Tabulae* was published, a professor in Cologne named Aegidius Macrolius published a single sheet—a drawing of the brain and cranial nerves—that he 'came possessed of,' as he put it. It was a plagiarized version of Andreas' missing drawing."

Tritonius scowled. "Wait—are you presuming . . ."

"I am beyond presuming. It was only years later that Andreas found out how it got into the hands of Macrolius. While on a campaign with Charles V, the royal camp passed through Cologne. Andreas sought out Macrolius and confronted him about his plagiarism. Macrolius confessed that while traveling through Padua in 1538 he purchased the drawing from a certain medical student who was desperate to settle gambling debts. That medical student was you."

"You cannot prove any of that."

"True enough. I have nothing in writing from Andreas, and Macrolius is dead. But tell me—have you seen the second edition of the *Fabrica*?"

"No."

"If you had, you would have seen that the kind reference to you, his 'dear companion in my studies' in the first edition, does not appear in the second."

Tritonius said nothing.

"At any rate," I continued, "Andreas must have been the last person you thought you'd see coming ashore on Zante, but unlikely things— even highly unlikely things—can and do happen."

"As we have said."

"But how is it that you did not mention the man who came ashore with Andreas?"

Tritonius flushed. "What?"

"The morning after our dinner, I visited the customs office, and while confirming the dates of Andreas' arrival and death, I learned that a German pilgrim also stricken—a Georg Boucher—came ashore with him."

The muscles around Tritonius' mouth and jaw tightened. "It did not seem important to mention him. He was hardly ill."

"Yes, it would appear so, as Herr Boucher left Zante two weeks later. A diminutive gentleman, according to the customs officer, with a birthmark on his face, though he could not say exactly where."

"I don't know where this is leading."

"I think you do. But there is one more confusing matter. The inscription on the gravestone is incorrect."

"Good Lord. If you are obsessed with the mistaken age, I can have a new gravestone made."

"Oh no, the problem is that the age on the gravestone is the only correct thing on it."

Tritonius stiffened. "Now you are making no sense at all."

"But the man in the grave was fifty-eight, was he not?"

Tritonius abruptly stood, and I stood to face him.

"For the past nine months, you have been keeping a terrible secret. The man buried there is Georg Boucher, isn't it?"

Tritonius took a step back, his voice quavering. "On what basis can you make such a wild claim?"

"When you next visit the grave, you may notice that it has been disturbed."

His eyes widened, and he lost all pretense of calm. "You don't mean—you would not have dared!"

My unblinking stare gave him his answer.

"You had no authority!" he cried, gesturing at the fortress. "If the grave has been violated, by nightfall you and your servant will be imprisoned within those walls."

I sat down and leaned back on the bench. "Think carefully before you act, Tritonius. I cannot prove it is Georg Boucher of Nuremberg buried in that grave, but I assure you I can prove it is not Andreas Vesalius of Brussels, and if I must I will reveal what I know to the authorities. And then, you will have to explain how you would mistake the identity of a man you treated and buried. I did commit a crime, but in so doing exposed yours. I think the authorities will be sympathetic to my motive."

"You have gone mad. I know the conditions of the burial—a simple shroud, head shaved, no clothes or possessions. Even if you did open that grave, you can prove nothing from a corpse rotting in the ground for nine months."

"You are right—almost. The soft tissues proved to be of no help; all we could say was that it was a male. But as you know, bones tell their stories for centuries."

"Meaning what?"

"Meaning this: As a child, Andreas fractured his right humerus above the elbow. It healed with a slight angle and a callus. The arm functioned normally, but one could easily feel this deformity below the skin. The corpse in the grave had no deformity of the right humerus. Need I go further?"

"No one will believe your story about his arm."

"Many people alive today will testify to it. He enjoyed showing it off—I'll wager he showed it to you, not that you would admit it. But I don't think you want to put me to the test. The proof lies in the ground at the church. You would incriminate yourself in a most unbecoming fraud."

He sank onto the bench and hid his face in his hands.

"Vesalius is not buried there," he finally whispered. "It is Georg Boucher."

I hesitated before I spoke. "And what of Andreas?"

"He is alive."

A shock passed through me at those words, even as I already knew the truth of them.

Tritonius lowered his hands to his lap, making no attempt to wipe away the tears that ran down his cheeks.

"It has been torture to keep this terrible secret, but at least it seemed safe—until you came. You forced me into a deception I was ill-prepared to carry out. Vesalius underestimated you. I owe you a full accounting."

Tritonius stared straight ahead and spoke in a measured voice.

"When I was summoned to the harbor that day, I was stunned to come face to face with Vesalius. He was not well himself, and wanted no more of the pilgrim ship. He used his attendance to Boucher's illness as the excuse to come ashore. The German was deathly ill."

"So it was Boucher who had sea scurvy."

"Yes, but Vesalius himself was showing early signs. He had some difficulty walking and had leg pains."

"Did Andreas recognize you as well?"

"Oh yes," he said with a morose laugh. "Even amidst the commotion on the dock. His eyes bulged when he saw me; he came up to within an inch of my face and growled, 'You stole my drawing, Tritonius!' I had not thought of the drawing in many years, and I did not know until that moment that he knew it was I who stole it.

"He set his anger aside for the time being to attend to the German with me. I wanted to take Boucher up to the fortress hospital. Vesalius agreed, but in the next moment he asked me where I lived. When I told him, he insisted we care for him in my house. I was so unnerved that I consented. I sent Selene away with instructions to prepare food for us and leave it at the door."

Tritonius became silent; every word he uttered seemed to exhaust him. I waited for him to continue.

"Boucher was delirious and could take no nourishment. He had lost several teeth and his gums bled freely, but he hung on doggedly. As for Vesalius, he devoured Selene's food and began to recover.

"When Vesalius learned that I had a supply of the laudanum of Paracelsus, he insisted that we use it to relieve Boucher's pain. I readied a typical dose, but Vesalius urged me to double it." Tritonius hung his head. "It was not long before his breathing stopped."

Tritonius' face was awash in agony. "What I did was a betrayal of my oath to abstain from doing harm, and a mortal sin."

"It is not for me to judge," I said.

"God will be my judge."

"What happened after Boucher died?"

"Vesalius revealed his plan to me. It must have come to him soon after he came ashore with Boucher—and found me here. He knew that Boucher was doomed, and his death would give him the chance . . ."

". . . to leave Zante as Georg Boucher."

"Yes—and to have the world think that he was dead. He did speak fondly of you, but he was convinced that you would not endure the Alps and a sea voyage to get here. And any random visitor would have no reason to question the circumstances.

"'Zante is the perfect place to die,' he said to me. So you see, we were never to meet."

We sat for a while without speaking. I was stunned that Andreas could devise such a scheme, let alone carry it out.

"And then, when he told you of his plan?" I asked.

He looked up. "I protested at first. He told me only that he still had things to do, but he could not do them as himself. 'But your fame is secure,' I told him, 'and any physician would be in envy of your career.' He only laughed at that. When I continued to refuse, he threatened to publish an account of the theft of his drawing."

"How could you have been swayed by such a weak threat? Your transgression was long ago, and he was plagiarized many times."

He gazed out over the sea. "My military record is not unscathed. My posting on Zante is a form of banishment, and any further trouble will have consequences."

I wondered what he meant, but said nothing.

"But I still refused," he continued. "So he made a greater threat. He would claim that I took Boucher's life with laudanum against his advice. Whose word would win out with the Church or the military—an obscure military physician with a blemished record or a world-famous physician and pious pilgrim? I was too shaken to think of a way out of his trap. And once he left the island as Boucher, any claim I made would sound too unlikely to be believed and near impossible to prove."

Through my anger I saw how unlucky Tritonius was to have the mentor he betrayed years ago appear on this remote island post at the edge of Europe, and then to be quickly ensnared in a brazen and desperate fraud.

If he did not agree to it, Andreas would place Tritonius at the mercy of the Church and the Venetian military. The sham burial was a serious crime, but worse was the possibility of being convicted of murder.

"Why was the wrong age put on the gravestone?"

"Vesalius wanted it. It was his way of paying tribute to Boucher."

We sat in silence. For Andreas to choose this path meant abandoning any chance of returning to any vestige of his former life—all to deceive the world that he was dead. But why? To what purpose? I considered the possibility that Tritonius was lying, but I dismissed it; his emotions were too raw to be contrived. Finally I stood.

"Farewell, Vitus. I am going to return to town. I am sorry for your suffering, but you have in good measure earned it."

"What are you going to do?"

"I have no reason to do anything. I have had enough of this beautiful, cursed island without any further adventures. I wish I never came here and never learned what I now know. My journey home will be taken up with what to do with Andreas' secret."

His sorrowful eyes met mine and then returned to the ground. I left him on the bench and walked into town as shadows crept across the road.

At dinner I told Marcus about my encounter with Tritonius. He just shook his head.

26 May 1565

We were taking breakfast when a sailor came to our table to inform us that the *San Lorenzo* would set sail that afternoon, and that a skiff would be waiting for us at the dock after midday. This was welcome news; I would breathe easier once back on mainland Europe and beyond the jurisdiction of Venice. Tritonius, in his state of mind, could be capable of anything.

We sought out Fra Pietro at the church for farewells and to make a donation in Andreas' honor. He was shocked by the amount and tearfully embraced us both.

"Will you join me in a final prayer at the gravesite?" he asked.

"Thank you, Fra Pietro, but we must make ready to board. The gravesite, I assure you, will be forever etched in our memories."

We went to the customs office for our travel documents and said goodbye to Sergente Penzi. While Marcus saw to our travel chests, I settled our bill with the innkeeper. I took a last look up and down the frontage before heading to the dock to board the skiff.

"Signore van den Bossche!"

I turned to see a distressed Fra Pietro walking briskly toward me alongside a young naval officer. I felt my face drain of blood; this could mean nothing but trouble.

"I am Lieutenant della Robbia," the officer said with a clipped bow when they reached me. "You are Jan van den Bossche of Brussels?"

"I am, Lieutenant."

"I must inform you that Doctor Vitus Tritonius was found dead in his bed this morning after not reporting for his clinic. On his nightstand was an empty vial of laudanum and an open bottle of wine. It appears that he took his own life."

I was speechless. I had not considered that Tritonius would resort to suicide to settle his own affairs.

"I am shocked," I managed to say.

"May I trouble you with a few questions, Signore?" he asked, glancing at a notepad in his hand. His demeanor made clear that I did not have the option of refusing. I fought to remain calm, clasping my trembling hands behind my back.

"Of course, Lieutenant."

"Guards posted on the fortress wall saw a man fitting your description with Doctor Tritonius yesterday afternoon. They stated that the conversation was at times rather animated, though out of earshot."

The guards! How careless I was to confront Tritonius where we could be observed.

"That was me with Doctor Tritonius. I went up to enjoy the view one last time and to thank him for having me to his house for dinner." I pointed at the galleon. "My assistant and I depart today. Doctor Tritonius has been tending the grave of my friend, who died here last fall. My friend was his professor at Padua."

"So I have learned from Fra Pietro," he said, nodding at the friar. "May I see your credentials, Signore?"

I handed over my travel documents and Antoine's letter of passage.

The officer examined the documents, glancing up at me several times. He then consulted his notes.

"The guards observed that you left Tritonius on the bench by the fortress. What did you do then?"

"I returned to the inn to join my assistant for dinner. He is on the dock; I can summon him . . ."

"That won't be necessary. The innkeeper vouches for your whereabouts last night. The doctor's housekeeper confirms the dinner you referenced, and that last evening Doctor Tritonius returned home alone, stabled his horse, and sent her off with his dinner unprepared."

He looked back down at his notepad. "It's odd, isn't it, that he chose to do this at the time of your visit."

He let his words hang in the air while he leafed through his notes. "Are you aware of any reason why the doctor might decide to take his own life?"

"None, Lieutenant."

"Did you know of Doctor Tritonius before coming here?"

"No."

"Then you are not aware of any . . . past problems Doctor Tritonius may have had?"

"None."

You taught me how to stay calm when I lied to Mother by biting the inside of my mouth.

With that he reached into his satchel and pulled out a piece of paper. "Doctor Tritonius left a note."

Della Robbia snapped it open, holding his stony expression. Does this note prove that I have just lied repeatedly? Have I walked into a trap? Tritonius, now free of earthly consequences, would have his revenge on Andreas and his prying friend. Soon I would be back up to the fortress again, this time in handcuffs.

"Perhaps you would care to read it," he said, holding it out to me.

How delicious a moment this must be for him, I thought. I braced myself and took the note.

25 May

I regret the trouble I have caused.
    My last wish is to have this notebook delivered to Signore Jan van den Bossche of Brussels before he departs Zante for Venice.

Vitus Tritonius

I reread it to be sure of its contents and handed it back to the lieutenant. He replaced it in his satchel. "As you see, he left us with very little in the way of motive. Do you know what he might have meant by the 'trouble' he says he caused?"

Regaining control of my breath, I said, "I am afraid not. Perhaps he is referring to the suicide itself."

"Perhaps."

He went back into his satchel, retrieved a familiar notebook, and held it up to me.

"The letter was left atop this notebook. Are you familiar with it?"

"It is his student notebook. He showed it to me the other night."

"Why would he want you to have it?"

"Probably because it has notes and diagrams from my friend's lectures."

Della Robbia, who until this moment played to perfection the role of inquisitor, smiled.

"Would it please you to have it?"

"It would."

"I have examined the notebook, and like the letter, it sheds no light on the incident. It seems we are often blind to the inner lives of people, even those we think we know."

"How true, Lieutenant. I have thought the same."

"Under the circumstances, I see no reason not to honor his wish. My report will state that after a thorough inspection I placed it in your care after our interview."

I took it from him, my hand shaking, and put it in my shoulder bag.

"Thank you, Lieutenant. I am sorry I could not be of further help."

"Well—I feel I can tell you that Doctor Tritonius had a checkered career. He was a fine physician, I am told, but plagued with gambling debts and bouts of melancholia. Being posted on Zante was a form of military exile, and a chance for him to improve his standing."

"I see."

The last thing Tritonius needed was to have Andreas arrive at his doorstep, and be drawn into his desperate scheme. Then I remembered something.

"Lieutenant," I said, "Doctor Tritonius has a book called *De humani corporis fabrica*, authored by my departed friend Doctor Vesalius. It is an important book and should find a suitable home."

"I will see to it," he said. "I regret that you must leave Zante under such a distressing circumstance. I wish you safe travels."

The lieutenant shook my hand and walked off. When he was a good distance away I sat down heavily on a bollard.

"You look a bit pale," Fra Pietro said, looking down at me.

Just then Marcus, with an anxious expression, came down the dock to join us.

"I saw you talking with that officer. Is there a problem?"

"Tritonius is dead—by his own hand, with laudanum."

Marcus crossed himself.

Fra Pietro shook his head. "I had no idea this laudanum was so potent. Within a week of your friend's burial, Doctor Tritonius gave it to Father Gregorio when he took ill with a fever and cough. It did ease the cough, but in a day's time God called Father Gregorio to His side."

Marcus and I glanced at each other.

"I don't suppose you can stay for the doctor's burial," Fra Pietro asked.

"I'm afraid not," I said. "Our ship is ready to depart, and we must be on it. But Doctor Tritonius will be in our thoughts for a long time to come."

"I understand. Your stay on Zante has been eventful enough."

"Quite so. But we take with us the pleasure of knowing you, and we will always remember your kindness."

"God be with you," he said as he embraced us once more and hurried away.

Fra Pietro, exiled to Zante by the Church, found his calling there. Tritonius, exiled to Zante by the Navy, found torment and death. There is enough room on one small island for many stories and many fates.

Marcus listened wide-eyed as I told him about the lieutenant's questions and the notebook.

"What about that Father Gregorio?" he said. "You don't suppose . . ."

"At this point I can suppose anything. Andreas was still on the island. If he and Tritonius suspected that Father Gregorio knew . . ."

My voice trailed off; I didn't want to think about it. We boarded the skiff and sat silently as it took us to the *San Lorenzo*. The captain greeted us warmly and had his first mate show us to our cabin, a marked improvement in size and comfort over our quarters on the *Trieste*.

Once alone, Marcus closed the cabin door. "No one alive knows what happened in the graveyard," he said. "No one will visit except perhaps Fra Pietro, but only to say a prayer. He may use some of your gift to hire a gardener, but there will be nothing to see. The thyme may die, but that will not arouse suspicion, if it's replanted; so much the better."

"I hope you're right. As Fra Pietro put it, our visit to Zante has been eventful enough."

"To say that our visit was eventful misses the mark."

I stretched out on my bunk. My body ached, and I was unnerved by the last-minute encounter with Lieutenant della Robbia. My head swam with the revelations we carried aboard.

"I need to sleep, Marcus. Wake me when we get to Venice."

Part Four

RETURN AND
RECKONING

This would have been a most tolerable sea voyage were it not for the cloud you hung over it.

I could not have imagined being grateful to board a seagoing vessel, but the *San Lorenzo's* speedy escape from Zante was welcome. After a few days I was rested enough to rise at dawn and go to the deck. After waving to the helmsman high astern, I listened at the rail to the rushing of the sea along the ship's hull as the first strands of pink and yellow light crept into the eastern sky.

In the early morning chill I grappled with the Copernican discovery that the sun's daily journey across the sky was an illusion, or marveled at the interplay of wind and sail propelling the ship. But these diversions were soon pushed away by the events of Zante; I could sooner believe that the Earth spun like a top as it moved around an immobile sun than I could believe what that island revealed.

The last-minute scare with Lieutenant della Robbia ended well; he would close the case listing us only as coincidental visitors, and the gentle Fra Pietro would be the unwitting guardian of a churchyard stained with foul play, some of which was our own doing.

The suicide of Tritonius weighed on me. In forcing him to relive the crimes he abetted under Andreas' threats, I doubtless pushed him over the edge; perhaps he could no longer see his tending to Georg Boucher's grave as ample penance. In the absence of Andreas, I made him the target of my hurt and anger. I was not proud to realize that it was easier for me to attack a compromised stand-in for Andreas than Andreas himself.

The final words of Tritonius—*I regret the trouble I have caused*— were haunting. I felt it was written to me, saying that he chose to take his torment and his secrets with him. I owed the man debts of thanks and forgiveness, debts I could never repay.

You may never know that Tritonius took his own life, silencing him forever, let alone that Marcus and I now possess your secret; Georg Boucher, with his right humerus showing no sign of injury past or present, lies in a grave marked with your gravestone. You would have taken some grudging satisfaction in my dissection skills.

I assume that when you got back to Venice and cleaned out Boucher's account, you got yourself a fresh identity to cover your tracks. You are well aware that it is easy to get new papers in certain quarters of Venice.

My thoughts ran ahead to Brussels, and to Anne, with as much apprehension as longing. When I left Anne amidst the fresh news of Andreas' death, it seemed that feelings long pent up within us had been set loose. Was there a different future ahead of us?

As for Andreas, my feelings about him were covered in confusion. In our lives I never held him to account—not even for coming between Anne and me.

Anne paces around your house thinking she is a widow. If she learns the truth about you, my dreams for her will be shattered; I will cast her into a purgatory in which her husband is neither dead nor alive, and what she will do then is anyone's guess. If instead I contrive a false account of Zante, then like Tritonius I become your accomplice. How could I abide a future with her built on such a deception? Remember my tapestry, and Melzi's painting? I would be Vertumnus to her Pomona.

I wish I had not followed my heart and gone to Zante, but I can't unlearn what I know. You abandoned your former life for a clandestine existence that cut me out without a word. It was a selfish and cowardly act, Runt. How can I forgive you for this?

8 June 1565

No letters awaited me in Venice—not from my brother Frans, which was no surprise, but neither from Anne. Before leaving Il Palazzo Piccolo two days later I dashed off letters to Antoine and my brother with our whereabouts, but my quill hovered over a blank page for a long time before I started a letter to Anne.

> *10 June 1565*
>
> *Venice*
>
> *Dearest Anne,*
> *Marcus and I are back in Venice and will soon set out for home. I will give you a full account of our visit to Zante when I am with you. It was a difficult visit, and words do not come easily now.*
>   *I trust you and Anna are well. You are ever in my thoughts, and I count the days until I am with you. A letter from you has not arrived here; perhaps it is late, or lost, or you have decided to write me at Ornans instead.*
>
> *With much devotion to you and Anna,*
> *Jan*

The note was sparse and vague. But what could I write that was not unspeakable on the one hand, or dishonest on the other? No, between Venice and Brussels I would choose between the two and summon the courage to say it with Anne in front of me.

Ornans

25 June 1565

The spire of the Ornans church came into view, and then its walls, this time without a field of dead soldiers to pick through.

"Remember, Marcus, Antoine cannot know the truth about Andreas until I decide what I will tell Anne Vesalius. As well as I know him, I'm not sure what he would do."

"I will remember. We sailed to Zante, visited the grave, paid our respects, and sailed back."

We rode quietly until we neared the gate.

"I know that you and Madam Vesalius have a complicated friendship," Marcus said.

I felt myself redden. "So you understand my dilemma."

"Aye, and I daresay few men have faced one like it. She thinks she is a widow. You know she is not. Whatever you choose to say to her about Zante, I will not judge you, and I swear I will not reveal the truth unless you do."

"If you were in my place, what would you do?"

"I don't know . . . but I have the good fortune of not being in your place."

As we rode up to the house, I saw Émile across the courtyard and waved to him. In return, he gave us a half-salute. And then I suddenly saw Émile as a missing piece of the puzzle.

Antoine and I walked in his garden as the sun set.

"Why did you make me the Count of Aarschot for our stop in Montbéliard?"

"I thought you'd enjoy being titled, if only for a day."

"It was a rare thrill."

"Odd, I hear no gratitude in your voice."

He laughed and put a hand on my shoulder. "It seems your journey was all you had hoped for. You rekindled many memories along the way, and you'll always remember Zante."

"Always, I assure you."

"You are weary to the bone and your clothes hang on you. Rest here a few days and let me fatten you up. And then, with luck, you'll be home in two weeks."

"Two weeks may as well be an eternity. I feel like I'm living Zeno's Paradox—even as I narrow the distance to Brussels by half, there is another distance ahead to be narrowed by half, and then another and another."

"Bah. Zeno's Paradox is a silly trifle. Only mathematicians and philosophers take it seriously."

"The paradox has crept into my work. I've yet to come across a satisfactory refutation, mine or anyone else's."

"Don't be a pedantic ass. The refutation is plainly before the eyes. Short of a mishap or change in plans, have you ever not *gotten* somewhere?"

"Until there is a refutation, I must say that I'm not sure." We laughed again and continued along the gravel path for a while. I broke the silence.

"I was hoping to find a letter from Anne awaiting me here."

"The mail can be unreliable. You will be face-to-face soon enough."

"I dread that moment as much as I long for it. Travel, when one is not aching, hungry, or drenched, allows time for idle thought. I'm stuck on something Anne told me before I left Brussels."

"And what is that?"

"In France, the day before Andreas sent her and Anna back to Brussels, a courier delivered a letter to him. Andreas told her it was from his publisher in Basel, but when I met with Oporinus, he denied sending a letter to him."

"Well, either Anne or Oporinus is mistaken."

"Either—or neither. She was quite clear about what Andreas told her, and Oporinus did not even know about the pilgrimage until the news spread of his death."

Antoine shrugged. "Perplexing—but what of it?"

"In Padua I visited the university. There I met Girolamo Fabrizio, the newly-appointed occupant of Andreas' chair. According to Fabrizio, after the Venetian Senate made Andreas the offer, he signaled Venice of his interest just before he left Madrid."

"But Philip had already denied Andreas the chair."

"Nevertheless, Andreas left Spain, it seems, with serious designs on it."

"It makes for an interesting situation."

"Indeed. And after the aforementioned letter was delivered to Andreas on the French frontier, he promptly sent his family away and went on alone."

"We can only speculate why," Antoine said.

"Here's more to speculate on. Fabrizio had it on good authority that the Senate became inclined to withdraw the offer when Andreas arrived in Venice. But they never got the chance because Andreas passed through Venice without even seeking a meeting. Why did Venice have a change of heart? Why would Andreas have killed his chances for a post that was his for the taking? I can't help but feel that the letter he got in France had something to do with it."

Antoine shrugged. "The timing is suggestive, but we don't know what the letter contained."

"Don't we? Anne thought she had seen that courier before. He was a big fellow with a red beard. And how many big, red-bearded couriers could there be in France? I have one in mind—Émile, your half-brother, the one who brought Anne and me the news of Andreas' death; the one who escorted us to Montbéliard; the one you entrust with important tasks. The letter to Andreas was written by someone who knew where to look for him. I think Andreas lied to Anne about who wrote it, and to be blunt, my dear friend, I think you are lying to me."

Antoine was impassive. "That *was* rather blunt. How so?"

"I have little doubt that you were the author of that letter."

We were nearing a bench. "Let us sit."

He buried his hands in his sleeves. "Enough cat-and-mouse. Yes, I wrote that letter, and yes, Émile delivered it. But take heed—by telling you I am breaching a royal confidence."

"What do you mean?"

"Just listen. Back when you asked me to intercede with the king about the pilgrimage, I did not tell you that the king was leery of Andreas' request, coming as it did soon after he refused to release Andreas to Padua. What's more, the king's snoops intercepted a letter Andreas wrote to a senator in Venice stating he intended to take the position. That letter was posted after Philip's denial. In his eagerness, Andreas revealed his hand to Philip. Fabrizio's account is accurate."

"So the king saw through the request for the pilgrimage."

"From the very beginning."

"And yet he sent Andreas on his way?"

"Indeed—with a letter of passage and a stipend. But Andreas did not realize that these were golden chains."

"You have lost me."

"King Philip is a petty bastard, but a cunning one. Our renowned friend was a prize that Philip would not share, much as a pouting child clutches a toy to his chest. He instructed me to inform Venice through diplomatic channels that were Andreas to reoccupy his chair, he would be a traitor in the eyes of the Spanish Crown, and that Venice would be complicit.

"These assertions—let us be frank and call them threats—were designed to cause Venice to think twice before picking a fight with Spain over a university professor. Venice still smarts from the Turkish War thirty years ago, and trouble is again brewing with the Ottomans; more hostilities are likely, and Venice will need Spain as an ally. For Philip, then, Andreas became a convenient test of his sway over Venice."

"My mind is spinning. Why didn't you tell me about this?"

"You remember our talk in this garden about secrets—of course you do, you remember everything—well, it was a moot point; Andreas was dead. It was my official duty to maintain the secrecy of the affair, and I doubted that your knowing would have changed your travel plans. But now you have earned the right to know."

I reminded myself not to let slip the truth about Andreas.

"The whole affair is ridiculous, Antoine. A vacant anatomy post should be beneath the attention of great nations."

"Diligent statecraft stoops to this level more often than you think. And it must; a single ember from an untended hearth can lead to a house in flames. Christian alliances are fragile, and of grave concern to the Church as long as the Ottomans remain a threat."

"But you knew that Venice would abandon Andreas."

"If only I could have been sure of that. Priuli, the Doge of Venice, is the equal of Philip in pettiness. I tried to convince Philip to let Andreas go, but he would hear nothing of it. I had no choice than to deliver the king's message; coming from King Philip, it would surely reach Priuli. Andreas was ready to defy Philip, and if Priuli chose to defy him as well, an ember would fly from the hearth. I had to intervene, but covertly— the king must not doubt my loyalty."

"Hence your letter to Andreas."

"Yes. Émile tracked Andreas down in Perpignan. The letter minced no words about the king's knowledge of his intentions and the king's threat to Venice—but also this: Affronted royals are vindictive, and Spain has assassins everywhere. Taking the Padua chair, I warned him, would be at his and his family's peril."

"Are you saying they all could have been killed if Venice gave the post to Andreas?"

"There was no way of knowing. However, I assured Andreas that were he to forego the chair I would make things right with Philip; completing the pilgrimage and returning to Spain would be proof of his loyalty and repentance. In the end, Philip would have flexed his muscles with Venice; Andreas, in snubbing the Senate, would appear to have changed his mind; Venice could let the incident drop without losing face."

"Incredible. All this in service to a distant fear of the Ottomans."

"I trade in distant fears, Jan, just as in chess you look for danger several moves away. The loss of the Padua chair was a great blow to Andreas, I know, but I reasoned that he would settle for staying alive and regaining the good graces of the king. Alas, he never made it back to Spain."

No, you didn't—but not in the way Antoine thinks.

"I hope you are not angry with me."

"I should be, but I am not. Probably because I will never fully understand what you do to earn a living."

He stood up. "Just as well. Come, let's go back to the house and have some Cognac. You can take retribution in chess. Or perhaps you'd like to talk about Anne."

"How much Cognac do you have?"

Much later, in my bed-chamber, I looked out the window at the Milky Way.

I see why you sent Anne and Anna away. You still clung to your hope for the Padua chair and wanted them out of danger. But you also knew they would not be safe in Brussels; as ruler of the Low Countries Philip had them at his mercy.

You concluded that it was too great a risk to accept the chair. The pain would have been too great to stop in Padua, knowing you would not return. You took Antoine's advice and sailed off to the Holy Land from Venice without a word to the Senate.

Philip had trapped you, but on Zante you stumbled onto an escape—your public death and clandestine resurrection. But then what?

Four days later, we made ready to go, well-fed and rested. As the stable-boy brought our horses, the familiar figure of Émile rode up along with them.

"Émile will ride with you to Besançon," Antoine said. "Just in case there's trouble." Marcus greeted him warmly. "We're getting to know you quite well, Émile."

"The pleasure is mine," he said with a crisp nod.

As we made our way through France toward Brussels, I more than once replayed the conversation with Antoine over chess and Cognac:

"What is your hesitation about Anne?" he said. "Widows remarry. Andreas has left her with reasonable assets, I'm sure, but you can support her and her daughter quite comfortably."

"I would hope that my appeal to Anne would be on more than financial grounds."

"Do not discount practical considerations. But look, you have had a long friendship with Anne, albeit fraught, and I would wager she is not without feelings for you. You are deserving of each other."

"Maybe so. But I still feel that Andreas is looking over my shoulder. Would he think I betrayed him if I pursued Anne now?"

"A peculiar sentiment coming from one who rejects the existence of an afterlife. By your own thinking, Andreas can no longer care about you or Anne; how can you betray him? And at any rate, if he could speak from the next world, why wouldn't he approve? Your heart took you to Zante. Let it take you back to Anne."

Antoine could not be faulted for assuming that Anne was a widow. Still, his argument held. Andreas had removed himself from his life and everyone in it, and by falsifying his death had slipped into another. How different was that from a physical death? For everyone alive on this planet save Marcus and me, the difference was semantic. And if Marcus and I could live with concealing the truth, the difference would become semantic to us as well.

In Leuven, the day before we entered Brussels, I made a decision.

You have burned the bridge back to your former life. If you feel it necessary to be dead to me and to Anne, be dead, then. I will not reveal your resurrection secret. I will wrap myself in your web of deception to win back the woman I lost to you. I will be her Vertumnus, then, and I will smother any regrets before they take their first breath.

I shared my decision with Marcus, as I would entrust him to bear the same secret.

Brussels

12 July 1565

Marcus' brother Henk, who had watched over the house in our absence, greeted us warmly, but immediately took leave. "Your brother instructed me to fetch him as soon as you arrived."

I sensed trouble; Frans had never gone out of his way to welcome me back from a journey.

I was in my study when he arrived. We shook hands and clapped each other on the shoulder.

"Welcome home, Jan. You're scrawny but not beyond help," he said, taking a seat in Andreas' chair.

"And if you're still alive, Brother, it must mean there's still money you don't have yet."

Frans did not parry my jest as he usually would.

"Something's wrong," I said. "It's Mother, isn't it?"

He pursed his lips. "I didn't want you to hear this from anyone else. Mother is dead."

I closed my eyes, picturing the last time I saw her—shrunken into her worn chaise longue, frail, tearful, and confused, a far cry from the goddess who ruled my childhood. Even as her powers faded into senescence, a part of me believed she was immortal.

"When?"

"A month after you left. She stopped eating and making urine, and slept most of the time. The doctor bled her; she died the next day."

I fought back tears. "I feel terrible for not having been here."

"Don't be. As far as she was concerned, you never left. Most of the time she thought I was you."

There was an edge in his voice. He always resented the attention Mother paid to me.

"We found gold tincture in her dressing table—several ampules of it. An apothecary had been delivering it to her for a year. Did you know about that?"

"No. What do you do with it?"

"You drink it as a tonic. I'm told it's popular in France." He shrugged. "Well, it matters little; the doctor insisted it was harmless."

"Did you have a mass for her?"

"Of course. She is buried next to Father. We can visit when you are ready, but we should talk soon about the disposition of her estate. Our wealth has increased considerably."

Frans saw that I was staring at the floor and had stopped listening.

"We can talk about that later, but there is something else."

I raised my eyes to him. "What is it?"

"Anne Vesalius is engaged to be married. The wedding is to be 24 July."

Frans left me staring through the window at my garden. Anne's husband was to be Hendrik van der Meeren, a minor nobleman from Zavanthem. I had met him not long ago on a day trip to Vilvoorde—a cheerful, marginally-educated man of leisure who liked to hunt. His parents and Anne's were friends.

Marcus came with a cup of chocolate.

"You haven't had one of these in a while." As he set it down, he said, "I fear that the news from your brother wasn't good."

"I'm afraid not. My mother is dead."

"I am so sorry. God rest her soul."

"That's not all. Anne is engaged to be married in twelve days."

"What? I don't know what to say."

"There is nothing to say."

He touched my shoulder, and I put my hand on his.

"You are the only one in the world who understands, Marcus."

Marcus left and closed the door. I sipped the chocolate, seeking some comfort from it. I took out a piece of paper.

12 July

Dear Anne,
I arrived home today. I will call at your house tomorrow to tell you
about the voyage.
I understand you have some news as well.

Jan

I sealed the note, drained the last of the chocolate, and threw the cup against the study door. The sound brought Marcus rushing. He surveyed the floor of the study, strewn with shards.

"It seems you dropped your cup."

I held up the note. "Leave the cup for me and deliver this."

I turned back to the window. Out from the leafy shadows of my little oak tree and down the trunk came the same scarred squirrel that passed through the day I decided to go to Greece. Once on the ground he reared up on his hind legs and stared ahead.

"So, Squirrel, you're back from your journey, too. You seem none the worse for your travels, but I can't say the same for me."

13 July 1565

I sat at the edge of my bed, dressed and ready to leave for Vesalius House, summoning the will to rise. All across France, I had prepared myself for an entirely different reunion with Anne, as of the day before rendered cruelly moot. Mother's death was sad but bearable; I knew it had been near at hand. But the news of Anne's engagement was an ambush that sent me reeling. Why didn't you write ahead, Anne, to soften the blow?

Marcus answered a knock on the front door. After a few muffled words he came upstairs.

"Madam Vesalius is here."

"Here?"

"In the front hall."

"But I—well, show her to the study. Wait—is the sitting room presentable?"

> *In the study, Anne would sit in your chair where you warmed your hands over the stove, where you argued and joked, where you cursed a chess move you came to regret. Not today.*

"It's presentable enough. Henk kept it dusted."

"In the sitting room, then. I'll be down."

I forced myself off the bed. I was counting on the walk to Vesalius House as a last chance to find words to use, but now I would rely on whatever sprang up unchecked by reason or caution. Perhaps it was just as well; I would soon know.

I stopped in the sitting room doorway as Marcus pulled back the thin summer curtains and opened the windows. Anne stood facing me in the center of the room, hands clasped at the waist, the light from the window illuminating her face. She was unchanged from the day I left, save that she was no longer dressed in mourning; the sleeves and collar of her patterned dress were trimmed with the Burano lace I sent her from Venice.

Marcus made for the doorway, nodding to Anne. "It is good to see you, Madam."

"And you, Marcus."

I urged myself into the room as Marcus closed the doors behind me. Anne and I held our places, foregoing the embrace of greeting that would be expected after a separation of five months.

"You look well, Jan," she said.

"As do you."

"And you are safely home."

"At least we can say that."

This awkward exchange made me cringe, but even so, desire for her rose in my chest.

"I was about to leave for your house."

"I thought it best to call on you to express my sorrow at your mother's passing."

"Ah. Thank you."

"I attended her mass. It was lovely."

"So I am told." Her eyes glowed deep blue in the light.

"*You can do better than Anne van Hamme,*" I heard Mother say. "*She is rather small-framed, don't you think, and quite free with her tongue.*"

Anne took a hurried look around her.

"It's been a long time since I've been in your sitting room."

"For me as well. It's a poor relation to yours."

"I prefer this one. In mine I feel lost." She glanced at a chair. May I sit?"

"I'm sorry—of course."

She retreated to the chair, lowering herself onto the edge of the seat. I took a chair opposite.

"I must thank you for the lace," she said, putting a hand on her collar.

"It becomes you. You should have plenty left for your wedding gown."

Anne looked down and pulled her handkerchief from her sleeve.

"Forgive me," I said. "It has been a difficult homecoming. I was unprepared for . . . all this."

"Yes. Better that we speak of it face to face."

Anne gazed past me, waiting for me to continue.

"It was long ago," I finally said, "but do you remember when you kissed me in Vilvoorde?"

"Of course I remember."

"You told me to take that kiss to Padua, and I did—like a jewel in a velvet case. Andreas teased me about our letters; I said only that we were friends. But I did not tell him that I was falling in love with you."

My words surprised me in their forwardness, but Anne's response was measured.

"Why not tell him? He was your best friend."

"It seemed pointless. I feared you would not find me worthy."

"Oh, Jan. Your fears . . ." Her voice trailed off.

"Yes, I had fears—and were they unfounded? When I came back to Brussels with Andreas, the time we had spent together seemed to count for nothing. I felt cast aside when Andreas was with us. After he left for Basel to finish the *Fabrica*, you went off to Vilvoorde for weeks at a time. And then, Andreas appears in Brussels to propose marriage to you."

"That hurt you, I know. I was worried that you would never speak to us again."

You didn't even let me know you were coming. You showed up at my door and told me about you and Anne. You hoped I would understand. I offered my congratulations. We went to a tavern and met up with some friends to celebrate, but I slipped out and went home.

"I was more than hurt. I was angry at you both. But could I lose the two people dearest to me? I resolved to move forward with whatever grace I could muster—and so it has been. But Anne, was I wrong to think that as we waited last year for news of Andreas, our feelings for each other were set free?"

"You were not wrong."

"Then why didn't you wait for me? Why are you marrying a shiftless dolt like Hendrik van der Meeren?"

"Your anger comes easily when Andreas is not the target."

"He was my best friend."

"No one knows that better than I. Let me test your memory, though it is never faulty. You recall when we first met, that Sunday after mass?"

"I will never forget it."

"You made a dispiriting first impression. I had no intention of speaking to you again."

"Then why did you?"

"Because my parents insisted on it. You were an eligible man from a wealthy family, and I was getting past marrying age."

"So, you were sent to seduce the addle-brained son of a rich trader."

She did not answer until she stood and walked to a window.

"To them my sole duty as an only child and daughter was to marry well; I fought them to choose my own path in life, and you were the latest battle. But when you found your tongue, I discovered a brilliant, disarming man. And I will add that you were rather handsome. It was not out of duty that I kissed you in Vilvoorde."

"That's no consolation now, especially as for what it's wrought."

"I agree that there were consequences. While you were off in Padua that year, your shortcomings—as seen through my young and fickle eyes—crept into my thinking. You were so retiring, so absorbed by your obscure studies, so indisposed to travel except when Andreas summoned you. Your letters left me unsure of your feelings—just as, I suppose, my letters seemed to you."

"Merely receiving letters from you meant everything to me . . . if you only knew, Anne, how I ached to open my heart to you, only to hold back for fear of rejection."

Anne looked out the window and then back at me.

"When you and Andreas returned to Brussels, I saw the special bond you two had, but also the contrasts. He was as engaging as you were retiring, and his interests had nothing to do with yours. You sank your roots in Brussels while he cut his own to follow his passion to Italy. I sensed he was taken with me, and I confess I was taken with him—with the idea of him. With his life at the other end of the continent, beyond the reach of my parents."

Anne turned back to the window.

"Andreas and I had . . . assignations. He knew you had feelings for me. So did I; your heart was on your sleeve. But I told Andreas it didn't matter; I loved him, not you. He was certain that you would understand. He would tell you about us before he left for Basel."

But you left without a word to me about Anne. You waited until you proposed to her.

"I escaped to Vilvoorde to avoid you. My parents did not approve of Andreas; his family was not as prestigious as yours, and they did not want to lose me to Italy. But when Andreas came to Brussels to propose, they gave in, seeing no sign that you would pursue me."

"Your parents were right," I said. "I was victim to my own self-doubts, and you chose the person who offered you the life you wanted. I had no right to interfere."

Anne glowered at me. "Listen to yourself! If you were in love with me you had every reason to interfere. You use your self-doubts as an excuse for the lifelong spell Andreas cast on you. You couldn't challenge him for anything—not even for me. If Hendrik were your rival back then instead of Andreas, would you have challenged him for me?"

A breeze came through the window and billowed the curtain behind her across her shoulder. It settled on her, draping her bodice and waist like the gown of a goddess. The vision of her drew me from my chair; I went to her and freed her of the curtain. Our bodies were inches apart.

She did not move, and she fixed her eyes on mine. "Would you have challenged Hendrik for me?"

"Then—and now."

I took her around the waist and drew her to me. She did not resist, but as our lips touched she stepped back and paced into the room. She stopped, her back to me, leaving me at the window frozen in agony.

"Do you not love me, Anne?"

She turned to face me, her eyes glistening, her expression pained in a way I had never seen it.

"My feelings for you are real but beyond the point. I will marry Hendrik. He is a baron with some assets, and for the most part an un-objectionable fellow. He will hunt and drink with his friends, and on occasion come to my bed. There will be other women, but I don't care; he will be what I expect him to be, no more and no less. Besides, I will be a baroness."

"You don't care about that! A title of little consequence can't be why you would—"

Anne cut me off. "You're right, it's not the crux of it. It's because he has never met Andreas."

"What do you mean by that?"

"I have thought hard on this, Jan. Andreas would be a curse on our marriage."

"How can you say that? We can move past him together. He is no longer in your life or mine."

"I wish I could believe that, but I fear you will not—cannot—leave him behind. When Anna and I got home from the pilgrimage, as we waited together for news, I could not stop thinking about what my life could have been like, here, with you."

I took a step toward her. "And I thought the same."

"But you will never escape his dominion. You were devoted to each other, equals in many ways, but in the end you served him at his pleasure. When you went off to Padua that year we met, you chose Andreas over me. When you went to Greece five months ago to visit his grave, you chose Andreas over me. A marriage to you would be a marriage to Andreas as well. Andreas will always be sitting on your shoulder—on walks in the park, at the dinner table, and in our marriage bed. One marriage to Andreas was enough."

I wanted to protest, but the words caught in my throat.

"We were not even married before he darkened the skies over us," she said, her voice rising. "When he took up with Emperor Charles right after our engagement, his promise of a life in Padua went up in smoke."

"Imperial service was a family tradition."

"Will you always come to his defense? I didn't marry his 'family tradition,' and that big house he built did nothing to make me feel any less betrayed. When military campaigns took him away from Brussels, I was grateful that you still offered your friendship. You know now that I dreaded his homecomings, and that you never saw the worst of him.

He refused to talk to me, his wife, about the campaigns, but I'm sure he talked to you."

"Not much. Sometimes he would write about them."

You wrote from St. Dizier, in 1544: "Our hospital is within earshot of the fighting, close enough for gunpowder smoke to burn my nostrils. I move around amidst the pandemonium deciding who will get my attention and whom I will let die, whose limb I will amputate before I go to the next. I am grateful when I discover that a new arrival is already dead."

I did not listen with care. I'm sorry, Andreas.

Anne retook her chair and leaned back.

"Did he ever write to you about the other women?"

"What?"

"You are as blind as I once was. Courtesans travel with the armies, and Andreas not infrequently availed himself of them. Secrets such as those are not well kept at court, and spread like foul air rising from a moat. In this indignity, at least, I was not alone."

"I cannot believe it."

"Believe what you choose. Still, we had some good years in Brussels after Charles abdicated, but then Philip called him to Madrid. The hostility against him there spilled onto me. I was an outsider, and I had few friends. I treasured the times he took Anna and me to the Low Countries when he traveled with Philip . . . when we would see you. But those visits just made me more homesick, more spiteful. And then the pilgrimage."

"I did not realize how unhappy you were. How unhappy you both were."

A silence hung over the room. Anne regarded me, calm yet resolute, as I sank into a chair opposite her. In weighing the circumstances of her life—what had come before, and what she could glimpse as yet to come—she made a fateful choice and delivered it without pretense or indecision. I would face a different future with her than I had so long hoped for. And as for Andreas, I would face a reckoning with who he was at his core. I sat looking at my shoes in a stew of anger, despair, and self-pity.

A fluttering of the curtains broke the silence.

"You haven't told me about Zante," she said.

I should tell her everything, if only to spite you both.

"It is a lovely island, with a delightful climate. The commerce is mainly fishing. A fortress in the hills overlooks the harbor. Andreas' gravestone is modest, in a peaceful spot under an olive tree in a church-yard at the edge of town. The inscription had him at fifty-eight years old."

Anne smiled. "If he knew he'd be furious. Did you meet anyone who saw him before he died?"

"Only the physician who treated him. Andreas was near death when he came ashore."

With a catch in my voice I said, "I cannot help but miss him, Anne."

"I know."

"So you will marry Hendrik."

"Yes."

20 July 1565

"Marcus, come here," I called out from my seat at the window. A sealed note was in front of me on the table. Marcus appeared at the door, and I waved him in.

"Marcus, I am dismissing you from my employ," I said, handing him the note.

The color left his face.

"Well, open it and read the terms."

He unsealed the note, read it, and shook his head in disbelief.

"I cannot accept this."

"What I've done is not up for debate. But in any event I'm afraid you have no choice but to accept it."

"But . . ."

"But what? The money is no longer mine. It sits in an account in your name. You've had more than enough of me and this house; go start your boatbuilding business."

"Who will see to you, and to the house?"

"I'm not yet an invalid, mind you—but your brother Henk has agreed to take your place. It seems that he was not looking forward to returning to the fisherman's life. I expect you to stay on until he masters the ledger and can make a decent cup of chocolate."

Marcus glanced down at the note. "This is far more than I need . . ."

"If there's any money left over I trust you'll make good use of it."

Marcus' eyes filled with tears. "How can I ever thank you . . ."

"All you have done in my service is beyond any measure of thanks you owe me. I have asked a lot of you."

I brought up a flask of brandy and two glasses from under the table.

"It's a little early in the day, but a toast is in order." I filled the glasses and handed one to Marcus.

"To your success and happiness, my good friend," I said, and we drained our glasses.

"That may have not been a good idea—I'm a bit light-headed," I laughed, and sat down, motioning to Marcus to sit in Andreas' chair. It would be the first time he sat there.

"I will miss this house, Master Jan," Marcus said.

"You are being dismissed, not banished. You'll have your own house to look after, but I expect you to visit and check on your brother. And from now on, you shall call me 'Jan,' as any friend would do."

I poured us another glass of brandy. "Let's take our time with this one."

Marcus twirled the glass in his hand. "It appears that you and Madam Vesalius will remain friends."

"In four days she will be Madam van der Meeren. I will be in attendance."

"This is not the outcome you wished for, but perhaps it is for the best."

A burst of activity out the window caught my eye. Two squirrels were chasing each other up and down the trunk of my oak tree. I recognized one of them, living a squirrel's life despite his old wound.

"I promise not to burden you with any more secrets, Marcus."

He cocked his head. "Are there any more to know? Because I'd just as soon be kept in the dark . . . Jan."

Hendrik van der Meeren was only too happy to install himself in Anne's house and make use of her inheritance and her pension from King Philip. By the wedding day the Vesalius family crest had been chiseled off the front entrance and painted over in the sitting room. Hendrik rather liked Andreas' hip-joint doorknocker, but Anne had it replaced with a conventional lion's head.

There would be plenty of room in the former Vesalius House to accommodate young Anna and her new husband, a lawyer named Jean de Mol, whom she was to marry in September. Her Uncle Jan would have the honor of giving her away.

Unbeknownst to Hendrik, who had never seen the painting, Anne had me take "The Extraction of the Stone of Madness" to my house. I wrote Antoine about the fate of his gift to Andreas; he was not offended, and insisted I keep it.

1 August 1565

The day before, Hendrik announced to his wife of seven days that he and his comrades would be leaving in the morning to hunt boar in the forests near Maastricht. I met Anne and Anna for an afternoon walk, and I had just returned and sat down at my desk when Henk came with a cup of chocolate. I took a sip and nodded my approval.

"Did you make this or is Marcus still prowling in the kitchen?"

"He's not here. He said I could make one on my own today. He is becoming a nuisance."

I laughed. "We'll send him on his way soon enough."

"By the way, Master Jan, two packages came for you while you were out."

"Really? Well, let's see them."

"You will need to clear some space on your desk."

Henk fetched the packages, one large and one small, postmarked from Venice.

"You can go, Henk."

I cut the twine that secured the large package, undid the wrapping, and peeled away the cotton batting underneath. Between two protective covers was a copy of the 1555 edition of the *Fabrica*.

Two notes were affixed to the cover. I drained my cup of the chocolate before I opened the first note, which bore the seal of the Fugger Bank.

16 June 1565

Piazza San Marco
Serene Republic of Venice

I bring you greetings, Signore van den Bossche.

On 22 March 1564, Doctor Andreas Vesalius, Count Palatine and Physician to King Philip II of Spain, presented himself to this office to request that we safeguard this copy of De humani corporis fabrica *until his return from the Holy Land. He paid for fifteen months of storage, and left instructions to forward it to you at your address in Brussels if he had not returned by then to claim it.*

He also left a small box that was to accompany the book in the event that the book was sent to you.

With the fifteen months' term approaching, we inquired at the Consulate for any news of Doctor Vesalius, only to learn of his passing in Greece this October past.

In carrying out his wishes, we send our warm regards and sincere condolences.

Do not hesitate to contact me if I can be of further service.

Lorenzo Castiglione, Director
Fugger Bank, Venice

The seal of the second letter was imprinted with three weasels stacked in full extension.

22 March 1564

Venice

Dearest Scarecrow,
I sail for Holy Land tomorrow. I have completely annotated this Fabrica for a third edition. Dragging it along did not make sense—it's unwieldy for travel, and it could get lost or destroyed.

If you are reading this, I am either known to be dead or disappeared long enough to assume that I am. I would entrust no one else with this. You will know what to do with it.

I am grateful to have a friend like you. Please see after Anne and Anna.

Forever your Astral Twin,
And.

Andreas was prophetic in that he was both dead and disappeared, but he could not have predicted what would happen months later on Zante.

How it must have pained you to abandon your Fabrica when you got back to Venice from Zante! But you had no choice—you were no longer Andreas Vesalius. You knew it was destined to come to me, and you would count on me to get Oporinus to publish it— posthumously, so to speak.

I paged through the book cover to cover, finishing long after the sun had set. Andreas had made hundreds of marginal notes, deletions, additions, and redesigns. Hardly a page went without comment. Despite his exceptional command of Latin, he strove for even greater textual clarity and elegance. I laughed out loud when I came across a passage in which Andreas softened a stinging criticism of Galen. Did he think that attacking Galen was no longer necessary to justify his own standing? Could he not quite free himself from the Greek master's grip?

As carefully as he pored over the text, the illustrations did not escape his scrutiny; he detected letter labels obscured by shading and indicated where they should be moved. He drew in corrected versions of anatomical details with which he found fault.

Given his favorable reading of Fallopio's *Observationes* and his own extensive response in his *Examen*, I was surprised that he had added only a few new anatomical findings, and those were based on his own work before he went to Spain. Was he too proud to include advances from other contemporaries in his *magnum opus*—even those that he had himself acknowledged?

Andreas wrote me after reading Fallopio's critique: *If I found Galen fallible, why should I not be so as well? This is how our science advances, isn't it?* And Guinter's great insight, in the lecture he read to me in Paris, echoed this sentiment:

"I prefer to think that across the centuries, Galen invited Vesalius to stand on his shoulders for a better view. And now behold the likes of Colombo and Fallopio, who in turn stand on the shoulders of Vesalius."

Andreas the investigator welcomed improvements upon his work; Andreas the man, perhaps not so much. If those who study nature—be they physicians, botanists, or astronomers—fail to guard against their human failings in the greater interest of truth and progress, then it will fall to others to correct the record.

In revisiting the *Fabrica* that day, I became aware of an aspect of Andreas' thinking that had escaped my full notice; throughout the text he points out the relationship of disordered anatomy to disease. These comments were signs that at his core, he held to the physician's mission to care for the sick, and he knew that the careful study of anatomy was the path to that end.

I closed the *Fabrica* and noticed the little package. I opened it to find, carefully wrapped in cloth, the bone-handled pen with the copper nib I had given Andreas when we were in primary school. I had no idea he still had it. I turned it over slowly in my hands. It felt lighter than I remembered it. The bone was worn smooth and glossy where Andreas' fingers gripped it. The copper trim was nicked and scratched. He had probably used this pen to make his annotations.

I set the pen down on my desk, not sure at first what I would do with it. It started out as a childhood gift to Andreas from me, desperate to win his friendship—but had come full circle to be a relic of a great anatomist who entrusted it to transfer his genius onto paper.

My eyes were drawn to my Brethren of the Common Life school bag, just months ago unearthed from behind my desk. I took it off the shelf and returned the pen to its original home. Just as the pen became a relic, the school bag became a reliquary.

I rewrapped the book, put it in a corner of the study, and went to bed.

2 September 1565

Anne hung her head and turned over her king. "I resign. Again."

"You played well until you took that foolish risk with your Queen."

"I need no reminding, and you need not make matters worse by gloating."

"I am trying to be gracious. Here, let me make a peace offering."

I called out to Henk. "Would you bring us chocolates?"

"Right away, Master Jan," he answered from the kitchen.

Anne and I sat across from each other in my dining room, she directly under the tapestry of Vertumnus and Pomona. I retrieved a letter from my pocket and handed it to her.

"This came in the day's post from Oporinus."

17 August 1565
Nadelberg 6
Basel

My Dear Jan,
I rejoiced at receiving your August 2 letter to learn that you had reached Zante and are safely home.

I am dictating this letter to a secretary; the shaking palsy has made writing impossible. My balance is failing me, and yet sometimes my feet seem to be stuck to the floor. I am told my face is without expression. I am weary of this life, but the smell of ink and the sound of the presses keep me going.

Old Number Two finally printed its last page. I cried for a week.

I was astounded to hear that Andreas' 1555 edition has come to you fully annotated. Doubtless, he intended a third edition, but I must tell you that I cannot consider embarking on that project.

Times are not favorable for the shop, and the cost of producing a third Fabrica *would be beyond us. Furthermore, sales of the second edition lagged behind the first, and I cannot risk the possibility of similar results.*

Be assured of my allegiance to Andreas and his memory, but I beg you to understand my predicament. If you wish to locate another publisher, I would have no objection.

In the meanwhile, my best wishes to you and Marcus, and my condolences to his widow; you have spoken highly of her.

With devotion,
Johannes

Anne handed it back.

"Number Two is a printing press?"

"The press that printed the first *Fabrica*. He believed it had a soul."

"He has the heart of the true artisan who loves his tools. And he is kind to think of me. But he leaves you with a dilemma."

"I cannot not fault him for his rejection. Andreas intended for me to get it printed if it came into my hands, and Andreas would trust no one but Oporinus with the *Fabrica*. Even if I found a publisher, transferring the woodblocks would be inviting a nightmare."

"What will you do now?

"I am thinking of telling Oporinus I would make it worth his while to produce the book."

Anne frowned. "If you carry on with this, I wish not to hear about it. The book is haunting you already."

"I'm haunted not so much by the book than by a duty to see to his legacy."

"Your duty to him was as his friend, and after your voyage to Zante, your devotion to him needs no further proof. You owe Andreas nothing more than to treasure his memory. Let future scholars see to his legacy."

Anne mistook my silence for hurt. "I'm sorry," she said. "I have no business instructing you on what you owe Andreas."

"No, no, you're right. I am struggling with just that—and the book has become part of the struggle. But my dear Anne, you've given me an idea for a solution."

15 October 1565

The new day's sun spilled over the wall of my fading garden and a breeze roused the scarlet leaves still clinging to the oak tree. It hadn't been cold enough to light the stove, but I asked Henk to have it going this morning. I stood by the window and re-read a letter that came the day before.

11 October 1565

Office of the Rector
University Hall
University of Leuven

Dear Master van den Bossche,
In accordance with our previous correspondence, and with great thanks, I write to confirm receipt of the 1555 edition of De humani corporis fabrica, *with handwritten annotations by its author Andreas Vesalius, a celebrated alumnus of the University.*

Under the terms of your bequest, the book will become the property of the University and kept under seal until your death (by God's grace many years hence), at which time it will be made available to interested scholars without precondition.

The University will honor your request to remain anonymous, and to destroy records of the gift if and when the University chooses to transfer ownership of the book to another individual or institution.

The University is deeply grateful for this exceptional gift, and for your unfailing generosity over the years.

May God bless and keep you,
Thomas Gozaeus
Rector

I would write my lawyer with instructions to file the letter from Rector Gozaeus with my estate papers, and to have it burned upon my death. Many minutes passed as I sat before a blank sheet of paper, glancing at the empty chair nearby. I took up my quill and started to write.

15 October 1565

Dear Andreas (to me you will remain Andreas, whatever you call yourself now),

Today is the first anniversary of your death and resurrection— your personal Easter. You are in rare company, but the resurrection of Jesus, if it is to be believed, was a miracle; yours was clandestine and all-too-human—you never even set foot in your grave. And as you have so thoroughly removed Andreas Vesalius from the living, your Second Coming is as hard to imagine as His.

I know the full story of the Padua affair. Philip imposed a terrible price for your impulsive and poorly-disguised pilgrimage ruse and made you a pawn, through Antoine, in a game he played with Venice. Antoine was concerned about your safety, but your safety was not his primary concern. Forgive him—he has a difficult job.

You may be interested in some family news. Sweet Anna is engaged to a young man who would meet your approval. Anne, however, chose to marry a minor nobleman of middling intellect who enjoys living in your house and spending your money. I was crushed to learn of the engagement upon my return, because I allowed myself to imagine that it would be me, not some crude country baron, who would take your place.

Losing Anne to you those many years ago left a scar that still tugs at me, though I tried mightily to disregard it. I share a good measure of blame for losing her, to be sure—but the cloud that hung over your marriage to Anne, it seems, was big enough to cover me. She feared you would haunt our marriage, and I could not convince her otherwise, perhaps rightly so. Despite myself I admire her determination to reach a solution for herself.

So then, by dint of our fraught histories and the vagaries of circumstance, Anne and I have managed to arrive once again at a place where a husband separates us. And yet, once again, we have found a way forward within the boundaries of friendship. I believe that speaks for something important between us, and I struggle not to cast the situation in a tragic light. Her country baron is often away hunting or carousing, so I see Anne and Anna often. The hurt remains, but the pleasure of having them in my life is ample compensation.

Meanwhile, I am considering a professorship-in-residence at Leuven. Young students may well keep my mind working a while longer. My knees are as bad as ever, no thanks to you, and my back does me no favors in sending a dull pain down the back of my left leg.

More news: Your daughter has far surpassed you in mathematics, and Anne would easily defeat you in chess. You may recall that Anne started a salon for women before you married her. It has been reborn in the sitting room of your house. About a dozen women attend, and I was invited to give a lecture on geometry.

The journey to your so-called grave on Zante reminded me of your greatness in the world, but also made me see how unaware I was of your despair, and of Anne's. I will always regret this short-coming, but I will no longer burden myself with it. Antoine believes that we cannot know others completely; that there are always secrets, even between friends. I have come to see that he is right.

I cannot resist wondering where you are and what you are doing. I have a theory: like Paracelsus, you are living a nomadic life of the alchemist healer armed with your knowledge of anatomy, a fugitive from your old life on a pilgrimage to nowhere. From Oporinus I learned of your chance meeting with Paracelsus, and later on you wrote me of your admiration of him despite his strange notions and personal failings. Anne told me of your alchemy experiments in Spain. I worry that the potions you concocted might have had an effect on your mind, as they might have had on Paracelsus.

I am in receipt of your annotated Fabrica. *Oporinus cannot work on a third edition. I will look no further for a publisher, but I have made arrangements for its safekeeping, and some future scholar may be inspired to bring it to life. By that time, it's likely that you will have died a second and last time. You will be angry with me about this, but you need not fear about your place in history.*

I was touched beyond words to see that pen again. Its journey back and forth between us seals our bond.

I don't expect that we will ever see each other again. I will live out my days in Brussels, and I will travel only as far as Leuven. You would not dare come here; no disguise could hide you in your home city or anywhere nearby. You would even need to avoid institutions of medicine; anyone who has opened your book has seen Calcar's likeness of you opposite the first page. With Tritonius dead, only Marcus and I are left to carry your secret. Rest assured it is safe with us; to reveal it would serve no purpose other than to invite chaos into all our lives.

Let me say this in closing: yes, at your bidding I traveled the continent against my will, and I allowed myself to be part of your grisly adventures. Yes, you hurt me when you took Anne from me; yes, you hurt me with your sham death and your abandonment without a word. But I forgive you all these things. Because of you I survived childhood on firm footing. Because of you I never felt alone. Because of you I was drawn out to see the world, the good and the bad of it. I took pride in being part of your success.

My dearest friend Andreas, as the tumult rose around you after the Fabrica *came out, you burned your papers and manuscripts in a fit of pique, an act you lived to regret. I hope not to regret what I am about to do this morning. I will miss you always, but I must let you go. Let us wish each other well.*

Forever your astral twin,
Jan

I sealed the letter, turned it in my hand, then opened the grate of the stove and dropped it onto the flames. I took all of Andreas' letters from the drawer where I kept them all these years and fed them into the stove one by one.

Afterword

*T*he *King's Anatomist* is a work of fiction, but my aim was to build the plot around what is known or widely accepted about the life and times of Andreas Vesalius. In the interest of storytelling, however, I have taken some liberties that bear mention:

- Jan van den Bossche is a fictional character.
- Vesalius' childhood fracture while stealing a dismembered leg from the gallows is an invention. I felt justified in using it to support the plot because I think Andreas was that kind of kid.
- The lecture of Guinter of Andernach is fictional, but I liked the idea that he could have been persuaded by the *Fabrica*, as others were.
- It is unlikely but not entirely implausible that Vesalius saw Leonardo da Vinci's anatomical drawings; the Milanese physician Girolamo Cardano knew Vesalius as well as Francesco Melzi, and had himself seen the drawings. Vesalius could have passed through Milan on the way to Padua.
- Many art historians favor the idea that Stephan van Calcar was not the only artist for the *Fabrica*. For my purposes, one artist was enough.
- Vesalius never met Paracelsus, but creating this encounter was irresistible, given that both had strong connections to Johannes Oporinus.
- Vesalius did not accompany his woodblocks for the *Fabrica* from Italy to Basel. I had a difficult time believing that he would let them out of his sight, so I sent him and Jan along.

- I invented King Philip's standoff with Venice over Andreas' retaking of his professorship at the University of Padua, and therefore Antoine de Granvelle's role in it.
- Vitus Tritonius, the former student of Vesalius, was never a Viennese navy physician on Zante, and I further sullied his memory to advance the story.
- I made my best forensic assumptions on the condition of the corpse in the Zante grave.
- There is no reason to believe that Vesalius survived beyond his stop on Zante, now called Zakynthos. I am convinced, though, that he wished for a life free of Spain, and I gave it to him.
- To my knowledge the 1555 edition of the *Fabrica* annotated by Vesalius was never at the University of Leuven. It was my way of setting it free from the story so that it could turn up centuries later for study, which it has.

I have omitted some notable details usually included in biographies of Vesalius. I ask forgiveness from professional historians of medicine, anatomy, or art who may be rankled by them, and for any other errors of commission or omission.

Bibliography

Books

Ball, Philip. *The Devil's Doctor*. New York: Farrar, Straus and Giroux, 2006.

Ball, James Moores M.D. Andreas Vesalius, *Reformer of Anatomy*. Medical Science Press, 1910.

Berengario da Carpi, Giacomo. Commentaria. Bologna: Yale University Medical Historical Library, 1521.

Cameron, Euan, editor. *The Sixteenth Century in The Short Oxford History of Europe*. Oxford: Oxford University Press, 2006.

Carlino, Andrea. *Books of the Body*. Chicago and London: University of Chicago Press, 1999.

Greenblatt, Stephen. *The Swerve*. NewYork: W.W Norton & Company, 2011.

Hale, John. *The Civilization of Europe in the Renaissance*. New York: Atheneum, 1993.

Johnson, Paul. *The Renaissance: A Short History*. New York: A Modern Library Chronicles Book The Modern Library, 2000.

Kusukawa, Sachiko. *Picturing the Book of Nature*. Chicago and London: University of Chicago Press, 2012.

O'Malley, Charles D. and J.B. de C. M. Saunders. *Leonardo da Vinci on the Human Body*. New York: Henry Schuman, 1952.

O'Malley, C.D. *Andreas Vesalius of Brussels*. Berkeley and Los Angeles: University of California Press 1964.

Reisch, Gregor. *Margarita Philosophica*. Freiburg: Yale University Medical Historical Library, 1503.

Saunders, J.B de C. M. and Charles D. O'Malley. *The Illustrations from the Works of Andreas Vesalius of Brussels*. Cleveland and New York: World Publishing Company, 1950.

Willemsen, Annemarieke. *Back to the Schoolyard: The Daily Practice of Medieval and Renaissance Education*. N.p.: Brepols Publishers, 2008.

Vesalius, Andreas. *De humani corporis fabrica*. Basel: Johannes Oporinus, 1543.

———. *Epitome*. Basel: Johannes Oporinus, 1543.

Articles

Compier, Abdulhaq. "How Europe came to forget about its Arabic heritage," *Al-Islam eGazette*. (January 2011).

——. "Rhazes in the Renaissance of Andreas Vesalius," *Med Hist*. 1, no. 56 (January 2012): 3–25

Hazard, Jean. "Jan Stephen van Calcar, précieux collaborateur méconnu de Vésale," *Histoire des Sciences Médicales*. 30, no. 4 (1996).

Lanska, D. "The Evolution of Vesalius' perspective on Galen's Anatomy," *History of Medicine*. 2, no. 1 (2015): 17–32

Mavrodi, A., Paraskevas G. and P. Kitsoulis. "The History and the Art of Anatomy: a source of inspiration even nowadays," *Italian Journal of Anatomy and Embryology*. 118, no.3 (2013): 267–276

Nutton, Vivian. "Vesalius Revised. His Annotations to the 1555 Fabrica," *Med Hist*. 56, no. 4 (October 2012): 415–443.

O'Malley, Charles D. "The Anatomical Sketches of Vitus Tritonius Athesinus and Their Relationship to Vesalius' Tabulae Anatomicae," *J Hist Med Allied Sci*. 13, no. 3 (1958): 395-97

——. "Some Remarks on the Significance of Andreas Vesalius," *Scientarium Historica*. 6 (1964).

Pagel, Walter and Rattanzi, Pyarali. "Vesalius and Paracelsus," *Med Hist*. 8, no. 4 (October 1964).

Siriasi, Nancy. "Vesalius and Human Diversity in De humani corporis Fabrica," *Journal of the Warburg and Courtauld Institutes*. 57 (1994), 60–88.

Symposia

The Four Hundredth Anniversary Celebration of the *De Humani Corporis Fabrica* of Andreas Vesalius. The Historical Library, Yale University School of Medicine, 1943.

Vesalius Continuum commemorating the 500th anniversary of Andreas Vesalius Conference Zakynthos (formerly Zante). Greece, Sept 4-8, 2014. (personally attended)

Acknowledgments

Writers speak of the solitary nature of their enterprise, but the wise and humble writer will allow trusted third parties to weigh in on their work in progress. Writers can be too close to their creation to reliably detect its flaws, or too self-critical to be secure in its strengths. I was fortunate to have learned this lesson early on, and this book has benefitted as a result.

My wife Selina Strong had the first crack at my raw output. We are still cordial.

My writer's group—Richard Anderson, Gerard Coulombe, Therese Dykeman, Judith Evans, Steven Gaynes, Joann Kalif, Todd Kalif, Ardeth Miller, and Millicent Zolan—gave me steadfast feedback and encouragement during the book's gestation.

When I felt the manuscript was a readable whole, a cadre of beta-readers—Irwin Berkowitz, David Bickart, Toni Bickart, Joette Katz, Martha LoMonaco, Jim Motavalli, Eben Riordan, and Cecily Stranahan—stepped forward to dissect it with diligence and objectivity.

Matt Coleman, PhD, Professor Emeritus of mathematics at Fairfield University, Fairfield Connecticut, kept me above water in the passages involving mathematics. Alexandra Mavrodi, DDS, of Zurich, Switzerland, and H.S. Compier, MD of Amsterdam, the Netherlands, both of whom have contributed to the literature on Andreas Vesalius, were gladly willing to offer helpful further insights.

Vivian Nutton, PhD, Emeritus Professor of the History of Medicine, University College London, and an international Vesalius authority, has been exceedingly gracious with his time in responding to my questions.

My friend Alan Neigher, JD, provided moral support and valuable counsel.

The staff of the Yale Medical Historical Library in New Haven, Connecticut—especially Melissa J. Grafe, PhD, the John R. Bumstead Librarian for Medical History—paved the way for me to examine the treasures housed there.

Sarah Ons of the University Archives at the University of Leuven, Belgium, tracked down the name of a former university official whose name, I suspect, has not appeared in print for five centuries. I was happy to give him another day in the sun.

I will be forever indebted to Colin Mustful, the founder of History Through Fiction, who saw value in my manuscript and leant his skillful and professional editing to it.

Last but not least I here celebrate the memory of Phil and Fanny Duschnes of Philip C. Duschnes, Rare Books and First Editions, in its time a prominent antiquarian bookseller. "Uncle Phil and Aunt Fanny," as I knew them, employed my mother, Dorothy Klatt Blumenfeld, for forty years, and introduced me as a high school student to Andreas Vesalius. Having the freedom to see and handle the extraordinary books and manuscripts that passed through their Manhattan store was a gift to me and my family that can never be repaid. Whatever skill I have with the written word came to life there.

About the Author

Ron Blumenfeld grew up in the Bronx, New York in the shadow of Yankee Stadium. He attended the Bronx High School of Science and the City College of New York before receiving his MD degree from the State University of New York—Downstate Medical Center in far-off Brooklyn. After venturing to the Southwest desert for his pediatrics residency at the University of Arizona, his family settled in Connecticut, but Tucson remains their second home.

He practiced pediatrics for twenty years while gradually transitioning to administrative positions, focusing on clinical quality improvement and health care utilization. Ron was a long-time physician reviewer for the National Committee for Quality Assurance, a prominent health industry accreditation agency. During his career, he did extensive health care and business writing, which taught him the virtues of economy and clarity. Upon retirement, he became a columnist for his town's newspaper, a pleasure he surrendered to concentrate on his debut novel, *The King's Anatomist*.

His love of books springs from his childhood years spent in an antiquarian book store in Manhattan, where his mother was the only employee. It was there, as a high school student, that he was introduced to Andreas Vesalius and his revolutionary textbook of anatomy, a cornerstone in the history of medicine and a masterpiece of the bookmaking art.

Ron's a long way from his glory days as an all-star catcher in the Stadium Little League, but still enjoys a variety of outdoor sports and hiking. He was a hands-on partner in an exciting but quixotic adventure with a French friend in a small vineyard in southwest France.

He and his wife Selina are fortunate to have their son Daniel and granddaughter Gracelynn nearby.

Printed in the USA
CPSIA information can be obtained
at www.ICGtesting.com
LVHW040315030224
770776LV00003B/247